Ra Legacy The Art of Nature

DAVID ZALTANA

For

Vera and Merna

Table of Contents

THE READER

Rule number 1: Think for yourself…

There are many things to say. Some are happy, some are sad. However, everything works out for its divine purpose. There is always a reason.

In this world, you must understand the nature of things. Whatever you see, hear, touch, smell, feel, or taste—the five senses are essential, and you witness them for a reason. If you understand these aspects of life and how they work, you will be able to see life from a different perspective. Many distractions blind us, stealing our minds from what is true in nature. So, you must understand what true nature is; it's far from difficult. In life, we also make mistakes, and that is all fine, as it is part of the experience called "life." If it doesn't break us, it surely has made us who we are today. Life will either put you into oblivion or mold you into the best version of your supreme self.

Once you get your wings, you will be divine. However, it doesn't end there. The choices you make are crucial with those wings. "Life" sometimes will make you see a realm that is all paradise; since it makes you feel delight, it can be a trap. Just like a beautiful sky with clouds in front of you, then a mountain waiting for you to mess up as it looks you directly in your eyes. You must make the right choices with humility, honesty, and in accordance with your true nature. This ultimately will empower you to make the right decisions. Be patient with yourself, as you become what you think or believe. "Life" is a journey. Learn from this, and you shall be free…

CHAPTER 1

My Life in A Sketch

Life is so great when you can just do anything you want. There's nothing better than Mother Nature protecting us all from all the dark forces. Dad always said my feathered necklace pendant would always protect me, no matter where I am or what bad energy comes near.

"Well, that's good enough. Just need my jacket and I'm out of here."

I hope Nova and everyone else is already there. I don't want to be the only one standing by the building.

"And where are you going, missy?"

"Out to paint, Mom. Y'know, my friends are waiting."

Mom making her frybread for later on. I kind of lost my taste for it.

"Razaiella…" Mom says, folding her arms with a frown. "Why don't you settle down today? I plan to take you and Lakia school shopping later on. The school year is right around the corner."

"Tsk, like we're learning anything. I'll be back before three. I promise."

"No way. You do know the clothing shop closes at five. You and Lakia both are worth four hours of shopping."

"Mom, the more we talk here, the less time I have," I smirked. "Let me enjoy the last days of my vacation."

Mom returned her smile at me, knowing my time was surely almost up. Back to daily mind torture, I felt like every time my alarm struck my ears for it.

"Alright, Ra, go on. Hey! Your breakfast!"

"Already had my blueberries and juice! Byee!"

I wish she would drop me off, but if I did that, she would just judge my friends as she always does. One thing I hate about New York is that it makes you wear a sweater in the morning and carry it in the after-noon. Then the creeps love to stare at a fourteen-year-old girl walking down the street. They don't know I have Mother Nature by my side. "Oh no! The train!"

If Mom hadn't asked those questions, it would have met me there. My book bag doesn't make it easier to run up the stairs, either. "Hey, wait! I'm coming!"

The people of New York eyed me as I ran for my life, as if the train was escaping hell itself.

"Eygh."

"You just made it," a much older man says, pulling me in.

He looked as though he was late for work in his suit, tie, and pol-ished dress shoes. His eyelids sat low on his green pupils, and his hair slicked back but long to his shoulders. Kind of reminded me of the Greek god, Zeus. "Woo, thank you," I panted and grinned.

Every time I meet someone new, it's like they are just drawn to look at me and ask me questions.

"You know, you may not get there wherever you are headed if you try too hard. What's the rush?"

"Just going out to meet up with some friends. Nothing special."

The soft-spoken, well-dressed man smiled while holding onto the handrail above him. Everyone just looked so depressed, going wherev-er the train was taking them.

"The way you ran up those steps tells more than that. If they are true friends, they will wait. I hope they are not leading you down the wrong road. You know how the city is."

I giggled. "Trust me, I know. Crime, weird people, addicts, crazy shit."

"How old are you, young lady?" the man smiled.

"Huh? Why does it matter? Oh damn, what time is it?"

"See, you did it again."

"Tsk, it's eleven O' three. This train needs to go faster."

"Never rush life, young lady. The right time is never wrong. Other than that, a beautiful soul girl such as yourself should not be using such foul language. It makes you ugly."

When will this guy just shut up like everyone else, minding their business? The lady holding her metal dog on a leash even looked annoyed. People would rather robots than the real thing nowadays. I have to text Nova to let them know I won't be there for another ten minutes.

"I remember back in the day when I first saw a cell phone. I have lived for a very long time, and when these things came out for kids… I believe that's when parenting went downhill. Then the internet. Back in the day was the golden age. The world was such a pleasant place—not perfect, but cleaner than this. People are like the dead walking now."

Me trying to find a place to sit was just out of the question. Maybe the next train would have been better.

"You know, you are a very beautiful young person. Just by seeing you get to this train, it tells me you are a go-getter. Just one thing, young lady. Never let this world tell you who you are or what you can or can't do. Take away your talents and leave you crippled by what the Creator has blessed you with. Even tell you how to feel. That is why so many in this very cab are just here. Not living—dead on the inside. They sin for the moment, and then the consequences come for a longer time. Demons are slave masters. Every addict is a slave, every alcoholic, every person into witchcraft is a slave. You can make yourself a slave just by thinking you can do whatever you want. That is when it comes, young lady, and then you are hooked to your desires. They become your slave master."

Thank goodness, my stop was in sight.

"Also, never take precious life for granted. Many have done this, and I have witnessed a man lose his wife that way, and his soul became ravenous for lust that never filled him."

Trying not to eye this guy, and I wonder why no one told him that I didn't care. Usually, they are that rude. "Because men are weird."

The low-eyed man grinned. "Not all. Man is not perfect, but you must know how these things work. Someone you love isn't perfect, and I know you know who."

Looking back up to the man as he smiled down at me.

"Your feelings will never lie. Usually, the first is correct," the man smirked.

"Please exit safely," the train speaker announced.

"Oh, thank God!"

I wanted to run like I never have before and just yell, getting out of that train. But the best thing in the world was coming to me in just a few minutes. One thing I can say positively about New York City is that everywhere is full of life, good and bad. People walking the streets, steam coming from the gutters, the addicts doing their own thing but not harming anyone. It's a mix of both worlds. So that guy, who took life for granted—that's him. Mom told me to be careful with those types of men anyway. I didn't need to hear it from everyone.

"Well, it's about time! What took you, Ra?"

"Sorry, sorry. I was on the train, and this guy—I thought he was going to ask me out."

"Girl, everyone wants to."

I grinned. "Someone sounds jealous, but you're pretty too, friend."

Lexus knew I cared nothing for guys. We're in a group of three boys and us two girls. If I were to have a boyfriend, I would hope it would be with someone in the group. Dante—he's a cool guy and has been with me and Lexus forever. Jordan—he just joined us from school. Then, Nova, Dante's older brother. I think he's over twenty years old. School didn't mean a thing to him, as he always said the streets taught him about life, not the schoolhouse. It kind of felt like it's nothing more than the truth. Besides, I prefer someone older and my circle small. As Lexus has been my bestie forever, I trusted her the most.

"Time for some music too," Jordan says, taking out his mini speaker and spray cans from his duffle bag.

"I'm in the middle, I think. Mine will take up the most space."

"What do you plan on making this time, Ra?" Nova asks as he stands behind me with his arms behind his back, spectating.

"It's a surprise. I want to do something on the wall no one has seen before."

"Hmph, sounds like a plan. Where's your sketchbook?"

I shrugged. "Forgot it. I don't need it anyway. I sketched it in class, and I remember what it looked like. I'm going to use just three colors, so it won't be so hard either."

Nova frowned with a grin. "What?"

"It's all in your head," I smiled. "Just have to have a good memory, I guess. Hey, Jordan. Turn your music down just a little. That speaker is so small but loud."

"Hey, you don't like music?" Jordan laughs. "Lex likes it."

"She likes it because that's her type," I replied, looking at her shaking her hips. "All that is nice is the beat."

"And that's all that is—is the beat," Nova says. "It's dark as hell, but I can ride with it. Just focus, Ra. It's just so dope someone can pull off something like you can. I've been with the murals for years and still haven't mastered it like you do."

"So that means she has you beat, bro," Dante says as he begins spraying the wall.

"Hey, I just do things. I don't know how, but it's like the portrait is already on the wall. Then, all I have to do is trace over it. Not hard at all. The only thing that might mess me up is that I have to rush this since my mom wants to take me and my sisters school shopping today. At three… and it's eleven-thirty."

"You're smart, Ra," Nova says. "You'll figure it out."

"You are too. That's why you should try school again, but I know that isn't your style. Maybe college?"

"Naaa," Nova shook his head. "My sister told me the other day that there is no such thing as a mixed person."

"What?" I raised my eyebrow.

"This comes from when the bullshit indoctrinates you, and you can't think for yourself," Nova replies.

Getting ready to paint on the wall, something bothered me about what I just heard. My sisters are mixed.

"What would make her say something like that? You told me she has a doctorate degree, right?"

"That's right, and that right there tells me I don't need anything that is going to mess with my head. Man, she said that to me because she claimed that they removed the term 'mix' from the ethnicity sheet long ago. You know, when you sign up for a job or something. Ha, so I asked er', as if she was right here—if they removed the word, wall, from the dictionary, this isn't a wall anymore? Remember, she has a doctorate, though. She's always right. Somebody like me, I'm always wrong because I'm a street dude."

"Street smart, homie," Jordan says, giving Nova a high five.

"Bet that. Tsk, what really stood out to me and got me thinking, though—they pay people like my sister to teach this foolery around the world. Lots of money, too. No wonder the world's fallin' apart.

Misinformation everywhere, but that school crap is for the birds and sheep. Better think for your damn self out here. Even our old man back then used to always tell us, if you can't think for yourself, your ass is grass."

"I don't know what to say. Anyway, I have to get this done. I feel good about this project… and it's… eleven-thirty-five."

"There's always tomorrow, Ra," Jordan says as he puts on his gas mask. "Let's get to work."

Doing art is just something I love to just take me away. The way you can express your feelings, thoughts, and soul. Nothing can take this from you. Every time a spray can was sprayed, the white-greyish smoke reminded me of my dreams of Mother Nature's destruction. My guardian angel that hung from my neck protected me from the vicious twisters. However, I see that there was always more to it, as revealed in my dreams and nightmares. As for Nova, education is necessary, and this is what they want us to know—for us to understand and create a better future. For his sister to say that she had to be joking. The crazy thing is, I had no memory of seeing it on the list. It didn't matter, though; it was his life. I only wish my art could come to life, just as this I am making would take me and fly away.

"Now… that's fire, Ra," Nova says, then removing his mask. "I know you always do your thing, but this is sick!"

"Sick?" I frowned with a smirk.

"Not sick, but wicked. Dope as hell. Talent at its finest, baby!"

"We all know she can draw and paint," Jordan says, standing with Nova as they admire my sacred skills.

"I just do it. Ha, Lex did good too. Just her shading is a little off."

The cartoon woman she drew was just the usual anime-style figure. I think she did well, but in the corner of my eye, she always kept looking over to my side to see what I was doing. Instead, she should focus on her own thing, as Nova said.

"You all did great, but Ra really fired it up. The angel hanging over the words just looks… wicked! With three colors, too? Now that's talent."

"Nova," Lexus sighs, "you all gas her up too much. It's cute, but she isn't even finished."

"Definitely won't be able to finish today, but there's always tomorrow. Right, Jordan? Then this mask… ugh, that's better. Feels like it's trying to eat my hair with it."

Dante, Jordan, and Nova did just simple graffiti wild-style writings. Since Nova is the oldest, you can tell he has more years of experience. Wild style, to me, was just abstract—nothing but just scribbles of letters combining with one another. Art, to me, is making life in anything you create on paper, board, or a wall. It must also mean something. That is why I am the queen of wall art. I will complete it tomorrow with just the last few letters under my angel: Z and A.

"We're out for some lunch, Ra, you in?" Nova asks.

"Don't think so—"

"Oh yea, Mom wants you back. That's cool, but I commend er' on at least letting you come outside. I know some dudes who never leave the household. With everything going on in my life, you have to know these streets. Shit out here is no joke. Hard to trust people, that's why we have to keep our circle small. Less friends, the better. Just like how you have to know good and evil. You can't just be a goody two-shoe."

"I beg to differ bro," Jordan says.

"Really? Well, mister honor roll. Tell me how that works how anything I just said is wrong. Better yet, one hundred dollars right now to prove me wrong."

I grinned along with Lexus as Nova always did his routine. It was actually interesting when he debated with anyone because he was always sure he was right.

"So, no money, or you just can't tell me how?"

"Man, I'm not debating with you today. It's my own opinion," Jordan shrugs.

"I'm telling you all. All respect homie, but when school has your head in the clouds, you can't think for yourself, and that is a big issue, trust me. Listen to this," Nova says, lighting a cigarette.

"If someone, anyone can't put their money on the table about anything they say, don't trust em'. My therey is—"

"Theory?" Jordan shakes his head.

"Okay, smart ass. See what I'm saying, you all?"

Daunte, Lexus, and I grinned together as it wasn't that serious. He was cute when he got upset or annoyed. I understood him, though.

"Why is it that in English, everything is said differently than it is written? Guess I'm talking to the wrong crowd. Anyways, in my... theory on this, if a person doesn't want to put their money on the table, they have no say in anything. Either they just want to debate and argue, or might just be a hater. Not saying you are homie, but it is what it is. Don't judge me because I made a simple mistake."

"I just stated an opinion, and for that reason, as you just did. For what you just mentioned, we all judge. That kind of talk is for the birds. As they said, they milked that titty dry with that word a long time ago."

Nova nods. "I can go with that as that's a fact for sure, but I actually meant, don't judge me for messing up on one little word, but you're right. We all judge since we have to make moves on everything. Making the wrong judgment could mess you up to the point of no return. Anyways, you coming, Ra? Time to get out of—"

"And there she is," I sighed.

She actually drove around looking for me. I never told her where I was. "Oh damn, it's almost three-thirty." "Razaiella! Get over here! Right now!" "Hey, Mom!" Nova grins as he waves. "See you guys later. Tsk, so embarrassing."

"Don't worry about it, Ra. Tomorrow then," Dante says.

I should have told her just to get me black shoes with cute tops and pants, but she would probably get me something ugly anyway. "Hey."

Mom pulling off fast, almost breaking my neck, along with Lakia and Munisha in the backseat.

"Don't 'hey' me, Razaiella. You said three, and I had to drive looking for you in the filthy streets alongside hoodlums. Why didn't you pick up your phone?"

"Why are you being judgmental? You don't know them. Those are my friends."

Mom shook her head, and I could sense her frustration deeply. "I used to be very judgmental of your father, and I wish I had not been so lenient with his actions. Ra, if you are caught doing graffiti on a wall and the authorities get involved, your father will be the one picking you up. Or would you like to be wearing the orange jumpsuit? No daughter of mine will be embarrassing me like this. I always tell you and your sisters to protect your aura. Bad energy rubs off so easily. Hmph, then he waves with a cigarette in his hand. You've got to be kidding me, daughter."

I didn't know why she was mad because she knew I was going out. Then Nova just complimented her about me being out without restrictions.

"Hi, Razaiella."

"Munisha is speaking to you," Mom hissed.

"Hey, um…yea."

I didn't feel like getting new clothes all of a sudden. I have friends who love art, so I had all of this bad energy. Nova waved, and she didn't wave back, but she told me to say hello to a half-sister.

CHAPTER 2

Family Matters

The days go by fast when you're not thinking about them. When school starts, the days pass more slowly, and it gets worse as the last days approach. I hated it since it meant nothing to me. I barely had any real friends, only the ones I did art with. I knew this school year would be a long, boring one. Even the teachers were being replaced by AI tutors, and they could never make their voices sound more like human voices. Lakia and Munisha didn't care; they just wanted to go to get out of the house.

"So, how was it today? Boring, huh?"

"It's the third day, so they're not giving us much work," Lakia says as Munisha walks, eating her chips.

"Well, you're in the sixth grade. Wait until you get in the ninth. They're giving me crap that we don't even need to be learning. Just in three days. Consider yourself lucky."

"Hey, Munisha, give me some."

"No! Get your own!"

Even just looking at those two, they seem to be more of mutual blood. I grew up with Lakia more, as she was ten years old, and Munisha was five. My last name was different, as it was Lozano. Her and Munisha had the same Dad, and all of us had the same Mom. I never felt any way about it, just that they were closer to who they were.

"It's always good to share, right, Munisha? Oh, don't pout, we're your sisters. Sharing is caring. Here, Ra."

I shook my head. "No thanks. Just give her back her stuff."

"Oh, so you're afraid to get fat?"

"I bought a crop top, and I need it to look good on me. So just know that. Now… give her, her stuff."

"You didn't have to snatch it, Ra. Geez," Lakia frowns, leaving Munisha with a smile behind her.

Lakia was always weird to me. I had nothing against her, but she always seemed to think I was blind or stupid about things.

"You don't like me, do you?"

I grinned. "Why do you say that?"

"Because… I don't know. You just seem to feel a way about me. I feel it."

I shrugged, as I didn't know what to say. She knows what she does, and sometimes, she makes me feel insecure about her.

"We are family. I'm your sister. You hang out more with those people doing graffiti more than us. Mom even said it."

"Tsk, we walk home and go to the same school. What do you mean?"

"She means you don't like us."

I turned and saw many people walking by, minding their business, while three girls stood between the big, busy city. "If I didn't like you two, I wouldn't be walking with you. I got your chips back, didn't I, Munisha?"

Lakia grins. "What I mean is, you don't act like we're family. You're always so… far away. That's what it feels like."

Thank God we're almost home. I needed a nap for my mind and body. How dare she say that when I am the one to lead us home? The things going on in this city, the type of people out here—we can be kidnapped, raped, and then killed. Maybe because I'm the one with a cell phone, she's just jealous.

"I didn't mean to make you mad, Ra. I just wanted to tell you how me and Munisha feel. Us as sisters."

"Ha, you're good, sis. Let's just go inside, and I'm going to sleep."

"Don't you have homework?" Munisha asks.

"Tsk, I don't feel like it. I feel like drifting off and going somewhere later. See you all. Oh, and no cooking. Don't want to hear Mom's mouth, then I would take the blame."

That's just maybe it. She is jealous of me having a phone, the key to the house, and being in charge. Probably jealous of my shape too, but we are all fairly thin. Though if she keeps stealing Munisha's or others' food, she may just become what she fears.

"I have my own bedroom, a bed with a headboard, and my closet to the side. Then my looks," I say as I look into my full-body mirror. "Of course she is jealous, Ra, and that's okay."

As of the moment, my bed was calling my name. Physically and mentally drained from another day of torture.

"Will you teach me how to draw and paint like you, Ra?"

"Ha, once you're older, Munisha, you may be almost as good as me. I was born with this. So, as you can see, I don't even erase."

"So, how do you paint it? I have to erase even with a pencil."

"It's easy; once you see something in your brain, imagine it on paper or a wall. Then, with all your perspectives correct, you just trace over it. Gosh, it's windy."

"If you teach me, I can draw this angel just like you did."

"It's not all of that. Besides, Ra can't paint us. You know who she wants to paint? The tall guy who was waving at Mom. She wants to paint them kissing in a tree."

"Lakia, that's mean. You shouldn't say that. You might embarrass her. Are you okay, Razaiella? Your cheeks are red."

"Lakia is just a hater, and I don't care. I already know. Ha, she doesn't even know who I like."

"I don't? So why do you stare at him while he paints? You like to pretend, but everyone knows. But guess what, he doesn't. Wait, your eyes are weird."

"Nothing wrong with my eyes. Again, being jealous, that's why-"

"Lakia! What's that?"

"No way, not here."

"What's wrong, Munisha? You scared? It's nothing but a twister. Ra's worst nightmare."

"Come on, you two! Run! It's tearing up the train! Munisha, run!"

"Eyyygh, Lakia, someone help me!"

"Oh gosh, Lakia, help her! Tsk, I'm coming, Munisha! Hold on!"

"Oh, now you're trying to care?"

"What's wrong with you, Lakia? Hold on, Munisha! Eygh, my necklace!"

"Don't let it take me, Razaiella! Please, please help me! Eyyygh!"

"Ra, Razaiella. Wake up!"

It was all a dream…

"Are you okay? You kept saying something but couldn't under-stand," Munisha says, standing by my bed, questioning her look.

"Just a dream. Just hate when they feel so real."

"I don't have dreams—I do, but I don't remember. Lakia won't let me go outside. She wants to stay in her room, and that's boring."

"Gosh, what time is it? Crap! I slept for two hours!"

"Where are you going?!"

Getting up quickly, I felt for my feathered necklace on my chest. Nothing can harm me.

"I'm going out since I haven't when school started."

"Mom is going to get mad again."

I smirked. "I won't be gone for long. Just tell Lakia I went to the store or something. Just don't tell her I left. Let her find out."

I didn't even check to see if the group was even there. Something was just drawing me back to my mural and telling me to finish it.

"Oh wow, five missed calls from Nova. Then three from Lex."

So I guess they are there.

If I was able to do art for a career, that would be awesome. It sucks that it would be impossible from the get-go. AI, scammers, and hackers took that over some years back. Dad told me that his work was the only survivor in the art field. Artificial intelligence may have stolen digital art, but it cannot steal it from the hands of a true artist. His paintings, drawings, and, as he calls them, bas-relief figures are one-of-a-kind. I can do as much as painting, but no one can touch his skills, not even AI.

It's funny how Munisha never cared about my art—only in my dreams. Then of course that Lakia had to walk in and harass me. Then the big bully came for me again. Killing Lakia first with the stop sign pole going right through her body. Then the tornado pulled Munisha and me into it. Dad gave me the feathered pendant, but Mom told me it would ward off the bad spirits and the dark clouds with the tornadoes in my mind. It snapped it from my neck like it knew I relied on it. "What am I saying? It was just a dream."

However, the tornadoes seemed to know something I didn't.

"Look who decides to show up."

"Chill, Dante. I overslept. You don't have to watch and walk your siblings home. Then coming here by myself is enough. I see my craft is still in one piece."

"Ha," Nova sighs. "I think I saw someone looking at it the other day really hard. We're about finished. Well, Lex and Jordan finished theirs. Once we all get done, I'll submit this to the Grand Arts of New York. Ra, we need that five G's. I know your piece will help us to get the prize for sure."

"Tsk, I guess."

"What's up with you, Lex?" Nova asks, but I pay no attention and take out my spray cans.

"I just, um… don't think it's all that. They have dudes who do stuff all on trains, billboards. We just did it on a wall."

"Notice you said everything that they would be disqualified for," Nova replies. "We did the least thing as a mural. Hey, no negativity, girlie."

"It's not about being negative. We have to be realistic. That AKX gang has some of the best artists in Brooklyn. Tsk, I'm just saying."

Nova grins. "Negative Nancy here."

Listening to them go back and forth, I just decided to put my headphones on and finish my work. The Art Killa' Xeno clan was good, and many did know about them, but they lacked emotion and love in their styles. AKX only did gang-related works and even had nudity with their characters. People's minds are just sick, and that's why there's no respect for many things. Whenever I put my talent to paper or a wall, I always finish it with a feeling of being alive and giving a sense of love. My father always said to me while I watched him work on his craft, 'Whatever you do, do it with love.' If people just had more respect for things, the world would be a better place.

"Now that's beautiful. So wonderful, young lady."

"That voice," I said. "Oh wow… you."

I thought the train took him so far away that day. He must have followed me here.

"I see why you were in such a hurry. When the Creator created, He knew what He was doing. That skill and talent are marvellous."

"Umm, yeah, thanks," I said, looking as if this guy were my dad or someone close.

Him wearing that suit definitely made him look like he strolled through the wrong area. But again, his hair was so unique—the slicked-back, greasy hair, Greek god.

"All of you, such marvellous talents," the middle-aged man says, walking slowly with his hands behind his back, observing our works. "The angel one, truly—that my friend here just completed—is definitely my favorite. Actually reminds me of someone."

"Who are you, man? Dressed like you lost your way to the wedding?" Nova grins. "She left you that quick?"

The middle-aged man just smiled. "I just come here and there. What is the matter? Dressing nicely is a crime?"

"Not at all, just making sure you're good, bro."

"Right. Well, I must be on my way. For you, young lady," the middle-aged man says, then comes to my ear. "Remember what I told you. Never let anyone or anything change you. Never gain a black heart; it will make you decide to make reckless decisions. Never forget who you are."

I smiled. "I don't know what you're talking about."

"You were distracted, of course. If you choose wrong, my young lady, you will see. Farewell, you all. Oh yeah, you should have given her your eyes so she could see. Still a marvelous portrait. Gooday."

I stared at this man, whose name I never really got. I wanted to ask so bad, but of course, the weirdos behind me would act stupid. His energy was just so different.

"Hmmm, do y'all see what I see?" Lex giggles. "If you don't want him, Ra, I sure will take him. That's a money machine right there."

I rolled my eyes. "I don't want anyone's money. But do you guys think I should have colored her eyes like mine?"

"Naaa," Jordan replies. "I like it just the way it is. He told you that just because he likes yours."

"And that's just to show you how y'all females need to be so careful," Nova says. "Whispering in your ear. I'm surprised the fool got that close to you and you didn't make a move."

"Come on, Nova. If he got close to my lips, of course, but I didn't get that energy from him."

"Right. I'll defend you, Ra!" Dante says.

"Aww, my knight and shining armor."

I looked at my finished piece one more time as her wings spread over Nova's letters. Then, her arm hung over my name while she relaxed. It looked good. Whether you stood or walked, her eyes followed. "My guardian angel."

"Girl, you look like you're going to make out with her," Lexus smiles. "You packed up and still looking at her. It's pretty and dope. Don't worry, no one will mess with it."

Lexus felt like she had something to say to me from her energy. I didn't get why she was acting funny lately.

"Here, someone wanted me to give this to you."

The folded white paper looked like someone had it in many pockets and bags.

"I hope not from a crush in school. I'll just look at it once I get home."

"Aye, fam!" Nova shouted out. "Almost forgot to take those pics. You all got your black and orange bandanas?"

"Is it okay if we just have a black one?" I asked. "My mom was being weird and said it looked like a gang thing."

Dante grins. "Technically, it is."

"Sure, Ra. Let's hurry up and take these. I know Mom will be waiting for you to get home soon."

It's actually the time she should be getting off—six o'clock. I'll be walking home once she pulls up.

"Alright. Tripod is steady… ten-second countdown. We're going to do this with and without the masks, oh yeah, gas masks on, too, for one."

"Damn man," Jordan says. "Should have put on a tux-like buddy earlier."

"Let's do this," Nova says, running from the camera to the group.

Of course, Nova posed as if he had a rifle in his hands as we knelt in front of our mural masterpiece.

"Second one without a mask. Ten seconds… and everyone say, Grand Legacy!"

"Nova," I hissed, "you don't need the middle fingers."

"And that gives it more reason why I said we barely have a chance."

"Ra, you're cute and all, but we have to take it again. Those golden eyes of yours are out of place. Come on."

Hmph, then he should be doing something other than being so hostile at the camera.

"GRAND LEGACY!" the best art group in New York, Nova shouted.

"Let me see because I have to go, Nova," I said.

"It's dope. Now, one mor—oh shit!"

"Everyone! Stop where you are! Stop! This is the N-Y-C Police Department!"

The gang ran, and my subconscious made me do the exact thing as the siren popped out of nowhere.

"Who are they looking for, Ra?!" Lex asks as we run through the alleyways.

"I have no clue, but they came out of nowhere!"

Trying to find a place to hide, but those sirens and footsteps of the cops sounded so close. Nova, Dante, and Jordan left us all alone. I just couldn't believe it.

"Ra, up there!"

We looked up as though heaven placed a ladder of hope for us. Except it was a bit hard to reach.

"Ra, help me up. Girl, come on!"

"Chill out; I don't do this every day. Alright, I'm ready."

"Eygh! Shit!"

"You got it, Lex! Just pull yourself up! Hurry!"

"I… I got it!"

"Great! Now unlatch it for me!"

"Hey, you two! Stop!"

"Oh, come on, Lex! He's coming—he's coming!"

"Ra, I can't… get it down. Run! Girl, run!"

My heart raced. "Lex?! Hey, don't leave me!"

Either I kept running, or I would be taken in for doing my precious art. The voice came to me: decisions. Continuing to run for my life and knowing that I was all alone.

"Oh no."

The alleyway would eventually have a dead end. I sighed, "Well, I tried."

Hearing those footsteps getting closer, and my heart beating faster. I knew this was it.

"Ra!"

"Nova?"

His face didn't even look worried, like he knew exactly where to find me.

"What, you just standing there? Alright," Nova says, standing by the wall and bending down with his hands between his stomach. "Run up to me, and I'll throw you over. Hurry it up, or we both might be getting locked up."

I definitely was not into gymnastics, but I was going to learn today. "Eygh!"

"Come on, girl, push! Push yourself up! You can do it!"

Gee, I swear that took it all out of me after getting up from the other side. "Nova?"

"Get out of here!"

"What about you?" I asked as I looked up to the tall wall.

"I'll catch up!"

"Hey, stop right there!"

After hearing that, I returned to my track and field, onto the train, and then to home base. I just hoped and prayed everyone made it. Nova saved me. Then, the greased-back hair Greek god would not leave my mind as I ran through the dead streets of the city.

CHAPTER 3

Explicit Harmony

Night falls, looking down on me, but my guardian angel is watching my back. I couldn't understand how a day could go so fast and then turn bad so quickly. "Weird, Mom isn't home yet."

Music was playing, and the only person I knew who could play a melody so intricately beautiful was him.

"Ra, you've gotten here so late. Mom said he has to go."

Listening to Lakia only made my heart rise with anger just by hearing her. Then speak about my own father that way. "Dad?"

"Shoosh-shoosh. Can you hear it speaking?"

Dad's fingers ran across the piano. It was just something so magical and not of this world. The music that could hypnotize your soul with its intricate melodies of pure art. "Um, when did you get here?"

Dad just kept playing and playing, even with his eyes closed. How was he so good at everything? "Hey…"

Hugging dad from behind as he continued to play. He loved his favorite cologne and always wore it for Mom.

"Dad, Mom. She's—"

"Where is she?"

"On her way," I replied. "Dad, can you show me this one day? I want to be good just like you."

Dad just smiled. He wasn't going to show me anything—I just knew it, since he had many things I just couldn't figure out, and his lips stayed zipped about.

"Where is your necklace?" Dad whispered as he continued to play.

"Oh no, tsk." My hand felt for it, but my neck was naked. "Dad, Dad, can you stop playing? I want to talk to you."

"Just like her, trying to tell me what to do, how to think, how to feel. But I feel… she should be near."

"Ra, Mom said—"

"I heard you the first time, Lakia. She is already going to be pissed that I got back late. You're going to snitch, I know it."

"Young girls, this melody that I cannot stop playing. This is called *Lacrimosa*. The harmony that can steal your dreams."

Lakia looked to me. "What the heck is he talking about?"

"Here… we… go," Dad whispered as the soft melody traveled around us.

"What in the ancestors' name? I called your phone multiple times, Rafael! Get out of my house!"

Dad continued to smile while he still played *Lacrimosa*. As his right hand played the high notes, I could feel the emotion coming straight from it.

"Rafael! I will not tell you again. Get out of my house. Next will be the police getting involved!"

"Mom, you don't have to yell. Why do you even have to call the police? What did he even do to you?!" I then shouted, standing near my father.

"Rafael, last warning! Get yourself and your bad energy out of my house and away from my children!"

"Mom, why are you yelling?" Munisha says, rubbing her eyes, which looked to be from a long nap.

"JUST GET OUT!"

Finally, the music stopped singing, leaving nothing but silence in the air. "Dad?"

A kiss on my forehead and his smile told me his energy was just fine. Why did Mom hate him so?

"Next time you come uninvited, the authorities will be waiting for you! You hear me, Rafael? This is totally unacceptable!"

Dad walked away like that. Something odd, but it felt like he was in a trance. Not even eye contact back to us, only to get in his truck, which I didn't even notice parked across the street. His body language after he left looked as if he was just not there. Almost like a robot who just got fussed out by a lady and showed no emotion.

"Did you tell him I was on my way, Lakia?"

"I told him, but he just kept playing the piano. I don't even know how he got in. I thought it was Razaiella."

"So, you didn't lock the door when you left, Ra? Oh yes, I know you went out."

I just looked at Lakia, then rolled my eyes at her betrayal. The worst part is that she wanted me to call her a true sister.

"Ra, you always be sure to lock the door before you leave or come in. This could have been so much worse. Praise be to the ancestors."

"Mom, this is my dad you're talking about. He's going to be dangerous toward me? How can you say something like that?"

"I always ask for the ancestors to guide you, daughter. I know who he is, and I need you to understand me. Right now, I am trying my best to be as calm as possible. I am tired, long day from work, and I need to make dinner before it hits eight. Now, cool off, and we shall speak soon."

Whatever Mom had to really say to me, it was nothing I really wanted to hear for the night, so I just stayed quiet. How can people be so judgmental, but then they have two faces that turn almost every time? He's my dad, and no one can tell me he is a bad person. No one is perfect, especially her. I felt I would see him again very soon.

Knock-Knock

"Lakia, can you see who that is? I have to get Munisha's lunch packed. Better yet, wait!"

"I could have gotten it, Mom."

"No-no. Finish up your breakfast so you won't be late. I don't want any issues like the last—Oh! Jonathooon! How are you?"

How can this be happening, and why was this happening to me, I thought.

"Daddy!" Munisha shouts out, then dashes from the table.

I couldn't even eat, as I lost my appetite to hypocrites. If only my dad were here. None of this would have been going on.

"Morning, Razaiella."

"Jonathon is speaking to you, Ra."

I shook my head. "I put up my hand. I said hello."

"Words are stronger, daughter. I need to hear you next time."

"Tsk, yeah, whatever," I mumbled.

If she truly knew how I was feeling, she would know that saying hello to someone who took my father's place was not worth the energy. How dare she not care?

Looking in the mirror, I see her face and my father's. I know who I am and who I belong to. Lakia and Munisha can have their father enter, but mine cannot. "What a life."

"Now, you all be safe going out. I'll be out in thirty minutes myself."

"Will Daddy be back when we come home, Mom?" Munisha asks, as I was the first to leave the house.

"Possibly! Remember, we love you all! I love you, Razaiella! Wait for your sisters!"

All I needed was for my day to go bad, then come to that person my mother wanted me to call a stepfather. Dad changed his number, which I should have asked for last night. So many things just going on in my head.

"So you mean to tell me, she told your father to get out? Damn, in your face too?"

"Yeah, and she seems like I am supposed to agree with it, like I have no heart or soul. I don't get a lot of things in life, Sarabi. I just need to… ha, run away someday."

"Don't do that," Dante says, but Sarabi, my new friend in school, couldn't agree more. "It'll be all right, so I wouldn't stress it. We have that crazy math test on Friday, and they already have us slaving with homework. Pushing us so hard to fail with these exams back-to-back."

"Then it's still the beginning of the year. This school is hectic," Sarabi grins.

If I were to pass it, I would pass it, I thought. Most of what they taught was not really important anyways.

"Ra, it's going to be all right. You're not even eating your lunch."

I shrugged. "Tsk, I don't even want this. I ate the bread roll and some cold mixed vegetables. All of it honestly tastes like it came out of a can."

Dante grins. "Technically, it did. You just have to imagine it didn't, then it will taste better."

"At my old school—well, it was a private school—we had cooked food. Not… this stuff."

"Why did your parents bring you here?" I asked.

"It just got too expensive for private schools. So I just have to deal with it. But it's not so bad."

I grinned. "Once you stay for a while, you will begin to see it. But just like you said, Dante: imagine what it would be of your liking, and you'll be okay. Some time ago… Mom told me the world was just so different. It just got bad really fast when people lost their minds. Then she started bad-mouthing my dad, saying he changed after I was born. Hmph, maybe it was me."

"Razaiella, you need to relax. Like Dante said."

"Yeah, we don't know what you're going through, but what it looks like is your ol' lady seems to be just overprotective."

"You have no brothers, right?" Sarabi asks.

"Nope, only sisters, and they are half-blood. Same mom, different dad."

Sarabi sighs. "Harsh."

"What? It's the truth. I'm pretty much the only child on my father's side. Because that's how it works, right? The heir comes from the father, not the mother, right?"

"I… believe," Dante replies. "I will tell you this again: you're going to be all right. Right, Sarabi? Just be cool."

I nodded with a smile. Dante was very nice. I sometimes thought he was like that because he wanted to be with me, but I see him as a genuine gentleman and a brother. So, unfortunately, we could never go as far.

"Changing the subject, Nova was arrested yesterday. Yeah, they got 'em. Aren't you shocked or sad?"

I wasn't smiling, but with so many things going on, I totally forgot he saved me.

"Nova, he, um… he helped me over a wall, and that's when they got him. I guess that's how it happened. Tsk, damn, I'm so sorry."

"Oh no, you're good, Ra. He'll be out soon. I thought Lex would have messaged or you all would have called each other to gossip."

"Lexus? She's the one who left me, and I had to run for my life. Then Nova had to help me, and he got in trouble."

Dante nodded. "I know, it's messed up. He's my brother and all, but it's no one's fault. Nova does stupid stuff sometimes. It wasn't even us doing graffiti art. It was for some gang here they thought was us. New York is big. They were only asking if we knew about them, and we got spooked."

"Werd," Sarabi says. "So, what he get arrested for?"

For helping me, and I could not help but hear it next.

"He had his gun on him, and that's why he got burnt. And there goes the back-to-slavery-again bell."

"I'm glad he's going to be out soon, but I'm still mad that good people always are taken advantage of. Lexus hasn't texted or called, and that was odd of her. Well, see you, Sarabi and Dante."

"Dale, oh, yeah, Ra!"

"Hurry up, Dante, we'll be late for fifth period. Take care, Razaiella."

I could feel Dante was going to ask me something strange, even though he looked at the floor, then to the ceiling, then finally to me.

"Have... um... anyone asked... prom."

"Come on, man," I grinned. "You're going to make me really late. I have to go the other way."

"Tsk, dammit, my bad. Um, anyone asked... you to the prom?"

I smirked, shaking my head. "Not yet; it wasn't even on my mind. It's so far away. Unless you're talking about the fall dance."

"That is what I meant, yeah. Fall dance."

"Hm, that is not really my thing, you know that."

"Well, once you agree on going, remember your boy is first in line."

I wanted to say okay, but honestly, dancing is not my style. My hands do the dancing on paper. "I'll be thinking about it. Now, let's get to class. We have... one minute left!"

Dante was the only guy I spoke to in school, mainly as a real friend. The others just looked and stared at me like a piece of meat. In this school, everybody lost their virginity—but not me. I don't think like how these lost souls do. Right now, I wanted to break up that crap with Mom and that going-bald Jonathon. The thing was, I would be wrong. I don't want someone to destroy my marriage in the future. I was not an evil person, but evil people and things seemed to gravitate towards me. Speaking of this dance with Dante, I think I should go, just to see Mom's reaction. She was always overprotective, but I will be out of school soon. I need her to see how I will start to make decisions on my own.

"See you later, Ra! And don't forget, everything will be okay!" Dante shouted out, throwing up the peace sign.

"Be sure to tell Sarabi I won't come tomorrow! I need to get that girl's number!"

"Aye, aren't you going to wait for your sisters?!"

"They know their way!" I smiled, looking back as I walked from the school.

I guess he thought I was the keeper. I don't feel like being around anyone as of now. Just go home and meditate on my craft. Then, should I really go with Dante? He is not all of what I see in the future. I know what he wants, but I don't want to hurt his cute little heart. Lexus would be better for him, but I don't know if our school would allow others to join. "She gave me that note—I totally forgot."

From everything, I just couldn't understand why her energy was awkward to me. We have known each other for years. It just doesn't make any sense. "Oh, here it is. *Just so you know. I see you, and I really really reeeally wish you were mine. Your eyes; they shine with fire and burn with beauty. From your secret admirer.*"

So, I already know who this was from. "Maybe he will just get what he truly desires."

If he were here walking with me, maybe we could have talked more. I prefer in-person to the phone. It's more romantic—the poor people of New York. No future, no hope, and dreams gone. A man who looks like he was just tired of it all. Lifting his arms and fighting the air with his eyes closed. His friends, sitting there and out of it, too. "Why does he keep looking at me? Oh gosh, what does he want?"

These eyes of mine—once they receive contact with someone else's, it's like they are just drawn in. That entire group was addicts. "Is he still looking at me? Thank God!" I sighed.

"He's gone. Too many weirdos in this city. Just the person I needed to talk to at a time like this. Hello, Lex? What's going on? Yeah, I heard he got locked up, but he should be out soon. Yeah, it sucks, but next time, if that happens again, put the lever down on the ladder. I would have been locked up, too, if it weren't for Nova helping me. Yeah, it's okay. Oh yeah, I read the note. Who was it from, exactly? Tsk, come on, you can tell me as if I don't have an idea. Really? I didn't see or hear from him today. Dante was with me during lunch, but was a no-show. I hope he's okay. Damn, yeah… um. Lex, someone's following me, and it's kind of creeping me out. I'll call you back."

Why is he still here? I could have sworn I saw him make a turn on another street. Someone in this restaurant should be able to help.

"Hi. How can we help-"

"Hey, um," I said, looking behind me and through the glass door. "I think…there's some guy following me. I…I don't see him now, but I was being followed."

"Oh, really?" the hostess said, looking behind me. "Have a seat somewhere, and I'll get someone who can help. Do you have your parents' number? Please call and let them know what's going on and where you are. Everything is going to be okay."

It sure was cold in the mini-Italian food place. Dad told me long ago, when we hung out almost every day, that upgraded restaurants must have it very cool since the robots that take orders won't overheat. They are cheaply made, though, compared to the ones in significant, fancy places. "Tsk, I can't call Mom because she will flip if I tell her I'm not with Lakia and Munisha."

My contacts are so small. I know who. "Please, please… please pick up, Dad."

I don't know why his phone doesn't work. It's not his number that changed; he just didn't care to pay the bill. "Gosh, this could be bad."

Then Lakia doesn't have a phone either. Makes no sense to see families walk by, some with children. All I could do was smile back, knowing everything wasn't really all right. I wish Mom and Dad would just come back together, but she hates him with every fiber in her body. Family is so important, and it hurts to see when your own blood doesn't want to see it that way.

"Hey there, are you all right?" a mixed Dominican-looking woman said, then sat down in front of me.

She wore a black hoodie and blue jeans. The first thing that stood out to me was her necklace with that unique pendant. Her hair was super long, almost like mine, but probably longer. "Yeah. I'm okay. I was just being followed."

"I see. You're a beautiful young woman; you shouldn't be walking these streets alone, you know?"

"I guess… I guess you're right."

Her voice even sounded like someone not really from here. Similar to a British accent. Definitely wasn't a Yankee. "And your eyes. They're just like mine, almost, but a true golden color. I had to really get a good look at them. Wow."

Destiny looked down and smirked, and then those hypnotizing golden eyes looked back up at me. "Your parents are on the way, I'm assuming? You have to be so careful, sister. This atmosphere can be dangerous for those who do not understand."

"Yeah, they're on the way. My mom and dad are coming. What's your name?"

The woman smiled. "Destiny. What's yours?"

"Ra. Razaiella. I know it's not really common, but I love yours."

Destiny smirked. "It's beautiful just the way it is. Just be sure you know where you're going and not to get into any trouble. Something told me I had no choice but to warn you."

"About what? The guy? I'm safe here, for now."

Destiny nodded. "Be sure to keep your friends close and your enemies closer. I have to go now, sister. Take care of yourself and wait for your father."

"Wait."

Destiny was so fast getting up, like she had thought about, and was late for her date. "Where did you get that necklace?!"

"My father gifted it to me. Believe it or not, it's more than a thousand years old. Take care, Razaiella."

She was in a rush, but very nice to check up on me. Why did she leave the restaurant? Guess I just have a special bond with people—or the food here was just trash. "My phone… oh, thank God. Tsk, it's her. Sarabi? He gave you my number? I'm at a restaurant. No, just here. Ha, I don't have a clue about that stupid math homework. No, I don't think so. Maybe when I get home. Did you see Lakia and Munisha when you left? Oh, okay. No-no, just checking. But yeah, I will see you tomorrow. I just came here to think a little, but I'll be here for another fifteen minutes. Yeah-yeah. Okay, Sarabi, I have to pee. Ha, see you."

I just hope they got home safe, or I'll be hearing from Mom forever. They're old enough. Just like I was old enough to go out and do art on my own, they should too. Mom can't be with us forever. "Gee." I frowned. "This restroom stinks."

One thing I will take from Mom—New York has become a filth hole. Nothing was sanitary about this place. As soon as I get enough money and live on my own, I'm moving to Miami. "Tsk, even the mirror looks like someone thought it was a coloring book."

"Hey."

"Wha-what? What are you doing in here? This is the ladies' restroom."

"I just wanted to tell you something," the junky-dressed man said calmly.

He looked to be definitely off the streets, and I knew I smelled rotten cabbage. "What do you want? Help?! Hel—!"

"If you scream again, I'll gut you like a fish," the deranged man said, pointing his pocketknife at me. "Now, me and you are going to get out of here—together. Come here. I said come here! I promise I won't hurt you."

"What are you going to do to me? My dad is coming soon, so whatever you're trying to do, it won't work."

"Shut up. Since he's on his way, we don't have much time, do we? But for now, I will take his place. Let's go."

The smelly man put the blade between his fingers. I knew if I were to say something, he would just slice me up. He had nothing to lose—I did.

"Don't squeal; it's all in your head for now. Be a good girl for me. Keep it moving toward the exit, baby bird. Remember, I have my blade with me, so no foolery."

All the families eating and having a great time. No one even looked up—except a toddler, who seemed to feel that I was in trouble. Once we get outside, maybe I could make a run for it.

"Hey, is everything okay?" the hostess asked.

"Yeah, my daughter is frightened. I don't know who could have been out here."

"Sir, I did not see you come in. Young lady—"

The blade poked my back slightly. "No, he came. It's okay."

The smelly man grinned. "You see, now. Let me catch that asshole who was harassing my daughter. He will wish he had never been born. Come on, baby bird. She'll be fine."

What should I have done? If I had yelled, he would have stabbed me. I could sense he definitely was not playing.

"We're going this way, baby bird."

"Please, just let me go," I said as the man pulled my hand. "My father is coming. Please, just let me go."

"I promise you, keep—no-no-no. Don't even try to pull away, baby bird. You're mine until after I get what I want. Down this way."

The dark alleyway, along with the dampness, made it feel like a horror movie. People were looking, but this guy was almost my height, so he looked like a friend or relative. I didn't think I could overpower him, but maybe someone would come and help.

"All right, right behind here. Get your ass over here! Don't mess around with me, baby bird. I mess around with you."

"Okay-okay. Will you let me go? What do you want?"

The man laughed in a crazy, awkward way. "Everything. Take off your pants."

My heart jumped. "What?"

"Do it!"

He kept looking over the dumpster, which had an odor that could have been the one from the home he had returned to—that knife—looking right at me. I was petrified, only to have a single tear fall from both of my eyes.

"Okay, if you don't do it," the man says, waving his knife back and forth, smiling at me, "I will just have to cut them from you. Would you like that?"

"Please, sir—"

"Please don't make me have to do it myself. I'm being more than generous—all righty. Here I come. Your eyes…"

The smelly man getting closer to me left me no hope but to close my eyes and wake up. I didn't deserve this. I'm not a bad person.

"Please, just let me go, man. I'm only fourteen. I'll be fifteen in two weeks."

"Oh shit, really? Even better! Consider this an early birthday present. Gee, you have bosom for a kid. Fifteen, you say?"

"Just let me go—mhmm."

"No-no-no, baby bird. Now, we're going to do this the right way. Pull those pants and panties down for me, or my blade will do it for us both."

I just wanted this to be over with. Maybe I could get away once he's off guard. I'm not weak.

"Now, panties. No one else is looking. Come on, don't be bashful. My patience is growing thinner by the second, baby bird. Oh, you're mad? Those eyes—they're even more radiant when they're watered up. I'm a lucky—AGH—AGH!"

A man came from nowhere, like he was from another dimension, tackling the failed rapist. I was just happy to get my clothes back on.

"Shit—all right—all right. What's up, man? I was, I was just… come on, man. Don't kill me."

That face—a face I will never forget—my guardian angel.

"Dad?"

His eyes were not even giving me contact, just holding the rapist against the wall with his own blade to his throat. "How… how did you?"

"So… you like to play with little girls… do you?" Dad's soft voice said.

"No-no, man. I was just checking to see if she was all right, that's all. I'm sorry, man. Don't kill me. The knife… it's going through my freaking neck! Help—"

"Shoosh, shoosh. A man like you is not fit for any woman," Dad says, with a continuous smile, as if he enjoyed it. "You see, I have my ways also. People like you are sooo dangerous to nature. People who take advantage of those who are unable to protect themselves. It's a shame someone like you even has the ability to roam the world, disrespecting and disgracing us, true men who value and respect nature. You, sir, are nothing more than a leech to mankind. What's your name?"

"My—my name? It's Chris."

"Chris. Chris, what?"

My father must have been going to get his phone number next.

"Smith. Chris Smith. You can ease off the—agh! The blade, man. I wasn't going to hurt anyone. I swear to you, man, it was like I was in a trance. I don't know how I even got with the girl. Let me go, man. I'm sorry, all right?"

Dad continued to smirk eye to eye with Chris and then shook his head. "You must know how nature works. Eye for an eye, as they say. I know you, and I know your family."

Chris and I both looked at my father with oddness.

"Smith, some things are worse than death. You do believe in the nature of karma, do you not?"

"Yeah, man, and that's cool. Just get the blade off of me, and I'm outta here! I'm sorry, alright!"

"Smith… Smith… Smith… you are a man who takes advantage of nature. Those who do this get what they deserve. Some things are worse than death."

"You fucking weirdo! Let me go! HEELP! AGH—AGHHH!" Chris yells, falling to the ground and rubbing his eyes.

"I can't see! I can't see!"

Having no clue what just happened, I just stared at the man yelling. Finally, Dad glanced at me, then walked away. He should have let me go while he had the chance. "Dad, wait! I'm coming!"

CHAPTER 4

A Nightmare Within

In life, there are many things that are just unexplainable. Circumstances we will never have answers to. All we have is our hope to never live in misery, seeing as the people of the city always seem so mellow. Some rich and some poor. Then, seeing Dad. He wouldn't even make eye contact with me, no matter what I asked or where he came from. He just seemed not to care about my questions. His old truck was the only thing he seemed to care about when it came to dodging potholes on the raggedy roads. All I wish is that he and Mom can fix things and live together again.

"You know… she will be my wife, this life and the next."

"Why won't you just talk to her?" I shook my head and asked.

"Do you not see I made numerous attempts, Ra? Her heart betrays her thoughts. Her vision is clouded with lies, and her beliefs tamper with her reality." Dad smiled. "Our bond will never end as we are a one blood family. Everyone wants to be something they are not in this world, but you, Razaiella. You are my heir, and Isabella is my sweet soulmate. My love will always be with her, and it pains me deeply that she cannot understand that. She has forgotten her place in my heart and mine in hers. Forgotten love is the number one road to sorrow in this world. Our love, our trinity, is foul and forbidden for separation. Never forget who you are, Ra. Never forget."

"I get you," I responded, placing my head near the door as the wind caught my hair.

Throughout the entire ride, he just didn't seem to realize Mom hates him. I wish I could tell him, but I thought it would just make things worse.

"Feeling sleepy?"

I smiled and nodded. "A little. The breeze feels so good."

"Rest, Ra, you will be home, and I promise you, our hearts shall be united very soon. Trust me."

No matter what Mom says about Dad, he is still that same loving man. I just think he is a very different type of guy, like the man who wanted me to place my eyes on the angel. Everyone is different, and I know I am unique in my own way.

The cool breeze definitely didn't help my drowsiness. Dad's A/C didn't work, but who cared? Nature always provides the best.

"How was your nap, child? We're home."

"Home, already? I thought we were going somewhere else. Oh no… tsk," I said, placing my eyes back from the open window. "I'm in trouble."

"Don't fear anything, Razaiella. Only the ones who can take advantage and steal your soul."

Looking at Dad, as he just kept his hands on the steering wheel, looking forward. All I could do was smile. "Thanks for everything, Dad. Wait. So, you're not going to tell me what happened? How did you know where I was? What happened to that guy?"

Dad smirked. "I have my ways. With that fool… let's just say justice was served."

"But he yelled he couldn't see."

Dad grinned, then shook his head and looked out my side of the window. "Look at my gorgeous wife. Your mother awaits you. Go to her, and we shall meet again soon."

"Promise?"

Always, Ra. Always and forever.

Hugging Dad, he just felt so warm and his energy was on another level. Nobody can ever take his place. Not even bald man Jonathon. "Love you, Dad. Bye, and thanks again."

"Don't tell Mom."

I grinned. "Of course not."

Mom, standing on the building porch with her arms folded, only told me that she didn't care what was going on, only that I was with my father instead of my half-blooded sisters.

"When will you learn, Razaiella? When it's too late?"

"Hi to you, too."

"There is nothing to smile about, daughter. Once life gets to you, that is when you will wish your ancestors could make you smile again."

Rolling my eyes and seeing that snitch Lakia looking so lost made me feel like I wasn't really home with everyone. If Mom had known about her earlier today, she would be on her knees thanking Dad, not always past dead people whom she thanks and praises.

Dinner with all of the women and no man here to protect us. I wonder if Mom ever thought of that. She just didn't want to understand.

"If you ever leave your sisters to walk home like that again, Ra, know that there will be severe consequences."

I nodded. "Uh-huh."

"I kindly ask you to walk your sister's home. So, you all can be home together. But you left them on the dangerous streets of the city. Then I wait and see—don't call—wait patiently to see if that man has taken you. My spirit told me so, and it was correct."

"Mom… isn't your food getting cold?"

Mom drops her silverware. "Who the hell do you think you're talking to? You see? That man—damn that man. He's already affecting you."

"Mom, you don't know what you're talking about, okay? He will be my Dad, this life and the next."

"Surely he will," Mom nods. "But he will be behind bars if he ever comes near the school again. So, that is that."

That is when I dropped my fork in shock and collected my thoughts. "You know what? Goodnight, you all."

"Goodnight," Munisha says, her eyes seeming so frightened and innocent.

"One more thing, Razaiella. Turn and look at me. If I catch you in his dirty, mismatching colored truck again, with your hair falling from the side door like Rapunzel's—the police will be on a chase. Believe it."

She thought she could scare me. She can't steal my soul. "That's it? Can I go to my room now?"

Lakia just continued to eat as if she heard nothing. Then Mom, with all of these threats. Maybe one day Jonathon will just leave her, and then her mind will change. My father is just so evil. One day, she will see things differently.

"Tsk, I can't sleep."

"Huh? Ra?"

"Go back to sleep, Lakia. I didn't mean to wake you."

"Why can't you sleep?"

"Not really sure, just can't. Something is keeping me awake. I just feel like I have… too much energy to sleep. I don't know what it is. I just feel. There…"

"There what?" Lakia asks.

"I have to pee. Then it could be this stupid night light."

Tonight just doesn't feel right. It's eleven thirty-three, and I should be knocked out. Then it's so cold in the hallway. Mom must have made it like this, but it's not even hot outside. The darkness of our home was on both sides, but the bathroom lights lit half the living room. It's just too dark, cold, and quiet. Seeing Mom and Dad in the mirror as they both reflected on who I am. A mix of uniqueness from both sides. Dad's uniqueness is unexplainable, and it is only evident in me that I have a unique nature.

Going back into the dark hallways, I can feel the energy—the same energy coming from my dream. That's what it was—the attic. I knew it was something my dream told me. If Mom catches me up here, she's going to be pissed. She told me never to come up here, but there have to be answers somewhere.

The falling dust came from the ceiling as I pulled the string to let down the ladder. Guessing no one has been up here for years. "Now, where's the light?"

Finding another string and reaching for it in true darkness suggested that answers were definitely within reach. "Hack, hack. It's so dusty up here."

The attic definitely wasn't big, but the smell of old materials everywhere filled my nose the second I came up. "Nothing really here but old books and smelly old clothes. Hmph, some dream. I… wait a minute," I said as I got on my knees quietly to move the old dusty books side to side from each other.

"I knew it was here. Mom put our photo album up here. Tsk, what is wrong with her? No photos? Weird."

I knew this was a waste of time. When I laid my head on Dad's truck, the breeze must have whispered nonsense into my mind. "Hmph, wonder what this is."

Pulling the long blanket from the old dusty wall, I saw something I had not seen in years. "Dad's sculpture."

His bas-relief was a beautiful work of art. This one, if I recall correctly, was called the Mystical Angel, which he completed when I was five years old. I begged him one day to teach me how to create these intricate designs. "So, Mom hid it up here, too."

I don't know how Dad did these, but not one mistake on the woman's face. Her eyes, lips, and hair were perfection. The artwork gave me a feeling that I knew who this woman was. Or not, she was too perfect. "Maybe one day I would be just as good. Put this back over you."

Seeing how Mom has Dad's stuff up here tells me she still loves him. That sculpture could be her, but it was so dark that I couldn't see her eyes as well as they looked at the heavens.

"I know Dad has something up here for me to keep. I should have brought my phone to show the gang how good he was. Where all my talent came from. These dusty books. This one has an upside-down star on it. Oh… wow."

From everything in this dark and cold place, I have found the only true thing to keep in my heart, and once again, Mom hid it from me in books. I must have been eight months old, with my dad holding me and kissing my cheek while I smiled at the camera.

"A photo so precious," I said, as I began to look up to the dark ceiling and hold the tears from raining on it.

"Eygh! Lakia? Mom?"

The sound of something falling near the ladder made me jump, but I was still able to hold my mouth from screaming. "Tsk, no one's up here."

"Just us."

"Who said that? Who's there?"

The darkness of the attic, with the light going only so far. Something whispered, coming from the walls. The only place to go was down. "Something… something isn't right," I said, as I looked at the blanket on the floor.

The Mystical Woman didn't have horns. "What's going on?"

The woman's eyes removed themselves from the heavens and looked down at me. Then, blinking with a smirk. My heart, mind, and soul ran as fast as they could back down the dusty ladder. I couldn't believe what happened. What did I just see? Was this all a dream?

"Hey, Ra? Are you okay? Why did it take you so long?"

Tears rolled down the side of my face onto the pillow as I covered my head. "I don't know what to believe anymore."

"What? What did you say?"

I needed to leave the night in silence, and I wanted Lakia to be quiet, as she would never understand anyway. Once the sun rises, I wonder if Mom would have ever told me those things are up there. It's so hard to believe anyone nowadays.

"Good morning, Razaiella. Looks like Munisha beat you to the table."

"Morning, Razaiella," Lakia and Munisha said as I sat down.

"Hey."

"They said good morning, Razaiella."

I shrugged. "Okay… I said hey."

"No one is causing any harm to you, daughter. Why must you be so nasty early in the morning? Why?"

How can I answer someone who hides things? Then tell me someone I love is evil?

"Since you want to be quiet this morning and be rude, I'm afraid on a beautiful day such as today, you won't be going out to your troublesome friends with that foolish graffiti."

"You don't like or trust anyone, do you? Then it seems you're trying to find things wrong with everyone but the people close to you. Well, some."

Mom smiled and shook her head. "No, no, daughter."

The sun's rays shined from behind her as if she were so perfect. It was a lie.

"I have a judgment on what I care to have on individuals. To not harm but protect you. It's a mother's duty."

As she lectures, I'll just eat my two eggs with bacon and find a way out of here.

"Mom, Ra is just upset," Lakia says, surprising me. "How about we go with her to watch her paint?"

Mom chuckled. "Absolutely not. She's already on thin ice, and if she keeps this up, her little gang might just have to miss her for a month, maybe two."

"Thanks for the breakfast," I said, getting up with all eyes on me.

Now she thinks I'm in a gang. It's more like my Dad is sane, and she's insane. How can she think everyone is dangerous? Everyone except her.

Knock-knock.

"I just came out of the shower! Lakia, hold on! I said hold on!"

"Hello there."

"Oh no," I mumbled.

"Just a little of your time, daughter. I promise it won't be too long. Just a second to have a little chat," Mom says as she sits on the bed.

Here come more lies and bashing. "So, what did I do now? Can you at least wait till I get dressed?"

"Come, sit. You're my daughter—nothing to hide. The towel is fine."

Luckily, I blow-dried my hair before coming out, or she would be trying to make me catch a cold.

"So, daughter. My spirit tells me you have learned more than you've been expecting. Tell me… what is it?"

"Mom, to be honest… I don't know. I just don't really feel like there are certain people I can trust anymore."

"Oh… is that so? Is this because of how I treat your father? Or is it my protection for you?"

I frowned. "Protection? Mom, you can't protect me from everything. You know Dad… tsk. Never mind."

"No," Mom hissed. "Tell me, Ra. What did he do?"

"He did nothing. Only told me he still loves you."

"Hmm, love." Mom nodded, turned her head, and looked at me.

"What else did he tell you?"

"He told me enough. He told me how basically it's you who left him. You're making him crazy!"

"Calm down, daughter. No one is doing that but himself. You want to know something? Something you should know about life? The forces of it?"

Mom smiled, but I could see the tears forming in her eyes.

"There are things that are in our world. Things we will never understand. Situations roam the atmosphere to seek and destroy good people. I know many who have been destroyed by dark nature. So many things to destroy us, to make our lives miserable."

I grinned. "So… what are you saying? Dad's miserable?"

"Listen to me carefully, daughter. Be aware that there are opposing forces in the world. Love and hatred, happiness and sadness, confidence and fear. You make the choices to live your best life. That is why we, as women—we are the most precious in Mother Nature's eyes. The demons out there, I believe, we have a scent they most desire, with our thoughts and emotions. That is why we must control them, or they will control us. As a mother, I believe you are special. I know you are. So, these demons more than likely will try to come after you."

"Mom—"

"Daughter, just listen," Mom insisted. "You are your own master in this world. Now, that is what your father taught me long ago. You must know what you truly want in life. Your father—he knew, but for some odd reason, forgot. He changed."

From her saying the word *changed*, I could see and feel it. "So he's a bad person?"

"Not that, daughter, but I will say this. Please understand me. Searching for certain spirits may lead you to seeing them, and soon, you cannot stop seeing them. Bear with me. There are things about Rafael I did not understand. I do know this, these forces never appear as they… seem. On the outside, they seem so pure, so innocent, but on the inside, they hide, and they are most hideous. Once they show their true selves, they are the most hideous things you will ever see."

My anger grew, and I felt my eye twitch. "What the hell does that have to do with, Dad?!"

"His heart has become heartless, daughter. Due to trauma and heartbreak, he uses his mind more than his heart, but in my opinion, you need both to go through life. From that, again, there are demons who want to lurk and destroy all of us. The ancestors' guidance can only do so much. These dark energies, these demons, will get so close to you that you can feel them. The worst is if they breathe on you. Just like an illness, you can catch what they have. These demons are real, daughter. They roam these streets, and I know you've seen them. Here."

Mom pulled out her phone and scrolled fast through her pictures. I just didn't understand why she was getting so emotional.

"Remember this?"

"I sure do. My baby picture with him holding me. How can I forget that? Looks like I've seen it recently."

"Good, so remember. If you recall, his spirit was never as it is now. Now, look at his actions, daughter. His thoughts, emotions. Search your natural instincts, daughter. You know what I am saying is true."

"You… you just say that because you know he's different."

"Ra, he is different," Mom said, making a serious face.

"I… I honestly think… It's because you left him. Anyone would be mad. Why would he be happy?"

"I left him because he is not who he used to be. He used to be a beautiful, creative man. I loved your father, but things changed. Please, understand this if you don't understand anything else."

Mom wiped the tears that started to flow. It made me want to be strong for him.

"Well… is he your husband still? Legally?"

Mom smiled, looking to the floor.

"Yes. That is why Jonathon, and I could never… doesn't matter. Listen to me, daughter, Razaiella. These dark forces that go around— you must always be careful. I don't want to lose you. I see you in him. He still lives in you."

"Lives in me?"

"Just know, daughter. Your dreams—the ones you always talk about—they will speak more of the truth through the ancestors better than I can. Someday. You just have to listen to your heart and listen well. They reveal more than your senses. In the past, as a girl, we said *rez* culture. We understood many things because our past ancestors would tell us beautiful stories of our bloodline reserves. However, many have lost their way because they lost their way of the beauty and culture due to… new ways of thinking. I don't want that for you, Razaiella."

"You're telling me things," I grinned. "But they are hard to understand. Just say what you have to tell me straight."

"I am trying my best, but even as a young girl myself, my grand-mother said to me many things I did not understand; now I do. It is something that you will come to comprehend and appreciate as you grow older. Not so much in the time you have heard it first. Your mind is still young, and you will see as I see when you are ready."

"Why am I not ready now? I'm basically fifteen years old now. Soon I'll be with someone, have my first child, and be living on my own, making my own decisions."

Mom smiled. "And, you are absolutely right, daughter. You will grow up one day and be with someone. I want the very best for you, and that is all I desire. So, as you see with your senses, you can understand that my husband is still in love with me. I love Rafael, but who he was long ago. Once you meet a person whom you truly love, there is no one else but him. No matter who comes by, the only person sent graciously by Mother Nature's blessing will be him. I lost him due to something I could not contain or protect him from. It broke me, and it definitely shattered him. I don't want you having to share my pain, daughter."

Mom was so emotional, which made me sad. I knew there was more, but she was too weak to say it at the moment. I wanted to know more.

"I think this belongs to you."

Mom stretched out a necklace and clamped it on the back of my neck.

"It was in your jacket. Remember, daughter: if you let true nature take its course in life, you will have all the answers, and not one force can break you."

Mom opened her arms, and the warmth of our hearts bonded. I love her as I love him. Never take your parents' life for granted. We only get one.

CHAPTER 5

Divine Instincts

The world is just becoming colder and colder, darker and darker. Nothing ever stays the same. They always said New York is the city that never sleeps. Why is it that people do not see that life shouldn't be just black and white? It should be filled with vibrant colors, just like my mural. Surprised no one has written on or tried to destroy my piece. The haters are real and will try to sabotage anything beautiful they may see. My Dad seems to know about people like that, and that is why I agree with him more. He doesn't want to give up on love, and love is what makes everything go smoothly.

"You still aren't finished, Ra?" Lexus asks, folding her arms. "It's good as it is."

"It is, but I just love to make my art perfect. You know I'm a Virgo," I smirked.

"So you think you're perfect?"

"Not at all, Lex, but I do know I'm different."

Lexus giggled as if I said the funniest thing. "I guess."

"Leave Ra alone, Lex," Jordan says. "Everyone is different in their own way."

"Tell her, friend. I'm glad to be different. That's what makes us all unique, no? If everyone were the same, life would be so boring."

That is why no one will ever be me or anyone to take my place. I am who I am. One thing about me—the thing I hate the most—is a copycat. Then, I can never see why someone wants to be like another person. You should love yourself for who you are. No matter what, you will always be who you are.

"Ra," Dante says, standing behind me as the group just watches me paint, "speaking of different—you've been different these last few weeks. Ya know, a little quieter than usual. What's up with you?"

I smiled, knowing this question was going to come, but not so late. "I'm okay. What? You think something is wrong?"

"Not really. Just… you've been odd since my bro got locked up. I know you feel some type of way about it, but he won't be in there forever. What's funny?"

"You didn't say anything wrong. I just… I…"

"She's just special, Dante. Like she told me, she's different. Sure is different now. If you wanted Nova, Ra, you should've opened up to him. I mean, date. Shut up, Jordan. Only your filthy brain. No offense, Ra, but you are a virgin, right?"

I frowned as Lexus smiled at me. "Whose business is that?"

"Wellll, you seem to never have a boyfriend, annnd you seem to be single forever. Sooo…"

"Lex," I shook my head. "Really?"

"Um, yeah. You should know none of us are virgins. Wait, Dante, are you one?"

"Aye, I'm fifteen… but I'm not."

"Exactly. So, girl, I'm not saying to be a whore or anything, but you need to stop being such a… what's that word?"

"I'm boring, huh? Well—"

"Not boring, babe, just a… introvert, that's the word. You are always to yourself and scared to let someone touch you. Jordan? Are you one?"

Jordan grins. "Shit really doesn't matter. As Ra just said, my business is my business. You, Lex, you need to chill with that. Everyone sexing each other. Not everyone is down to catch something. You feel me?"

"That's why you should strap up, babe."

"Let me tell you something," Jordan says. "In this world, shit gets real. You see how people are. My dad told me to always strap up, but to be honest, I don't want to get involved. Kinda scared, to be honest."

"Of what?" Lexus asked.

"The stuff out here. You're not hearing me? Aye, I kinda feel like it's not worth it when you do something, and it messes you up for life. Y'know, getting an STD, being busted by the police, or even failing school. The future matters to those who want it."

Dante clapping and cheering Jordan—and I could definitely agree.

"That's what I'm saying. J-R for president! My brother was locked up, and the family kept telling me to stay out of trouble. I know I should stay away from stupid stuff."

"What your problem is, Lex, is that you made it a bad habit."

"What'd you say, Ra? Hey, I don't care. I'm me, and that's how it's going to be. I'm a bad bitch and no one can tell me otherwise."

I knew Lexus was a little wild, but not so sexually active. People are just sometimes stuck on stupid. I cared about myself and was too beautiful to let any man touch me. If she just knew how life is still good without all of that. "From what I learned in school… Tsk, let me start packing up. From what I learned, I am not a girl who wants to catch anything out here. Jordan is right. They have things out there that you can catch, and it grows out of you. Everybody is just going around giving it to one another; it's gross, Lex. That's not for me. The worst part is that you can never get rid of it. I can only imagine if I meet a guy, and he's my first, and he gives me something that I can't get rid of. That's the really messed-up part. You should think about that, Lex."

"Girl!" Lexus laughs while we all just look.

"Don't worry about her, Ra," Dante says as he shakes his head but smirks. "I thought about it too. What if, um, my first gives me something—my sex life is over. Shoot, they say eighty percent of people who are hitting this, or hitting that, have something. I can even look it up for you when I get this paint off my hands."

"You all are just lame! Eighty percent of junior high has done it. It's normal. Like… I don't know, you just do it. It's 2032. No one is really thinking about it the way you lames are. I know Nova for sure ain't a virgin."

"Speaking of the devil!" Jordan says as we look over in his direction.

"Aye, bro! You out?! How?!"

Nova walked up with the same clothes he had on when we last saw him and a sack bag over his shoulder. He looked untouched.

"You all thought I was going to do life or something?"

Nova's face turned to me, with his eyes meeting mine as he hugged and clapped up everyone.

"I see you made it, friend. I'm glad," I smirked.

"Really?"

I could see his blush—even felt it. I knew what he wanted, but what about his younger brother?

"You missed me?"

"Oh, don't flatter yourself," I smiled. "We all missed you."

"Especially you, Ra."

Lexus was the one acting weird. "I don't know what's wrong with her. Anyways, what did the police say?"

"Just some bull. Basically, they think I'm a criminal for smoking a little weed around minors. Told 'em that shit is a part of our atmosphere. Ha, am I wrong? I also see you got what's rightfully yours. But! I need you to have something else. I know you need to go before Mom calls."

The only reason I wouldn't date Nova is just from what he said—though whatever surprise he had for me, I knew it would give Lexus more of a reason to act weird.

"Just a little something-something."

"Nova?"

"Shoosh, this is between you and me. You need this going back and forth from home. Trust me."

"Nova," I whispered. "I don't need it. Plus, if my mom sees me with that—"

"That's why she won't."

"Aye, goodnight homies! Tomorrow!" Jordan says, walking away and leaving Lexus and Dante with their eyes on us.

"Ra, just take it. After the other day, I couldn't stop thinking about if another gang had us on the run or anything crazy like that. You getting hurt is the last thing I want."

Him looking into my eyes like that, with the sunlight falling—I knew he was sincere and was truly honest. "Oh gosh, this could be only one person… and it is. Hey, Mom. Yeah, I'm on the train now. I'll be there in a few. Tsk, they said they could walk the rest of the way home by themselves. I walked them, oh gosh. Mom, I'm not responsible for them. Tsk, alright."

Nova smirked, but I could not help but, as he looked down at me.

"You see, I don't need any more trouble. See you tomor—"

"Please," Nova says with his puppy eyes and a smile. "It's because I care."

"Ha, whatever," I blushed. "Just be sure you teach me how to use this thing. Guns are not my thing. Only the ones that paint on walls."

"That a girl," Nova says, kissing me on my cheek. "Now, you can go home. Safely."

I knew he cared, but not that much. Then, right after prison, he went to get a pistol. I wanted to throw it away, but I heard these things have serial numbers, and if somebody finds it, he would be going straight back behind bars. Because of me. Again. Life is just so weird—just like how Lex is also so interested in my sex life. Since assuming she's not a virgin, she wants me to be just like her. She should hate copycats.

The entire city has gritty areas, alcoholics, addicts, and rapists—I think most of them are on the train with me right now. In my view, it's safer to be in a place with many people. That day, when that idiot tried something, my dad stepped in. That was the first time, but I guess Nova would have said that if I had the gun, it might have ended better. Still, I wonder how my dad knew where I was and how he managed to find me. The only explanation was that he had traced the phone line, but his own phone didn't work. There was something about him I just couldn't quite figure out—how he did what he did. Mom was right in a way; he changed, but not in a bad way. He loves us too much and wants to protect us from all the people she claims are bad for our spirits. Even getting out of the train car, they walk past you and stare. These demons are everywhere.

"Hey."

"Hi—oh. Thanks," I said as a man gave me a rose, but kept walking.

Where the hell did he come from? "Another note?"

The more beautiful the flower, the faster it withers. Bloom on your own timing, not with others. Never let anyone take your beautiful shine. You are divine.

Looking back to see where the man was—of course, he vanished into thin air. My smile couldn't be any wider. Everyone in the train station saw me, and I wanted to ask if anyone had seen him. I suppose I looked sad, and he wanted to make me happy. I wonder what Mom would say once I got home if she read this. There are good people in this world; you just have to be careful. You never know what people's intentions are. "Time to hear the noise."

Knock-knock-knock

"It's me, Razaiella!"

CHAPTER 6

Look Me in My Eyes

Being in the cold and boring classes is the worst. I always like my mind to have a mind of its own, as if something or someone tells me what to say is true or false. School? No different. Everyone pretty much says that seventy percent of what we learn, we'll just forget by next year. Only thing is—why must we fill our heads with some pointless, difficult lesson and then just forget it all? My art always mattered more to me. "Thank God class is over."

Everyone got up faster than lightning, dodging the eye.

"Razaiella. Will you come here, please?"

"I have to get my sisters and be home soon. My mom already has me on thin ice."

"It will only take a second," Mrs. Valdez says with a smile. "You're not in trouble."

"Oh, trust me. I try not to be."

Something was telling me it was something that she wanted to speak to me about. Maybe something at home bothered me, and I was eager to tell her the truth.

"Razaiella. I know you are not a stupid person. Why have your grades been steadily declining?"

A familiar paper Mrs. Valdez pushes to my side of the desk. "What? A C isn't bad. Stands for cute."

Mrs. Valdez smirks. "Not quite. You should know when you get too comfortable, C's turn into D's, and D's turn into F's. It happens, and once again, you know this stuff."

If only she knew. I couldn't care less about this stuff. "Mrs. Valdez. I'm not good at math. I tried, really, I did."

"Then you should also know that this won't cut it for passing my class. A C is not for those who want bright futures. Once again, your grades are declining—zero tolerance for slackers. I just want to be sure a beautiful person, inside and out, succeeds. I know how much you love your artistic works, but they will always be there. Oh yes, I know that is your first love. However, your studies come first."

The quiet, echoing classroom definitely made me feel as though I was the one who was stupid. I'm singled out because of a silly grade.

"Okay, Mrs. Valdez." I grinned. "I'll do better, even though this stuff in a few years won't matter at all."

"And you are correct, somewhat." Mrs. Valdez nodded. "As women, we must succeed in life, no matter how pointless things may seem."

Mrs. Valdez caught my eye in surprise.

"You are talented and very much a unique person, Razaiella. Have you heard of type A people?"

I shrugged. "Not really."

"They are the ones who have a personality that is as solid as a rock. I know it in you, as you are clever in your thoughts and mind, as you are an artist. Type A people are strong people who are hard to break; they don't give up easily. I am a type-A person, and I know and feel you are one as well. As a woman to a young lady, I only want the best for all in this man's world. So again, zero tolerance for the slackers. You can do this, Razaiella, I know you can. If no one has ever told you so, then I'll be the first."

Mrs. Valdez reached her hand out, and our hands came together. Her energy was always brighter and more understanding than these arithmetic's. "I'll do better next time. I promise."

"So you shall. I'll hold you to that. You may leave," Mrs. Valdez smiled, but gave me the feeling she would be watching me even more closely.

"Oh, Razaiella. Focus on your blessings, not your curses."

If Mom were more like Mrs. Valdez, I would definitely be in a better state. Or maybe it's just me. I'm a bad girl who just wants to go out and get my artwork on the wall—expressing who I truly am. Mom… she can be just stressed out. From Dad being who he is, her raising us on her own. Then her being a doctor is really what could make her stressed out. So I can get all the best grades in the world, go to college, become a high-paid worker, and still hate my life? That is why I want to do what I want to. Nothing more but be a creator, a designer. That is who I am. "Munisha? Hey, Munisha, come on! Time to go home. Oh gosh, really? Bullies? Give my sister back her book bag! Snotty brat, gimme! Now go away."

The teachers in the playground didn't even look my sister's way. They just kept their eyes glued to their phones. All the kids did was play and be stupid, so I guess that was a good reason. They probably just did it because they liked my sister, and they gave me the same treatment when I was younger, but I had no one to help me.

"Ra, they took my juice! It's not in my bag."

"Let them have it. There's plenty more at home. I swear to myself, I'll never have kids. Especially at a young age. Then if I do, I hope it's my own gender."

"Lakia's not coming?" Munisha asks, putting on her purple and black backpack.

"I don't think so. Mom said she has practice or something. So, just us for today. Not really in the mood to be out on the streets today and hearing Mom's voice like last night."

"You love your art. You love to draw. Mom is, umm… are you mad at me?"

I grinned as we both walked onto the sidewalk and into the world of misery.

Never left my mind the guy who yelled out he couldn't see after Dad got to him.

"No… I'm not mad. Just… wondering."

"About what?"

"Many things," Munisha replied, as she just kept looking down the way.

"Okaayy… good or bad things? Hey, I just noticed Mom didn't do your hair right."

"Lakia did it. She's too rough."

I shook my head and rolled my eyes—as of course she would be messy with it. Should have known Lakia made crooked ponytails.

"Mom shouldn't even have you leave the house with that. That's not like her. Tsk, I don't know what's wrong with that girl, though."

"I told her I wanted your hair. Like how you have in—"

"Ponytails, yeah, I know. Ha, my texture is a little different. You have good hair, but not like mine."

Munisha's face just went from jolly to a sour second grader. It was cute. "Hey, tell you what. Once we get home, I'll give you my style. I hate to see sad faces."

"Because you're the nicest."

I smiled. "Only if Mom sees that like others do."

I know me and Munisha will be better sisters than Lakia and I. Judging how she did her own full-blood sister's hair, she didn't give a rat's ass, as Dad would say a long time ago. Maybe because she heard someone wanted to copy me. Something I hate, but my little sister is an exception. Lakia, not so much. "At least our house isn't too far from the school. That's why I don't know why Mom got so heated."

"How long will you stay? Mom won't be home until tonight with Lakia."

"Forget already? I said you'll be with me today. I'll surprise Mom by being with you and spending quality time with you. Home, and not out being bad."

If anything, I should be praised for caring for myself and another person as we walk through the city. Jonathon claims he works so much—he should be here for his children. Dad was always here for me, even when he argued with Mom. He always came to me and acted like everything was okay. Then Mom would say he was always here because he had no job. Munisha's hair is so curly and wavy that I thought she would need more oils. "Do you like it?"

Munisha stared at her pigtails in the mirror. "I…"

"You like it? No?"

"I… love it, Ra. How did you do it so fast?"

"Ha, I pretty much braid my hair with my eyes closed. Now you can show off to those bullies at school and prove to them I'll always be there if they bother you again."

"I love it, Ra. I love it so much—so much."

I can tell she just wanted a little more, but didn't want to say it. Her hair is hers. So important to love who you are first. Mom constantly reminded us that.

"So how about something to eat?"

"Yeah, I'm so hungry!"

"Who could be calling me? Probably Mom. Lex? Hey, Lex, what's up? Come to the spot? I don't feel like it today—what? Not just got out. Why are they arresting him again? What witness? Um, that makes no sense. I don't understand… why would he be getting arrested? Tsk, okay, I'll be there as soon as I can."

"Are you okay, Razaiella?" Munisha asks with a smile.

"Yeah, uh… just… let's get something to eat, and I have to go out after."

What could it be that they released him and then wanted someone to say we were all together and Nova was not out committing a crime? Nova just isn't that type of guy. Something just doesn't feel right. "Watch the hot dogs, Munisha. I have to go to the restroom. It's four twenty-seven."

Putting the dogs on high definitely was a no-no. Mom would be thinking I'm trying to burn the house down. "Wait… that music."

Right after the restroom break, those gentle sounds came from the attic. Not knowing whether to go up or stay down. Something definitely is going on up there. There had to be something that I could give to Dad at least. "I can't be scared. Dad needs me, and I need him."

The ladder inviting me to go up gave me the chills, though something was definitely drawing me in. Something that was left behind, and I needed to see. That statue—her eyes back to where they were, pointed to the heavens. I believe that is where they were before. Something whispered, and it wasn't coming from the statue this time. The books I ran through. They seem even to be restacked neatly. I can hear the voices, but where are they coming from? "Where are you?"

My head turned swiftly to a book falling on the floor. Something up here definitely wanted me to see more answers that I needed. "What… the hell? A book with eyes staring right back at me. Okay, Razaiella, don't freak out. Just… calm down."

The skull on the book's front cover, with eyes that seemed to watch my every move, gave me the impression it wanted to take my soul and suck it into the green and orange pupils of the cover. The back was more common. "I've seen this before, but where?"

The back cover of the old but not dented book featured a man with his arms and legs out, showing them in different patterns, like a clock ticking swiftly. "A book with no title. Interesting—ugh, the inside smells so old."

All the pages with amazing text. Old English letters. I definitely needed to learn these intricate styles. "Woah, what the hell is this? A man… with a… goat mask… even what… B cups?"

"Razaiella! The hot dogs are on fire! Razaiella!"

Tripping on the books, scattering them all over the place. I had the food on low. Other than that, I needed to tell Dad about that stuff up there. There was no way he had any idea about it. "What happened?! How did the fire start?!"

"You took so long!" Munisha says as the kitchen swallowed her with smoke. "I thought you weren't coming."

"Are you okay? You didn't get burned, did you?"

"No. I just moved it off the hot thingy."

"So weird. I was just gone for like five minutes. Not long at all. It was on low, wasn't it?"

"I think so. Mom says you're supposed to cook hot dogs for fifteen minutes."

"Yeah, and I left at four-thirty. It's… four fifty-eight. How can that be?"

"You were away, Razaiella, but I helped. No problem," Munisha smiles with my complete confusion.

"And why do I smell air freshener?"

"I sprayed it on the hot dogs. I told you they were on fire."

"Oh God, Munisha," I grinned, but frustratedly shook my head. "That's not a fire extinguisher. You could have blown us to hell. Tsk, now who's calling me? Yeah, Lex. I'm on my way."

"You're leaving?"

"I'll be back, Munisha… in an hour or so. Mom shouldn't be back by then. Just… take a nap or something. If she comes, tell her I forgot something at school."

Munisha's smile turned upside down. She's been home alone before. I just hope when I get there, the police won't arrest me for something stupid. The graffiti in this city is everywhere. Making the world a colorful place shouldn't even be a crime. The busy streets of New York, going home to go back to slavery tomorrow. That same guy fighting himself was getting old; it must be the way of life. "Lex! Lex?"

"Yeah, that's her there! She told me to wait here so she could fight me, or she would shoot me at school!"

"Wa—wait? What?"

"Drop the bag, ma'am," the officer says as he keeps his gun on his hip while a female officer does the same.

"I just came here because she told me to."

"You have any weapon on you, young lady?" the female officer asks. "A girl like you should not be out here making threats."

"I didn't make any threats!"

"Is this it? What are you doing with this?" the male officer says with a frown. "Hands behind your back."

"Lex, tell them the truth! You told me to come over here!"

Lexus just stood quietly, and the worst part—I could almost witness a smirk on her face.

"You're a damn trick, Lex!"

"Ma'am, get into the car."

Not knowing if my encounter with that book was scarier. Why would she do such a thing? Seeing a bird flying over the car—could it be my guardian angel with me, my ancestors letting me know everything will be okay? I'm not a bad person—just had terrible luck.

CHAPTER 7

For A Peace of Mind

Not knowing whether to have so much hate in my heart or fear. How can you trust anyone in this day and age? Everyone just seems to be out to get you. Their hearts are colder than the prison cells, which is enough to make you sick. Lexus—I always felt something odd about her, but I just didn't want to think anything of it. Not really a friend, but a person to watch everything you do. Why couldn't I see that these were always her intentions?

Then Nova. Why? Thinking about it all night long in the prison realm. Things didn't make any sense.

"Lozano, Razaiella?" an officer says, looking through the small glass in the door. "You're free to go. Lucky for you, there was no misdemeanor. Your mother is waiting for you."

Having been blamed for something I didn't do, I wanted to ask, *What about the gun?* It could definitely stay. I just couldn't see how all of this happened so fast.

"She's free to go. I told her she is lucky for certain."

"And I told you all that she lied."

The officer sighed. "That's fine if she lied, sweetheart. The major problem is, you were carrying a firearm, and you're just a minor. In New York City, that is automatic probation, house arrest, and, of course, a criminal record. Since we are being a bit generous, as you told us, someone gave it to you for protection, and we will investigate it. We will have to do a few more investigations to make our streets cleaner."

"I surely appreciate you, officer. Get over here, Razaiella. You embarrassed me far enough."

Mom's face was a face that I'd seen before, but her energy was beyond furious.

"Mom—"

"No. I don't want to hear a word from you. Not a word. Wait, so where did you get that weapon from? Since the officers are here. Someone gave it..."

Mom's eyes glued to mine, almost as if she wanted to see who it was in my head.

"I told you. I don't know. Someone."

"Oh, so it just hopped and skipped into your bag?" Mom hissed, arms folded.

"Mrs. Lozano, we have suspicions that it was someone considered a close friend. Your daughter doesn't seem to be the aggressive type. However, she needs to be aware of her friends. Razaiella, as the sheriff of the county, I warn you with all honesty—never, ever take what does not belong to you. If your story is true and it is a friend, he or she could face many years for granting a minor a weapon. Child's play is no joke, especially out here. So I beg you, stay away from the crowd, please?"

"And she surely will, Sheriff. I thank you all for your forgiveness and time. Ra, you just don't know," Mom says, picking up her purse with a grin of frustration. "I've given you exact instructions to pick up Munisha, then go straight home."

"...I did."

"Then left," Mom shakes her head. "Are you trying to make life harder before you even hit your twenties? Just like your father. Get in, and I don't want to hear anything from you. You are more than on thin ice, and you should be praying and thanking the ancestors for aiding you to be free."

So much for them. If the ancestors would have seen what happened, one of them would have told me something—not just let me walk, take a train, and end up in a trap. Like I told Munisha, I'm not a bad person, just had bad luck. I try to stay away, but trouble always seems to find me.

Dad could have been the same way, and it passed right down to me. So maybe one day I'll be just like him—the greatest artist, and show my skills all over the world. Not working hard for a job I hate.

"I think it's time for us to leave," Mom says as we pass by the stream of lights that passed us in the car.

"What do you mean by leave? Leave home?"

"This city… this place. It is all too toxic for my family."

"…I don't know. This all seems so unfair."

"You are correct," Mom nods slowly as she drives. "You went and got a weapon from someone, or they gave it to you—a weapon of destruction. You really thought something like that would protect you from these dark forces of nature? You are highly mistaken, daughter."

Hearing those words—and her not believing me—made me just want to jump out of the car. I again was trapped.

"Mom… what do you think? Tsk, forget that. So, what about you? Are you perfect? Because you don't see how anyone is good enough."

Mom just nodded her head with her lips pulled in together. I heard the car accelerate, but that didn't scare me. "What about Jonathon? So what is he? Good? He barely even sees Lakia or Munisha. Then you don't even try to see my dad."

"Razaiella… daughter," Mom says calmly. "When you finally understand the true nature of life, one day—maybe just one day—you will. Where were your true friends when this person did this to you? I may not understand the mentality of the streets, but I do understand the ways of nature much more. That is what is important. Believe it or not. People are unpredictable, Razaiella. No matter what they say, or how they make you feel, they can switch up their thoughts and feelings about you in the blink of an eye. For your own protection, daughter. You should know this."

I didn't know what or who to believe anymore. Too many questions that needed answers. All I want is someone to be true and genuine with me. As blood, as a friend, neighbor, artist. If anyone is out there who is true—one hundred percent—that is the person I want to be around. Yet, I know that was a lie, even at a young age. No one is perfect. Everyone has something bad about them. That is why I don't judge. *Just be your true self* is what I believe, and everyone in the world would be more loving, kind, and truthful.

"Hey, Jonathon. Yes, we just arrived. No-no… she's okay. A little bit of trouble, but praise be to the ancestors, she's fine. I don't think she'll be in any more trouble. At least not anytime soon. There's a new plan. Yeah, see you when you get here. Love you too. Where are these damn keys? Here we go. Yes, daughter. There is a new plan. As a mother, I feel I must protect my family from all bad energies. Know that I, again as a mother, want the best for you."

"I just don't know why we have to—"

"Wait… someone's here," Mom says, as she stops me with her hand and looks straight forward without a blink.

The beautiful melody could only be played by one person I know. I could even feel his energy from the musical notes once again surrounding me.

"What are you doing in my house again?!"

"Dad."

"Rafael! Get out of my house, or I am calling the police this time without hesitation. I mean it!"

From our window, lights pulled up behind Mom's car. This was definitely going to be an interesting experience. Even with my heart beating faster in excitement, I could not help but smile.

"Oh God. Rafael… please just get out. Not tonight. Please."

Seeing that guy, Jonathan, get out with his expensive car, just like Mom's own, and then open up the back door, smiling.

"Those half-bloods are here too."

Mom frowned. "What did you say, Ra? Goodness, Rafael. This is not good. The problem will be much bigger this time without authorities. Please, leave… for your daughters' sake. Come on."

Dad continued playing that beautiful melody and showed no signs of being bothered.

"Hmph, so he does have a scent," Dad smirks as his fingers ran across the keys. "You smell it too, don't you, Ra?"

"Rafael," Mom begs with her hands folded. "Please, just get out. If you love me and your daughter, you will listen."

The doorbell rang, and Mom's face was petrified in fear. This ugliness and hate needed to stop.

"It's over between us, Rafael. Stop playing that piano! JUST GET OUT!"

Dad stopped and smiled to Mom and then to me. He started playing a song I'd heard before. The melody was so hypnotizing but beautiful.

"You love this melody, don't you, Razaiella? *Lacrimosa*… never forget it."

"Hey, I heard yelling… what's— you?"

"Jonathon," Mom pleaded, pushing Jonathon back.

Dad was still playing and never missing a note to my ears. Jonathon could only be kept in his confusion, and it all felt so good.

"Hey, man, I thought we settled this a long time ago," Jonathon says. "You get crazier by the days or what? Answer me, damn you!"

"Jonathon, please. Just go upstairs. I can handle him. I don't want any trouble. Please… not in front of the children. Just… go, okay?"

Jonathon definitely had the energy to attack, but my Dad would make him suffer just like the guy in the alley.

"Rafael… okay. We both know this isn't going to work. You—this isn't you. I can help you get treatment. But now is not the time. I promise to do my best to help you. I promise, okay?"

Dad smiled and changed the melody of the keys to another beautiful song, I swear I heard on a classic radio station.

"You know this song, don't you, Ra? Don't you?" Dad says as he closes his eyes and rocks slowly back and forth.

Mom, Lakia, and Munisha all just looked at each other as all the songs were just for me.

"She's with some other guyyy. I don't want to do this anymore, I don't want to take away his life. I don't want to be… a murdereeer."

Dad's smile turned to a frown—a face I haven't seen in a while. His energy was like it flipped an entire three-sixty.

"I told you, freak! Get the hell out of the house, and you're still here?!"

"Jonathon! No, please, don't shoot him! Stop!"

Mom cried with her hands on her mouth as the loudest scream may have woken the neighbors. For some reason, I knew he wouldn't pull the trigger. My heart raced, yet it was also at ease. Dad and I just looked at him with no fear in our hearts. Almost like we knew he was just showing off in front of Mom.

Jonathon, aiming the shotgun at my Dad, with me beside him. I still felt nothing, without a blink or shake. To me, he was the one scared.

"Just so you know, buddy, this is a twelve-gauge. I'll blow you out of your shoes. Get the hell out of the house. It's late, and I'm tired of this shit."

"Some things are worse than death," Dad says as he gets up.

Dad warmed my soul with a kiss to the forehead. The idiot was still aiming the shotgun.

"Hmph," Dad grins. "Pitiful mortal."

CHAPTER 8

The Eighth Sense

The days were getting colder, and the months of snow flurries began to fall every now and then. It was a hassle getting it out of my hair. Unfortunately, time has gone by, and still no sign of Dad. Mom is skipping Thanksgiving and, this year, not even thinking of putting up festive décor in our home. Mom, along with that bald guy Jonathon, probably moved Dad out for good. Then, that so-called friend Nova—he'd call me, but I would definitely leave him on read, along with everyone else. No one can be trusted in this world. That is why art will always take me away from all these harsh realities. "My angel, sitting as a princess above my world. When people die, I wonder if they grow wings."

When I leave this world, they can paint me with black wings. Just like my angel, Zara. Her sitting on her name—it's just so her nature.

"Razaiella," Mom says, standing by the doorway. "Almost ready? We leave no later than fifteen minutes."

"Yeah, I'm ready. Just can't believe we're… what?"

Mom smirked. "Just looking at your beautiful drawing, daughter. I love it. Since you're all packed up, I'll see you downstairs. The home movers will get the rest. Jonathon will be here when they come later on today. Razaiella? Come on, you can finish your drawing in the car."

She knew that would be the last place for me to even place my pen to paper. And it's five in the morning. Getting up at four a.m. to be on the road, leaving my home, my father, school, my so-called friends—I didn't know how to feel, but I was sure enough to know my life would change. Would it be for the better or worse? Even seeing myself in the mirror that watched me for many years—something here made me feel like I was leaving my soul behind. "But why does it always feel like something is after me?"

Grabbing my backpack—the last thing I marked on the list on my phone. Just to be sure I didn't leave anything. One thing I wanted to ask my mom: the stuff up in the attic. Those things the movers might see, and they may just leave it. Or they might just take what rightfully belongs to my father. I knew there was more up there to find—answers for me—but I was too late. I definitely needed more answers.

"I see you're up and ready to go."

I wonder why he thought it was okay to even speak to me again.

"Dad, are you coming to visit us?" Lakia asks. "Mom says where we're going is far away from here."

"Of course I'll see my girls again. Never think I won't."

Jonathon was holding his daughter tight, his eyes tearing up, but also closed tight. I had no father to hug or say goodbye to. He could have been under the Brooklyn Bridge, hiding from the cold.

"Jonathon, we're almost set," Mom says, holding her purse and expensive tote bags. "So, just as we planned. Check on the house every now and then, and give me a call if anything is out of the ordinary. The movers should be here at ten o'clock sharp."

"You know I got this place protected, my love. Only issue—you know I may not be around as much in the area. Work during the peak season gets a little aggressive."

Mom nodded. "That's fine and understandable. My agent is looking for me to sell this place soon enough. A buyer will come—praise be to the ancestors in advance."

Mom hugging and kissing the ugly man right in front of me and his daughters—that's when I needed fresh air.

"See you, Jonathon. I'll give you a call midway."

I just wish my father had been here, just so I could see those happy, lovey-dovey faces turn upside down.

"All right girls. We are out of here and off to a much better place. A place where we can finally call peace. This will be the best for all of us. I promise. Oh no, did I forget something?" Mom says, slamming on the brakes.

Jonathon dashed down the porch stairs and to us as if we had stolen something.

Mom grinned, rolling her window down. "What did I forget already?"

"Just a good luck kiss for both of us. We'll need it. Good luck, my love. Goodbye, Munisha, Lakia. Daddy loves you all. Razaiella, everything will be all right. Much love to you, Isabella."

One day, I know Dad will be back in the house—I can just feel it. Jonathon will be so clueless. He will need more than prayers and luck.

"Mom?" Munisha says as she sits quietly in the back with Lakia. "When will we go back home?"

"Oh, child. You will see it again someday. Our new home will be so much prettier and quieter. You will meet new people in school and in the neighborhood. Most importantly, you'll see more of what true nature is. The city has blinded many with lies and false realities, and I do not want that for my family. We all will be in the new atmosphere of civil civilization. Just wait, you all. You will finally see."

Mom made it seem like we were going to the most perfect place in the world. I could feel it from her, as she just seemed so eager to be there. "What do you mean by civil?" I wondered. "The people in this new place are perfect?"

"Not perfect, daughter. They have more of a… cultured way of living, if you will. New York… ha, this place is just too toxic. The air is even filthy. You can't look down a road that lacks someone who has littered on Mother Earth. An environment where my three children must make a life for themselves? I think not. Our ancestors would like us to be in true nature, where life is more dominant. As I said before, better for all of us."

Mom knows this wasn't something I wanted, and she knew why. One thing Dad always showed me was that we are born alone, and one day we will die alone. As he never really had any family or friends. So, no matter where we go or how far we move, something about life will never let us have what we truly want. With me, I kind of felt it—to be alone even with one hundred friends. The family was not great, but they were there.

We exited the big city, and I looked to the passenger mirror, seeing where I once lived. The tall buildings stood tall, and I felt like they were just looking back at me, saying I would be back one day. I turned on my music player as Mom listened to nature music with flutes, guitars, and other instruments in the mix. My melodic beats were more soothing and gave more energy. Then, we saw the tall trees standing side by side as we traveled down the never-ending stretch of roads. Of course, Munisha would say she had to use the restroom. I just wanted to see what Mom was saying about this perfect place. All I felt as we continued to journey was the coldness of the air as it continued to drop quickly.

"Hey Jonathon. Yes, how are you? We stopped at a station on the way. Giving the car some juice before we arrive. Yeah, it actually had about twenty-three percent left. We have about three hours to go, and so far, it's been going really well. Yes-yes, they're fine. We grabbed something to eat, and we're all excited. The weather is getting a bit nippy, but I felt it before when I was on the train the first time coming up. No, I don't want to leave my car in New York. You need to save your money, love. Buying a new car is not what I need or want right now. Ha—for Christmas? An SUV would be nice. Jonathon, no way. I don't need it. Thank you, love. We need to save, not spend. Well… we'll see."

Arriving in the city of Boston, it wasn't a bad place. Much cleaner than New York. I could stay here, but this wasn't perfect enough for Mom.

"Are you cold, Ra? Tsk, I am," Lakia says as she wraps herself tightly in her jacket.

"It's okay."

"I know you'll miss New York. I will too. Hey, but Mom said she would take us back every now and then. So it shouldn't be that bad."

"Ha," I shrugged. "It's whatever. If she wants us to be in the cold weather, that's what she wants."

"Munisha, let me get some chips."

"Nooo, get your own!"

"Mom, can we go now?" I asked, as I didn't feel like watching those two fight, and I didn't feel like saving the day.

"We're ready. Yes, that's just Ra telling me she's ready to see our new home. She's right. I'll call you once we reach the mainland. Love you too."

The sky was getting darker, but the light rays were trying to peek through the clouds. It already felt gloomy enough. Comparing the two places so far and where it looked like we were headed: New York, the big city—dirty and lively. The forest areas, which we stayed in between, just showed how there could be something or someone hiding in them. Next thing you know, you wake up, and the bear is opening your refrigerator. The birds looked so angelic, even the black ones. They seemed to have more friends and family than people. It would be funny to see Dad just pop up at the place and smile and wave as we pull into the driveway.

"Here we are, family. We made it. The Maine land."

Seeing Munisha from my left peripheral vision knocked out.

"It's nice. The ocean is glittering from what's left of the sun."

"That is our sun, Lakia, kissing the ocean goodnight. Mother Nature gives all, as long as you give her a chance. There is so much more to see. Let me give Jonathon a call."

The scenery was nice—just so old-fashioned. Some buildings looked new, but others appeared to be made of old wood or had been standing for a hundred years.

"Yeah, Jonathon. This place is amazing. A bit of overcast here and there, but the sun manages to get through certain areas. Yes, Ellsworth, Maine. It's a paradise; I can already feel it."

One day, she will say this place is not what she thought. I could feel that too. All I know for sure is that my graffiti days were over. Not a wall I know I could do real artwork on. Then again, they're made of wood. "Who could this be? Tsk…"

Nova still doesn't get it. If I keep ignoring your calls, what makes you think I want to talk? If I were to block him, he would know he's out of my life forever, even though it was Lexus who caused the trouble. I felt like it was her mainly, but the gun from him started it. It was nothing but trouble, and I hated that I had to agree with Mom on that.

"Oh yes, Jonathon. If I didn't tell you before, this place has a guard gate—a sense of security and peace of mind. Hold on… Happy Holidays! Isabella Lozano. Just moved in. Thank you. Gosh, did he have his tongue removed?"

I grinned. "Maybe."

The houses were definitely not like the ones back home. They all looked expensive with clean white walls and brown trimmings. All had upstairs rooms, too. I wanted my room away from everyone else.

"Here it is, family. Jonathon, I wish you were here. Yeah, we'll talk. It's time to get settled in. I love you too."

The feeling of this new house definitely did not get me excited. It made me want to see Dad open the door for us and start life over again—the right way.

"The ancestors blessed us with this new home, and you girls get to choose your rooms."

"Munisha? We're here! Get up!" Lakia shouts, then runs past me.

"You like it?" I asked as Lakia beat me to the door.

"It's amazing, Ra! Come on, Munisha! It's so amazing! We have a pool too? Right, Mom?"

"And that is what I don't want for you all. I only believe Ra and you can swim, but Munisha cannot. I need you all to be extremely careful. Never go out there without my permission."

"I'll teach her," Lakia says.

I guess our home wasn't perfect now. A pool in Maine—it's almost always cold here. So, whoever gets in it will wake up in the morning with the sniffles.

"Welcome home, new family," Mom smiles, standing behind us three.

"Wow!" Lakia says, stepping in first. "This is so—eygh!"

"Good evening to you all. My name is Sansa."

I giggled. "That's what you get for always trying to be first."

The hologram on the wall was so realistic, but it was nothing new to me. I've done graffiti on billboards with multiple holograms that move and talk.

"Sansa. This is Isabella Lozano, and my family. My children."

The digital woman smiled. "Welcome, family of Lozano Isabella. I am sure you will find a cozy space and magical comfort that meets your true desires."

Munisha's face definitely didn't like it. It had no pupils. Just a blue face with lips, nose, and tacky eyebrows. If a burglar comes, that's enough to tell him or her they picked the wrong house. "Now this is a bedroom," I said, throwing my luggage on my white and gold bed.

A huge, almost vanity-style mirror. The gray-white walls needed color. Maybe if Mom isn't so strict, I could design my own room. "At least this bed is… it's amazing!"

"Don't get too comfy, daughter. We have one more stop."

I wondered where we could be going after riding the entire day. Mom should have been tired, but somehow she had all the energy. She even felt like a brand-new person.

"Lakia, I want you to watch Munisha."

"Wait, we're not going?"

Mom smiled. "Not this time. Me and Razaiella have some business to attend to. I want you to show me how mature and responsible you are. No cooking and no going outside until we return. You and Munisha can unpack and get organized."

I could already hear Munisha's little feet going up and down the stairs. She looked tired, and it made more sense than the others. Wherever Mom has us going, it better be worth the time and energy.

"How do you feel about the neighborhood, daughter?" Mom asks as we both sat in the car.

"It's… okay. A little too quiet."

Mom grinned. "That is what we want, daughter. Peace, love, fresh air, and tranquility."

"That's the only thing. The shower won't be our best friend with this weather."

"I love it all. Just as you know, I love coats and boots. One of these days will be a day of shopping. I know you're not into all of that shopping, and art is your main passion, daughter. As an artist, I can already tell—you will be into fashion. I know it. I see it and feel it."

Mom knew I didn't care to shop all day, yes. However, I like my attire simple. My friends would call me gothic, as my appearance was always in dark styles. Black—my second favorite color—with fuchsia being my first but second love. Darkness makes everything stand out. That's why an orange-golden color surrounds the pupils of my eyes. That's why I am satisfied with who I am and never change for anyone. "So, where are we going?"

"To another realm, daughter. A place where nature speaks and shows out the most. Once we arrive, you will truly understand how I learned the ways of Mother Nature."

"I hope it's not too far. I want to sleep from all the traveling."

"Patience, daughter, patience. Once we arrive, you will see as I see."

I just needed to ask, as I wanted to do the entire eight-hour ride. "Aren't you upset about leaving Jonathon?"

"No… not at all. Why?"

I shrugged. I just really wanted to know what Mom would say. She seemed so calm about things—I knew something bothered her.

"When your spirit is at peace, you will know nothing to fear. He will come someday to see me and his daughters. Fear is a sickness, and I try to stay immune to it. Now, I have brought you out here not to speak on circumstances dealing with Jonathon and that part. I've brought you here so you can, once again, see as I see… feel as I feel. We're almost there, daughter."

She trusted him—that's what Mom said. She trusts a man so far away. She once screamed out, *Men are all the same*, saying that to my dad's face, too.

We, as women, need to protect our hearts. Another reason I didn't want to have a boyfriend. I trusted no one—especially now. The beautiful ocean with the sun's face still standing high. The beauty of the forest was incredible. They seemed more alive than people.

"We're here, daughter."

"What is this place? It's so… beautiful."

Mom smiles as she also looks out the window, left to right.

"This, Razaiella. This extraordinary place that the creator created for us, I call it *the Motherland*. Welcome to Acadia Park. I want you to open your mind and heart with me."

Mom parked on what seemed like a mountain. The feeling even made my ears pop a few times.

"Now, let's see what nature has to say for today," Mom says, getting out.

We definitely were high up, looking down from the edge. There should have been a rail just in case some idiot decided to shove and push while others tried to pass. The ocean tides rammed up against the rocks, with some splashes hitting my hair. This place was more than beautiful—it was special, with all the emotions whispering from the waves. "Mom?"

She didn't even tell me anything. Could have thought the water took her. Mom stood alone with her arms behind her back as the ocean faced her calmly.

"Believe it or not, daughter," Mom chuckled, "your father brought me here. Brought me to this extraordinary place from the heavens."

"Wow," I said, inhaling the pure winds.

"Tell me something, daughter—wait. Do you hear it?" Mom says, lifting her head and closing her eyes, with the wind blowing her hair.

"I… I don't really understand."

"I know you will someday. You are still too young to understand many things, and that's okay. Your father tried to corrupt you, but praise be to the ancestors, my prayers worked, and he lost."

I frowned. "Why do you say that? Is it because of the things he has? Or how he acts? Mom! I need to know. Please! Tell me!"

Mom unloosened her arms from her back and then shook her head.

"You see, Razaiella. Daughter. Forces of nature have already revealed to you the truth. He was not strong enough. You just have to see and listen. Don't be like me, please… don't. I beg of you."

"To be like you?"

Mom looked up at the sky as if the answers were in the clouds, then back down. "Listen to me, daughter," Mom sighed. "Your father, Rafael—you know he isn't who he is. I know you can feel it. I can, and I know you can too. He's your father, for God's sake. His spirit… his spirit has been devoured by something that is not of this world. A warlock, daughter."

I frowned, as I'd never heard of such a thing—but she called my father one. "A warlock?"

"Yes. A warlock is what and who he is. Though he is not there, as I used to feel him in his old body."

I shook my head and wanted to say *shut up*, as the pain of tears began to sprout. I knew it was all a lie anyway.

"When Rafael proposed to me, in this exact same spot, the ocean whispered to me—and I didn't want to listen. I truly loved him as he was. Such an exceptional man. Though when the dark forces of nature tell you something, it's best you never ignore them and heed the warnings. Tell me, Razaiella, do you see more than your eyes?"

Mom brought me out here to tell and ask me the weirdest questions. "Why are you asking me these things? I just want to know why you feel so much hate for Dad."

"Stop trying to avoid it, daughter. Try to understand where I am coming from. What did you see when you went up there? Oh yes, the attic. I knew something would eventually call you from up there."

Mom's face went from serious to a smile. "Tell me, what did nature speak to you while you were up there?"

"I… I… Mom, okay, I believe. You say Dad is a… warlock or something but—"

"Razaiella. You can't keep running from your fears all your life. I've learned that a long time ago. Those dreams you have, along with your talents of seeing things before they appear—you inherited more than just looks. You, my daughter, have been gifted the eighth sense."

Mom nodded with tears flowing down, with a serious smile. "That is why so many things in life may come after you. The demons of the earth hunt people… they hunt people, especially those with that gift. For me, I only feel as if I have a sixth sense. Your father—he knows."

So much to take in, I didn't really know how to respond.

"I don't know, Mom," I shrugged. "I'm just me."

"No, daughter. You are a unique spirit in this world," Mom said as she held my chin up. "You are one of a kind. Never forget who you are. These things in nature hunt souls, and they managed to take your father's. Someday, I know they will come after you more severely."

I nodded. "So… it's like a… hereditary disease?"

Mom wiped away her tears with a smile. "Please, just don't let it cripple you. I still see your father's aura in yours. I don't want them taking that too, daughter. They can steal your identity, your dreams, and then your life if you let them. Again, Razaiella… my beautiful and extraordinary daughter of many gifts, blessed by the ancestors. You are loved and surrounded by the angels of nature."

CHAPTER 9

State of the Art Learning The Atmosphere

The new school Mom brought us to definitely had a new feeling throughout the day. Nothing was the same—not even the teachers, as they were about forty percent automated and sixty percent human. For a school that's so quiet in Ellsworth, I never would have guessed there could be anyone here, but surprisingly, the school held seven hundred students. Everyone goes to lunch at the same time, and that annoyed me because I hated crowds at times. At least the area was peaceful and far from the roughness of the big city. One thing I loved and I could thank Mom for was that she allowed the school bus to take Lakia and Munisha home. I still loved to walk, and she said she felt safer knowing I was in such a place. When the snow began to get heavy, I would just tag along on the bus and be with the family. Just like today, we are together again.

"Ra, I really miss Dad."

"Oh, trust me, I know. Me too. My dad."

"One thing, Ra, I was kind of scared to ask. Why was he acting so weird?"

I grinned while looking out the window. "I…tsk," I shrugged.

Dad and Mom—I had so many questions myself, but Mom still didn't tell all of it. Almost comparing my Dad to some type of monster or something. The only monsters I knew were the ones who told lies and hid the truth.

"Here, what do you think?" Lakia says, showing me a sketch of what I couldn't make out at first, but eventually recognized.

"Um… at least you tried. An angel, right?"

"Grade it."

"It looks like a carrot with wings. C-minus. Hey, I answered honestly. I know some who would have given you worse."

Lakia giggled. "I wish I could draw like you."

Since she didn't have my gift, I wondered if she would be jealous of it. I wasn't always so good either. The only thing I really have is that I can see it before it's there.

"Have a good day, girls, and stay safe!" the bus driver says as we exit.

"Notice we're the only ones to get off here."

"It's because we live here, Ra," Lakia says. "And live in a rich neighborhood."

"Mom is rich?" Munisha asks.

"Yup. And Lakia and your dad are too. Oh, look—the fair. Does it ever open?"

"It always looks closed to me," Lakia replies as we all stare into the strange feeling of the park. "Mom will take us there; I know for sure."

"Tonight, then. I'll tell her I want us to go. Since I'm the oldest, she'll listen to me."

"But Ra, you don't even like rides," Lakia says.

"I don't. I just like the feeling of the park itself. The feeling of everyone being so happy. Seems like nothing bad ever happens there. It's Friday night, so no school tomorrow. I think it should be open."

The gloomy sky was overcast over us, and the city of Ellsworth may be peaceful, but it always had a melancholy feeling in the atmosphere. Maybe it was just too quiet. That's why I love sunshine, the ocean, and wind. If I'm ever rich one day, I would love my house to sit right next to the ocean with golden sands and the soft voices of the wind surrounding it.

"Hurry up, Ra. I have to pee!" Munisha says, twisting her legs together.

"I'm looking for the key, and I could have sworn I put it in my pouch. You should have used the bathroom before we left school."

"Ra's right, Munisha—"

"Hey, if you have to go that bad, just go on the side of the house."

"No! No way. Mom will be so mad. Just—"

"Got it! Now go before you mess up the front door carpet. Mom would kill us then."

"Welcome home, Lozano family."

"Hey, friend. How are you?!" I grinned as Sansa smiled back from the wall.

It's always good to be home. For some odd reason, I could feel a strange presence about to happen—just the feeling of being surprised, and it wasn't Sansa.

"Do you have a lot of homework, Razaiella? I sure do. Way more than my old school assignments."

"I have some, but I'll do it tomorrow or Sunday. Since we're in a private school, we have to wear a uniform, and we can't go outside as much—at least me. Then we're told if we fail one exam at the end of the year, we have to start all over again. The dumbest thing ever because I'm definitely not a test-taker. Tsk, Mom put us in this crazy crap."

"If you do—or keep doing it—we can be in the same grade," Lakia giggles and claps.

"Yeah… right. Okay, sis. I'm going to take a nap. I'll tell Mom about tonight because I do want us to go."

The uniform was so tight. Even as a fifteen-year-old girl, my physique makes me look more mature. If I were to just wear my shirt, they may say something. Having to wear a blazer every day with black stockings was definitely beginning to annoy me. Trade peace for control.

A much-needed nap brought the dark force that Mom spoke to me about. Although these things in my dreams appear when they desire, they always tend to have varying levels of aggressiveness. The tornado—they seem so amazing but so scary at the same time. The grey and black string of wind forms in the small city, making it almost look like a leg forming from the sky to the ocean harbor. My father told me that when they form from the ocean, they're called waterspouts. They swung swiftly side to side, along with the tornado that learned to walk. That one just started to become bigger, as it looked like it stayed in one place, facing me. The beauty of Mother Nature. There was not a soul outside; I felt the coldness of the city. Then the ocean that Mom said spoke to her, then talked to me with sounds of hydro aggressing. The book, the same exact one from the attic that watched me wherever I went, rose from the sea of oblivion. Those eyes stared straight down at me. Never allowing me to leave its sight. "What is wrong with me?"

The mirror I saw myself in could never tell. It only gave the reflection of a confused person who desperately needed answers.

"Ra! Mom said yes! We can go!" Lakia shouts at my door.

"Calm down. I haven't even eaten anything yet. What—how long was I asleep?"

"It's eight-something, and Mom ate earlier."

"I slept for four hours? Time flew by."

From everything in my dream, it felt like it had been longer, honestly.

"Come on, Razaiella! Get ready so we can leave!"

"You two better calm down up there, or no one is going anywhere!"

I smiled, closing the door in Lakia's face. She just ignored the fact I said I didn't eat anything. They usually have food at carnivals, so I don't mind. The only question is—why did the book look at me in reality? Was it alive and now in my head? Seems like the only person with the answers was really Dad.

The snow stopped, and it seemed to be right on time. Of course, the only fun thing in the city of Ellsworth was having everyone come. Just as I said—you can feel the happiness, and I definitely needed to be the one in the atmosphere.

"Look, Lakia!" Munisha says, pointing as we approach the entrance.

"That right there, I am passing on. I still need to eat, and after I do, I'm not getting on anything. Ha, maybe the Ferris wheel."

"You sure, daughter? I thought you liked rides. You're growing up and seeing it's not for everyone. If I were to get on, I'd be on a stretcher getting off."

"Let Lakia and Munisha have it. See how it feels after. Ha, and I think they call it The Waves of Carnage. No thanks."

That contraption had people swinging back and forth like a huge pendulum. The worst part of the ride is that the people are upside down and spinning like a tornado. "Just like my dreams…"

From that, everyone was minding their business, with families walking by with smiles and laughter. Some had ice cream cones served by robots, while others were staff members working the food stands. This is the perfect place, I would say, to come to if you feel alone—in your head, in your life. Just be happy with others, and you should blend right in.

"That's the first ride you two are going on?" Mom says. "How about you all get something before you do that?"

"Then they'll be sick after, Mom. Come on."

Mom grinned. "Sorry. A mother's instinct comes first. Have fun, you two, and be safe."

The way Munisha's little body tried getting through the crowd—I can only imagine if she got lost tonight.

"Sooo, daughter. How do you like the new atmosphere so far? Very different, I know—but it is time for a change."

"A big change. This right here smells so good. Turkey leg? That big?"

"Hello. How may I help you?" the silver robot with four arms says.

"Two turkey legs, please. Not too much salt, either." Mom looked at the menu on the wagon cart and shook her head. The only problem with places like this is that the food is a bit toxic.

"The amount will be… twenty-three dollars and sixty-five cents. Please pay with card or wrist pay."

"Wrist pay?" I asked in my cluelessness. "Then from a robot?"

"For twenty-three dollars, my money better not go to waste. You think is bad, daughter. Take a look over there."

From all the people walking, I didn't see what Mom was talking about. Then I saw it and realized it was something new and I had never seen before. "Wow…"

"When I went to places like this, they actually had humans doing the drawings, not machines. They are here to take your talents, Razaiella."

"But you can tell AI, you can tell when I do it."

"These things advance every other day," Mom nodded.

You have to understand that this beautiful place, with so much energy, will become gloomy once they have it entirely under their control. At work, we were first excited as we had the machines at our disposal, but they lacked something."

"What?" I asked as the balloons popped from the mini games.

"Heart, daughter. They lack heart. Even though the couple is having their picture drawn, the artist lacks emotion. I know you understand.

Other than that, Razaiella. Tell me again, daughter—how do you truly feel about all of this?"

I didn't really know the atmosphere, as I was new to it.

"Not so good, not so bad," I shrugged. "If New York had more places like this and quieter neighborhoods, it would be perfect."

"When I was a girl, there were more theme parks in Arizona. Then shopping plazas took it all over. I didn't think of it then because the boys wanted to go there more than the girls wanted to."

"I wonder why. It's boring without it."

"Greed, daughter. A child's amusement isn't enough for those who are in high power. I've seen this a long time ago, as I did enjoy being out. New friends at school?"

"Not really. Just this girl who likes to watch me draw. We talk a little, that's all. And no, I don't miss my old friends."

Mom nodded. "This is just for a better opportunity, Razaiella. I want you to feel at peace with your studies. Perhaps she can come over, and you all can help each other with homework?"

Mom knew I was okay with being alone in my room. I never had any friends come to my house. Then, with her always being so strict, I was surprised.

"Meal completed. Two turkey legs. Receipt code, three-one-three."

"Damn—I mean darn," I giggled. "This is too big to be a turkey leg. More like a baby calf."

It must have been twelve inches long, with the meat being thicker than a night's worth.

"This will take me at least three days to finish."

"I want you to know, daughter—you are so beautiful. Pose with it for me," Mom says, holding her phone up.

Hearing screams behind Mom came from the Wave of Carnage, which kept distracting me.

"Make sure you get Lakia and Munisha hollering. Oh," I laughed. "Look who got too scared. What happened, sis?"

"They said I was too short. Tsk, that isn't fair," Munisha says, folding her arms tightly while walking slowly toward us.

"Cheer up, Munisha," Mom says. "One day, you will be old enough to feel as bad. However, never rush anything. There is a time for everything, a season for all your desires. Patience is key. Razaiella and I are feeling great. She has matured significantly, and I am incredibly proud of her. This new place in Maine will be a step toward a better future for all of us. Now, how about a turkey leg for you, Munisha?"

CHAPTER 10

Project Demolition

Maine's atmosphere has grown on me, and last night's fair was spectacular with all the good vibes and emotions. For some strange reason, the sky seemed to love dressing in overcast conditions. The sun hides its face, or the clouds are just jealous of its light. So calm and peaceful, though. Drawing my favorite things was never a problem with the atmosphere. "Hello there. Are you an angel?"

The bird being so friendly with me, almost like he or she wanted to look at my drawing. "A gold, orange, and red bird. Never seen anything like you before. Gotcha."

It even allowed me to get a surreal shot of it. "Let's see if you're from this world. I... guess you are."

The AI explained the bird of limited regions in America. The Scarlet Tanager. "Definitely never seen you before in New York. Guess you don't like that place either. If you stay with me a little longer, I'll add you to my portfolio."

The Tanager flew to my shoulder and looked down at my sketchpad as if to say, I want to see how good you are first. Don't mess up my beauty. "I'll just draw you straight from my mind then. How about that? Wait... there's a bird on my shoulder. No! Don't go!"

A beautiful angel landed on my shoulder just like that. It took my mind totally off doing that, but it also showed me nature knows all. "Gosh, what's that noise?"

The echoing skies sounded like rolls of thunder coming straight for my body. Jets, I believe they called fighter jets, flying right over my head. About six of them, with one in front and the back, then two on each side, giving a V shape in the sky. "Wow, more? Then Mom says we would never hear noise like that again. I can't draw with this ruckus."

Of course, Mom would be on the phone talking with her so-called lover.

"Ra, did you hear that?" Lakia asks. "It sounded so loud, the house was shaking."

"They were just jets flying over."

"I never heard planes that sounded like that before."

"Um, where are you going? This is my room," I frowned.

"Oh… I just um."

"Just kidding, you can come in."

I have never allowed anyone into my room since we moved in. Something just told me to be a little bit more open and not so much of a recluse. Maybe my friend, the Tanager, spoke to me. Lakia, I felt, needed to tell me something, though. "Are you okay?" I grinned.

"Yeah… I just wanted to sit and see you draw. I told you I want to learn."

"You sound bored to me, but okay."

I wanted to tell her how that Tanager flew on my shoulder and just sat for a few seconds. However, sometimes it just feels like you should keep extraordinary things to yourself. People like to jinx your divine blessings since they lack them.

"You mainly draw angels. Ever tried drawing anything else?"

I frowned. "I like what I like. Then I'm learning this and already good at it."

"Oh yea," Lakia's eyes widened in surprise. "It's so pretty. I love how you use different colors for the letters. How did you do it?"

"Calligraphy Black Letter Fraktur style."

"But you can't do that with a pencil, can you?"

Getting up to go to my desk, which was filled with schoolwork and art. A little bit embarrassing, but I was a busy girl. "I got this from my dad a long time ago. I was probably seven when he gave this to me. This is called a calligraphy brush set. Some are hard to use, but I will learn to use them all someday. So hey, I'm not the best… yet."

Lakia just looked so lost, as if I were speaking another language. "One day, I'll show you."

"Ra, why you um… talk in your sleep?"

"Talk in my sleep?" I asked in surprise, but I knew there was some truth somewhere.

Lakia nodded. "Yeah… you do it a lot. When we were in New York, I used to hear you at times… you were saying something."

"I…"

"Then you did it yesterday before we went to the fair. Before Mom came home, I heard you mumbling something."

Ninety percent of my dreams felt so real. I probably couldn't tell if it was reality or not. "First of all, you shouldn't be coming inside my room without permission. Mom said no locked doors, but I guess I need to."

"Ra, I won't tell anyone. Trust me. I just want to know why you do that. It looks like a bad dream or somethin'. Yeah, that's what it is."

When she said that, it was like she was able to almost see something in my head and plugged it to the TV to see precisely what it was. Since she was so interested in knowing, perhaps she could learn a little more about me. I knew she wouldn't believe me anyway. "Can you… do you believe dreams can come true?"

"Um… yea," Lakia shrugs. "Why not? That is what they say when we want to have a good life, right?"

I grinned, shaking my head. "Not so much like that. In my dreams, there are many tornadoes, even though I have never even seen one before."

"Me neither."

"So in these dreams, they kinda' seem like… It's hard to say. Like they are trying to tell me something."

"Like what?"

"Like something bad is about to happen," I shrugged. "Hey, that's how it feels."

"Wow. That can be true. I believe you."

My eyes opened. "Really? I mean… that's great. Now, time to get something to eat. Lunchtime sounds…"

"Those planes again," Lakia says as we both look up at the ceiling fan that shook.

"They must be practicing. In New York, they did those stunts under the bridge and stuff. Dad took me to the airshow, I remember. They're cool but loud. Angels in the sky. His favorite was the Blue Angels."

So many things have changed over the years. I remember when he had me on his shoulders, and I was hanging on to his head while we walked by the waterfront, watching the jets fly around the Statue of Liberty and under bridges. With the millions of people there watching the show, I wouldn't stand a chance of seeing the angels fly. The only thing I hated about them was that the sounds seemed to make your insides shake, just like earlier. However, his bond with me, as father to daughter, was truly unique.

"What is this... what is this?" Mom says as she holds the phone to her ear. Her body is like a stone as she gazes at the TV on the wall.

"S.I.L.O initiation," I read from the bottom of the TV.

People who resembled soldiers in black and gray uniforms, with helmets, and some wearing ski masks that only revealed their eyes. The ones in the black chrome-like helmets with two black eyes looked like they were made to scare people late at night. "Who are these people?"

"How could they let this pass, Jonathon? Isn't this against everything?"

The seventy-inch TV was then showing many different ethnicities sitting in a conference room with flags from various countries.

"So you mean to tell me this is all over the world? Just how? Then, no one ever said anything about this? Okay, don't be late. Please give me a call once you're free. Love you. Bye."

Mom's face just looked so horrified as if these people were coming for her. "Are you okay? Mom?"

Mom smirked, then shook her head. "This is against nature itself. This is what I tell you, daughter... these dark forces coming for what is beautiful in nature."

Mom's face, a face I haven't seen since we left New York. To me, it just looked like a new army. What could they possibly do to us in this little town? Those futuristic-looking guns and trucks are for the bad people. Just something new, that's all. We should be safer anyway. My phone will tell me more. "S...I...L...O, initiation. Oh, so this has been a thing... just a day ago?"

All the videos that I scrolled down showed how it had just been released to the world a few hours ago. How could no one know about this? "The New World Order, Systems In Lives Omniscient. The beginning of the end."

****

A month finished with our first Christmas and New Year in Maine. Mom didn't even bother to decorate the house, just like Thanksgiving. With it being so quiet, it didn't seem like the holidays existed, especially in the neighborhood. Everyone was so tranquil with the snow falling on their faces. This place may be so peaceful, but it definitely wasn't alive. The black icy streets seem like they would never defrost. The day I chose not to take the bus back home was the day of sub-zero feeling. I just felt like tagging to be sure my skills weren't fading away. "The theme park looks deserted. Perfect."

The itching feeling of doing some real artwork was finally going to be relieved. If Nova had never taught me to jump a fence, I would have been a goner in this city. Speaking of him, he finally gave up calling me and the other fake friends. "Just can't believe they did that to me."

Just to show you, you never really know who your true friends or family are. I just can't see how people can be so evil.

The miniature theme park to me still lived without a soul walking inside. Somehow, I could still feel the energy of happiness, laughter, and excitement in the melancholy atmosphere. The empty seats of the rides to the offline robot with its head bowed. I loved it here. "Now, where do I start?"

Looking around in the somewhat spooky place with overcast snowy skies, looked like everything was just frozen. The paint wouldn't stick well, probably. Seeing the wave of carnage looked like a good first candidate. "A place where they will know, Razaiella was here."

When the ride swings back and forth, they will see, "Ra Rulez. Right in the middle."

"This place could use more designs anyway. Basic colors are so boring."

The tagging in the big city made more sense. Though Mom told me that people would think I'm in a gang once they saw it in Maine. Mainly, old heads would see it and not even care. "Heh, hey?! Who's there?!" I said as I heard a can hit the floor. Definitely a bit scary with all the clown faces and characters smiling at you. "I said, who's there? I have a gun, so don't try anything stupid!"

"Hey, it's me, well us."

"Trinity? How did you get in here?"

Trinity grinned. "The question is, how did you? Travis had to help me out. Oh yeah, this is my crazy brother, Travis. Travis, Razaiella, but she likes people to just call her Ra. She draws so much better than you can."

Trinity's brother was just an inch taller than me, and his eyes gazed at me, and I could sense he was already the shy type. "What? I won't bite. I'm Ra," I said, giving out my hand.

"Yeah, um… yea. I'm uh, Travis. You, you like to paint?"

I looked around as he just couldn't stop doing it. Was I that intimidating? "Um, are you okay? Trust me, I'm not bad, but if you test me, then you should be scared."

"No, no. I'm not scared. I'm… um."

"Stupid, that is what you are," Trinity says as she puts herself in front. "He's a bit weird, so don't mind him. I think he likes you," Trinity then whispered. "Anyways, let me see the gun."

I grinned after the smile from Travis. "I don't have a gun. I was just trying to see who you two were. I was about to get ready to go, though. Just wanted to walk around a little."

"Yeah, it's boring in Maine. I don't know why your mom took you from the fun place to this. Ellsworth is the worst in this state."

I rolled my eyes. "Tell me about it."

"Hey, get down," Travis says, getting behind a popcorn machine and then us following behind anything we can.

All I needed was to get arrested for being in this place. Mom would say I'm the cause of all troubles. "What happened?" I whispered.

"S.I.L.O trucks, coming from over there," Travis replied.

Looking over beyond the fence, the black trucks with the S.I.L.O logo and a white logo of a robotic rocket turned down my street and towards my direction to go home. Even the trucks looked creepy in person.

"These guys are the worst. I can't believe this is happening."

"My brother is right. Wait, you heard of them, right?" Trinity asked as we continued to duck.

"A little, but didn't pay enough attention. Someone in the online comment said, they are the beginning of the end."

Travis stood up slowly as there seemed to be five trucks left. "The beginning of the end sounds about right. This is a new military, so I heard. Dad told us that they're not like any other military, and they are all over the world."

"He said something… law?" Trinity says.

"Martial law. The police don't even like them," replies.

If what Travis said was true. What army was hated by the police? Authority is authority. "So why are they in Maine? This place is too quiet for them."

Travis grinned. "They're everywhere. All over the world, to the point where they need control. That's where they are. That's what Dad told me, and I can kind of see what he was talking about. Saying something about… um, Figure Eight people or something. We should get going, Trinity."

"Right."

We were safe in the park for now. I would be scared if we hopped back out and got caught by them. "You both are so scary. Besides, we're kids; why would they bother us?"

"Well, I'm leaving. See you later, Ra," Travis says as he continues toward the gate.

"See you," I smirked and waved as he looked so awkward walking away. Maybe my eyes scared him.

"Don't worry, Ra. You should get home without problems." Trinity grins. "I think he's in love, but hey. Let's hang out more. Let me catch up with this idiot. See you tomorrow!"

"Definitely!"

I couldn't tell if he was more scared of me or those trucks. To me, the fear of both, but S.I.L.O seemed scarier. "Martial law meaning. The temporary substitution of military authority for civilian rule. When in effect, the military commander is in control of an area or country. Leading to unlimited forces to make and enforce laws. Tsk, I rule my own life. As long as they don't bother me or my art, I'm good."

CHAPTER 11

Take Me Away

Being in a school with four walls and no windows made it seem like just another prison on some days. However, it was definitely safer than my previous school in New York. Trinity, along with her brother, was one of the few I spoke to. That is all I needed. "So, yeah, the big city is not as bad. You just have to watch your back."

"And someone really tried to rape you? That's crazy," Trinity says as we sit face to face in the lunchroom. "Then you said that you haven't seen your dad since. Our Mom and Dad have been married forever."

"And that's a good thing. If I ever do get married one day, I want it to be with one guy. I can't see how I can be like my mom. It sucks, honestly."

"Hey-hey, that's your mom you're talking about," Travis says.

"I mean, I am just telling you how it is. If I have children with a guy, then he might leave too. That to me, if you really think about it, is the worst. Lexus, who I told you guys about. She said that I need to be more like her. Loose."

"Loose?" Travis says with one eyebrow up. "Yea… nasty all over the place. Well, um, I'm proud of you, Ra."

I grinned. "Thanks. Basically, she just wanted me to be just like her. A whore—like her. If I didn't care about myself, I can see why, but she wasn't even ugly. That city, New York, is full of diseases. My mom is a doctor, and she showed me some… stuff that's out there. Yea, new viruses that if you catch it, you will have it until the day you die. Um, no thanks."

Trinity just looked at me as if I were speaking another language.

"It's the truth… I understand you, Ra… and there goes our lunch break," Travis says, getting up with the loud bell ringing in our ears.

"From what you said, Razaiella—"

"No-no, Trinity. I told you, just Ra," I smiled. "I like things simple for people. Besides, I don't need too many others to know me like that."

"Understood. I was just saying that you talk about New York like it's a dungeon. With tall buildings and crackheads everywhere. Kinda' scary. We can talk more after school. See you, friend."

"Trinity. Let's go to the fair tonight. You, me, and your brother. I want to get out of my house a little more, and I think my mom will be okay with it."

Trinity placed her finger on her lips and looked to the ceiling. "Hmm, that sounds good, but it's a school night, so we will have to go early. If they are open, of course."

"Yeah, they're open Thursday through Sunday. Tomorrow would be a better day, but I have a feeling about tonight. Know what I mean?"

"Okay. After school, then."

Something just told me tonight that I needed to be surrounded by happy faces and good emotions again. Being in the prison school didn't help at all. When I first came to the school, I would try to stay in the computer lab away from the crowd, but they mandated that all students be in one room during lunch. I didn't really care to sit with Lakia or Munisha as I didn't need everyone to know we were related. Many eyes from boys and even girls followed me, and I tried to stay off the grid. Maybe it was because I was a new student, or maybe my eyes seemed to glow brighter than theirs. As long as no one bothered me, I would be just fine.

"Free at last, free at last!" I grinned, hearing the last bell of the day ring and Travis's hands to the sky.

I knew he was glad to be in my last period, an elective.

"Razaiella, I mean, Ra. You like to show off in art class, I see."

"You know, art is my first love, right? I can't see myself without it. Imagine waking up and forgetting how to walk. That is how I would feel if I lost my hands or forgot how to draw."

"You know, Ms. Money is going to get you that art award of the year."

I just smiled as he and I walked out. I would have loved to be honest with Travis. I felt safe as he walked with me. Some creep of a guy might just try to talk to me all the way home. "Trinity! Over here!"

From all of the kids coming out, it was almost like millions instead of hundreds. "I asked my mom and dad if it's okay about the fair. They were hesitant at first, but we're good to go. We don't live too far from it either."

I was happy to have new friends to hang out with. I just hoped Mom wouldn't mind. "Let's go now. I know they're open. Let me just give my mom a call. I already have a funny feeling about something, and I just needed to be sure with her.

I wish I could also call my dad and let him know. It seems so odd, but there were times I was becoming afraid that my memory of my father was slowly but surely fading away. I haven't heard his voice in this new year of 2033. All I wanted to know was if he was okay. That was the only wish and prayer I asked from the ancestors.

"Ra, you're telling me you never had a boyfriend," Trinity says. "All of this time I wondered and… wow. Girl, I thought you were lying at first."

"Why should I lie? It is what it is. I don't really see anyone… I like—quick story. Two years ago, yea, I was thirteen. Just turned a teenager." I grinned. "This guy who I like, and he likes me, was just so weird. That Lexus I told you about saw our weird relationship and told us we had to stop."

"You two were trying to do the nasty or what?"

"Travis?! Sorry about him, Ra. Continue."

"Okay, and no. Nothing nasty. Only in your head. Anyway, Lex had taken me and him to the back of the school so we could have our first kiss. Yeah, a kiss. She had him and I stand in front of each other behind a bus like we were about to get married. So… the boy. He just stood there. He said he was mixed Islander and Native American Cherokee. One thing I liked about him was his height and long eyelashes."

"Yes-yes. Come on."

I grinned. "Sorry, Travis. Trinity seems to like it so far. So, um… he just kept looking around, and Lex told us, well, do something. He looked at me and then walked away."

"Whaaat? Oh my gosh, he got that scared?" Trinity asks. "Or was he just weird?"

"I don't really know. I liked him, and I was waiting for him. I won't lie; he was my first, and we eventually made it happen… once."

"Wait-wait-wait!" Travis says, walking in front of me. "You mean to tell me, you kissed him, but you said you had no boyfriend? How does that work?"

"Okay, calm down, sir."

"No, it's okay, Trinity. It's quite simple. I didn't consider… it a real boyfriend and girlfriend thing. A kiss can be from anyone, no? If there is no feeling between the two, then I don't think it's real. My eyes, like I told you guys, they scare people. Once they look at them, you may just fall in love quickly."

Travis folded in his lips and nodded. "I can go with that, but he still was your first kiss."

"Aww," Trinity laughed, patting Travis's back. "Sorry, bro. You all do know prom is coming up in a few more months. A guy asked me, and I said, maybe."

"Well, my mom, how strict she is, probably won't even let me go. I don't care."

"She might," Travis replies as if to have hope for me. "If she were really strict about you, she wouldn't let you walk home."

"That's only because I am the oldest of my sisters, and she wants me to love Ellsworth. She'd let me do the same back in New York, but that was because she didn't care as I knew many other people, I guess."

Trinity sighs. "If she knew about that behind-the-bus thing, you would've been done for."

"Exactly. To be honest, you guys, she's a weirdo. Telling me weird things about my dad, saying he's a warlock."

The twins just stopped and looked at me, then looked at each other. Now they may just think I'm weird too.

"Did you just say, warlock?" Travis asks. "Those people are, technically, witches, but the male versions."

"That is what she called my dad."

"Damn," Trinity says. "That's messed up. Why?"

Something that made me think about it too hard gave me a slight headache. "Listen, I don't want to talk about that. I will say this… I feel like I don't belong in this world. The way how people think, the way how people do things. People are just so weird… and evil at times."

"Girl," Trinity smiles. "That sounds like a guy broke your heart. Don't—"

"No-no. No one broke my heart, except my own family. Hey, we're almost there. Let's have some fun, yeah?"

I could feel the energy that one of them felt so bad for me. Travis, I know. He understood everything from me and listened. If more people were like that, instead of knowing it all, the world would be just a little better.

"Looks like they're setting up," Travis says.

"Hey, is the park open?" I asked the lazy operator as he lay back playing on his phone and his legs stretched on the table.

"Just in a few minutes. Shit, you all can go ahead in. Hey! Thirty bucks."

We all looked at each other and just grinned. "We don't have any money," I whispered.

"That's okay. Follow my league, Ra."

Trinity smirked as though she knew exactly what she needed to do. If we had no money, we definitely wouldn't be getting rides or playing games.

"If you let us in, we will give you your money."

I looked at Trinity and never knew that was in her.

"Ummm, naaa. You've got to do better than that."

"Oh, not just me. How about us both?" Trinity says, pulling my arm.

The man looked into my eyes, and I just stared back like a cat. I wasn't doing anything with this buck-tooth man. He even smelled like onions.

"Hmph, we'll see. Pretty eyes, I want my cut once you all come back out. Alright, slide through."

I didn't really think it would work, but it did. All you have to do is lie. If Trinity is about that life, she'd better pay him in full because I never said I was with it.

"See, now we can go and have fun," Travis says. "What did you tell him anyway?"

"That he can have you once we're done. Now, let's go."

The mini park was still lovely and energetic yet quiet. I didn't want to get on any rides anyway. They wanted to, but none of the operating robots were online.

"That reminds me. That new S.I.L.O. has something they are telling people to take. They said they would pay… what was it, Trinity?"

"Travis is talking about S.I.L.O. and some new medicine they have."

I thought to myself, *medicine*? "What does it do?"

"Nobody knows," Travis replies. "I think they said like five thousand dollars if you take it. Then, since money is going towards currency, it's eighteen thousand in O'C'—omni credits. That is the new currency of the world, they say. It started from the east side, and the world agreed to it, so now it's going everywhere."

The remarkable thing is that Nova spoke about this a long time ago. I swore I heard it before, but couldn't remember when.

"Now that's impressive," Travis says, looking up at the motionless Ferris wheel. "How did you get that high and spray your name that high?"

"Um, I rode."

"Duhh, of course she did. How else would she do it? My brother likes you so much, he doesn't know what to say," Trinity whispered.

The park's lemonade was good, but too bad we couldn't get that ridiculous turkey leg that took me three days to finish. Just walking around in the place made me feel happy.

"Hey, I'm going to use the restroom real quick."

"Ra, he would have me do this, and he really thinks we girls like this," Trinity sighs, shaking her head. "He told me to ask you… would you go to the prom with him? Tsk, I know, right? That's pathetic, and I told him—"

"No, that's not it. I'm surprised he doesn't think I'm weird, after all I've been through. Hmm, I'll have to think about it."

"Well, he wanted to know today, but you can tell him once you know your answer… and what do you mean by weird? Friend, you are… amazing. You are, you are beautiful, honest, and I'm lucky to be your friend. I respect you for that highly. Those friends you had in New York may have been bad, but you deserve better. Never let anyone make you feel down about yourself. Especially a guy."

Trinity's eyes looked in mine, and I felt her warm presence. "Um… are you lesbian?"

We both laughed and hugged as friends, as friends should be. My hardened heart began to get just a little softer as I didn't even know what to call a true friend.

"What are you two giggling about? Not me, I hope."

"Not at all, brother. Why do you look so awkward? Oh, I was supposed to say something?"

"Hey, give him a break, Trinity. Yes," I said as I smirked and put on my scary cat eyes. "I'll go with you to the prom. I'll be your lady for the night."

Travis couldn't stop blushing; it reminded me of long ago when, for some reason, he started to scratch his hair. I wanted to ask if he was okay. He may just poop himself next. "Only one condition, though."

"One condition?" Travis's eyebrow raised.

I knew exactly what to do to see if he indeed was for me. To see if he can be my brave knight and shining armor. "You see that rock climbing thing over there? I want you to climb up and spray your name at the top."

Trinity laughed. "Ho-ho. You know darn well he's not doing that."

"Of course, I'm not. I don't have any spray cans."

"Oh yes, you do," I said, pulling off my backpack.

"Whaaat? You actually carry around spray cans in school?" Travis asks with his eyes stretched.

"Hey, all you have to do is go there and write, Travis. T, R, A, V, I, S. That's all, and I'm all yours," I smirked. "Come on, you can do it. For me?"

Travis took the red spray can from my hand while I continued to smile at him. I felt every single bone in his body trembling.

The climb was only about twenty feet. I could do it in a minute. We did billboards and stationed trains back at home, and the trick was: never stop focusing on what you're trying to do. That's when you might fall.

"You're really going to do this, brother? I don't think you should."

"Yea, I know—"

"If you fall, Mom is going to ground me, and Dad is going to kill you! You'd better know what you're doing!"

"And hurry up, someone may come," I said, looking around the pretty much empty park.

"How the hell do you get this on?"

I sighed. "Forget that. Just climb up there. Don't be such a wimp."

Travis looked up to the top as if his life depended on it. "Alrighty', here we go!"

I told him it wouldn't be hard, and it looked easier when he was already halfway up. Then it dawned on me that I might be going to prom with someone I don't really see as a boyfriend. He may try to kiss me, thinking so.

"Oh shit!"

"Travis!" Trinity shouted. "That's enough, get down, now!"

"I'm good, I'm good. I can… almost… reach it."

"Wow, I guess my eyes really do hypnotize people."

Trinity frowned. "Ra, that's not funny. He's my brother."

"Ra, Razaiella! This is for you!"

He actually did it. The scaredy cat actually did as he was told. Well, I was a girl of my word. "Now, Ra Rules with a Z' at the end, and we're good to go."

"Ra… really?" Trinity says, rolling her eyes.

"Hey, you two! What are you doing?! Hey, you fool! You have no safety belt?! Get your little ass down from there now! Slowly! Better yet, wait, I'm coming."

I ran as fast as I could, not realizing that I had left my only two friends. "Tsk, we're busted."

Looking back and seeing Travis get down with the security man keeping his hand on his back, and then finally to the ground. I couldn't just leave now, especially noticing how his name and mine remained.

"Where are all your parents?" the security asks, holding and pulling Travis's shirt. "How did you all even get in here? The park is still closed."

"Well… we," Trinity says, then looks towards me.

"You sir, you are in the most trouble. That, sir, is called vandalism. Your parents will be paying for the damages, I'm assuming."

Poor Travis. He did all that for me. "Hey, wait. It… it wasn't him. I mean, he drew it, but I… but I told him to do it."

"Oh, is that true?"

Travis looked so scared, but when he looked at me, for some reason, it was like he knew everything was okay since he had won his ticket with me to prom.

"My friend, you have a lot to learn about life, especially women. They're both full of tricks. Let's go. You too, ladies. You, Miss Troublemaker. Get your parents on the phone."

As darkness falls came with my mom, I knew it would be another long night. It didn't even make sense how so many forces seemed to be against me. All I try to do is be honest, respectful, and loving. I'm not a bad person; I just have bad luck.

"I thought getting away would change things. Getting away from the sin city would help my family to see that life out there is still better. So, they won't be corrupted by the foolishness of the demonic ways. Jonathon was right. It really doesn't matter. However, I still believe in you, Razaiella… that you will never fall to the dark forces of our world. That the sun's shining face will never set on yours. The rays of the sun are spectacular to us, only if we truly want to understand. People tend to open their eyes and hearts when it's too late. Please, do not be like this, daughter. Someday… once I return to the planet, you will take my place as a mother of dignity and excellence. I know you will, daughter."

I just continued to stare out the window as it gave a better show. Mom had enough money to pay them back, and I had already said I was sorry. I guess she wanted me to beg for forgiveness, which I would never do for anyone in that matter. I am who I am. She dragged us up here and thought things would be perfect. Who knows, tomorrow may be the day something else happens, or next week. That is just how things are. I guess we would just keep moving and running away.

From the darkness falls to the morning sunshine, I surely felt the sun on my face. It was going to be a brand new day. Despite what happened yesterday, I feel like it was just a mistake, and I will tell Travis we are still good. At least they let him go along with Trinity. Most importantly, he didn't get hurt. I'll even skip breakfast today. Let my mom relax and know that I'm trying to be the best I can be. "I wonder who that can be," I said as I heard the doorbell echo upstairs to my room. "Probably Jonathon," I sighed. "Be positive, Ra, be positive. Maybe it's Dad."

Lakia and Munisha were already up. They never stayed asleep.

"What do you mean we have to comply to go out with you all? I don't know anything about this, and I need the real police."

"Ma'am, we are here on protocol. All will be clear once you and your family arrive at the facility."

The same metal faces of the people made it to our home. Why? "Mom?"

"You can't just take us from our own home? This is outright absurd!" Mom says, pulling out her phone in frustration.

"Since you have relocated to this town, we mandate that you come for observation and screening. All we ask is your cooperation. All will be clear."

"Jonathon? Hello? Oh my gosh. Why isn't he answering? Jonathon, please give me a call back. These devils, S.I.L.O., are at my house and trying to remove us."

"Mom?" I said, walking up close slowly. Seeing the man and woman with those metal masks made me a bit frightened. "What's wrong?"

"Ra, please. Go back upstairs."

"Wait," the female soldier demanded. "Her eyes. Have you been screened before?"

"No, what do you want?"

"Ra, please go back upstairs with your sisters. Please, listen to me, daughter," Mom said, with tears beginning to build up.

Walking slowly backward and looking into the darkness of the eyes of the soldiers. They looked scarier in real life altogether. Mom said they were here to take us, and that wasn't going to happen. One man I knew could get these trespassers out of our home. I know he's around. "Come on, Dad. Please… please… pick up. Try again… try again."

Dad knows me and knows when I need him. He can sense where I am. "Dammit. Dad, come on. I need you. Mom needs you."

Having too little or no contacts in my phone. I never even thought about giving Trinity or Travis my number. She told me her parents were strict about the toxicity of social media as well as mine. "Okay, maybe him. Nova, hey! Yeah, I'm okay. No, no. It's okay. Listen, S.I.L.O, um, they're at my house. Yea… yea, tell me, what should I do? Run? What do you mean?"

I placed my hand over my mouth. "Are you serious? Yeah, okay. I'll try. Thanks, talk to you later. I have to tell Mom."

Test subjects. We're not frogs. Nova said it's a martial law effect, just like Travis said. I didn't know we were being experimented on. "Egh, the stupid window… tsk, locked tight."

No matter what. I always tend to be alright. I have nothing to be afraid of, nor my family.

"Razaiella… can you come downstairs, please?"

My tongue felt like needles, hearing Mom's voice sounded so weird. My heart also raced. Maybe we could run away somehow.

Mom's crying eyes looked to me, "But it just isn't right."

"We will take her, and our systems management team will decide what protocol to follow next. Since she is the firstborn. We can settle for now," the female officer says, looking at me as I slowly walk to my mom. "Yes, we will take her."

"Take who? Take me?"

The metal ghost-faced soldiers just looked down at me.

"Get out of our house!" I shouted. "We don't know anything about you people, and we didn't do anything!"

"Razaiella," Mom says, holding me from behind.

"Razaiella Lozano. Is this correct?" the male officer says as he points the tablet at me.

"I thought if anything, we all would be going. Why me? By myself? Why?"

"Daughter… it's going to be alright, sniff. They can't harm you. They won't, okay? Just… I promise you, you will be okay."

Mom's face just looked so broken, but that wasn't enough for what was happening to me. "This can't be. Mom, please. They can't just take me. Why would you let them?"

"Please," the male officer says, behind me as I stare down into my mom's eyes. "Come with us. All will be clear."

"You evil people! We can't even see your faces! You all are like a gang, and I won't go!"

Looking up the stairs and seeing Munisha and Lakia looking down at me. They both looked shocked, but Mom didn't even stop them from seeing me like this. It's so unfair and cruel. "Just leave us alone!"

The soldier grabbed my arm and pulled me, and with all my strength, I tried to break free.

"Come now," the female soldier says. "You will see your family again. Just be a good girl and cooperate."

The evil gang pulled me to the porch, and I saw a neighbor's light go out in front of us. Why me? Mom followed, still crying and seeing me being dragged. I can get away. "Dad, where are you?!" I shouted, looking side to side, hoping he would come out of another dimension to get them all.

"I thought you said her father was not around," the female officer said as the male continued to pull me towards the black van.

"Agh. Shit! She bit me!"

Again, I was running from the true evil spirits Mom warned me about, and I did not know where I could possibly go. "Eygh."

The feeling of something shocking, physically and mentally, knocked me to the cold sidewalk. I couldn't move at all. Seeing my mom run and holding her mouth with complete fear. It was all her fault. The sun was shining, but the clouds covered its light from me. They all did this to me.

CHAP 12

The Beasts Realm

My head throbbed with aches and dizziness. My senses had become so weak. What was happening to me, my life, and this crazy world? "What? Where… am I? Is this… a dream? Why?"

I woke up again and saw my arms and legs strapped to a bed. This is reality. They put cords all over my body. What were they doing to me?

"Hello-hello-hello," a man says, wearing a long lab coat, accompanied by a short-cut brunette woman wearing a gray blazer and black skirt. "Ra… Razaiella? That is your name? A name very unique. Definitely not from around here, no?"

The doctor smiled, looking at the other woman. "How are you feeling?"

With all my strength, I tried to make out some words. "Wha... what have you done to me? Where is my mom? Dad?"

"Here safely, child," the doctor replied. "Now, there is nothing to fear, Razaiella. Nothing at all. You are not here to be harmed or harassed in any way. You have been chosen, and you should feel quite happy and proud of yourself."

"But… why?" came my weak voice.

"Because you are of a rare breed. Oh yes," the doctor nods.

"Rare... breed?"

"Yes, my dear. I think you have already noticed. Let me first introduce myself. My apologies. I get excited when I see new patients. My name is Dr. Sarban, and this is my assistant, Ms. Ava. We will be your best friends while you are here, so we can learn from each other."

As my eyesight became clearer, I paid no attention to this man. This place seemed to be from the future, with glass doors that appeared impossible to break. "What is… this place?"

"You are in S.I.L.O., Missy," Ms. Ava says with an evil smirk. "Now, pay attention. You will be released soon so that you can look around."

"Let's actually do that now," Dr. Sarban implies. "There are no prisoners in this facility, especially my guest."

Dr. Sarban loosened the straps on my arms and legs. I wondered if I could try to get away. I wouldn't even know where to go. Then they might shoot me again.

"Now, since that is done. The cables linked to your body are nothing but to test your heart and pulse. EKG. You see, you're fine," Dr. Sarban smiled. "We are here to help."

My mind was feeling a little more stable. When they walked in the room, whatever they did to me seemed to start to wear off. "To help with what?"

"We wish to see and check about who you truly are. As before, there are specific genes that we can recognize, indicating that a patient may hold the key to the future. Our world, Razaiella. As a human race, we are unfortunately declining. Thousands of years ago, we lived much longer. We were essentially… superior to our present time. What we seek is what we need for a brighter future. So, we need to do a little catching up, yes? Artificial Intelligence has given us ideas that we would have never thought of. Now, to save our human race, we will need those of…special blood. Rare breeds… one of a kind."

Dr. Sarban loved to look into my eyes and smile as I laid down on the soft white medical bed. I felt safe, but that was probably just to make me feel that way for the moment.

"Here," Ms. Ava says, giving me her tablet.

It was light as a feather and looked as though it were made out of the same glass as the walls surrounding me.

"Answer every question accurately. Your ethnicity-race is most important," Ms. Ava says.

Holding the tablet, I noticed that Roman numeral text had been written on my right wrist. Looking at the list, the ethnicities had more than fifty, which seemed like. Whenever I signed for an application, it only had about five or six. For some reason, Black and White weren't on there. For me, Native American, of course. My eye color wasn't on here, so I guess, other. Everything else looked good.

"Finished?"

I grinned at Dr. Sarban's accent. "I'm sorry, you just say, finished, kinda' funny."

"No-no, my dear. It's quite all right. I am not native to this place. I am from, they call, the Middle East. English is not my first language. As I said before, Razaiella. We are your friends, and no harm is to be done to my friend. Now, before you step down, are you able to walk properly? Can you feel your legs one hundred percent?"

Trying to lift my legs, which felt like they hadn't moved in months. I finally got down, and the shock of the vibration from the numbness hit me. I definitely was out for a few days. They didn't even tell me. "I think I got it."

"Good, good," Mr. Sarban said, helping me up. "Now we must go to get a little sample from you since your body is online now. Do you care for needles?"

"Umm, not really."

Dr. Sarban grins. "I see, as you don't have any tattoos, unlike many of the younger generation."

"I'm only fifteen."

"Here, put this on," Ms. Ava says, handing me a silver bag.

Opening the compact pouch was a silver jumpsuit that felt like nylon fabric and was very comfortable. I was so traumatized that I didn't even realize I was just in underwear. These bastards saw everything.

"Feels good, doesn't it?" Ms. Ava smiled.

"It's okay. Silver isn't really my color."

"Then we will just have to order you a black one, my dear," Mr. Sarban says, holding the door open for Ms. Ava and me.

I have never seen what the new world government building looked like. It was like a futuristic mall with glass everywhere and weird-looking metals. There were many glass doors with people walking around wearing the same outfit. There were elevators everywhere, and not a speck of uncleanliness was on the walls or floor—like they polished it all. The only thing that was missing were the masked demons.

"Here we are," Dr. Sarban says, again holding the sliding door for me.

There were many men and women sitting and waiting, like in a hospital, though they all looked so depressed.

"Since you are my new and favorite guest, Razaiella, you get to skip these people. VIP access, yes?"

"I… I could have waited."

Ms. Ava grins. "We give you VIP clearance, and you turn it down? You can't be ungrateful."

"Now-now, Ms. Ava. We want our patients to feel welcome. I will tell you a little trick, Razaiella, about times like this," Mr. Sarban says as he turns and looks down at me. "Your heart may be racing, but you do realize you can make yourself feel better? Just by getting things over with faster makes it better. It's a mind thing, my dear. I love always to say, it either makes you or breaks you. You choose. Wait, let the fear take over… or finish it now? Your choice, Razaiella."

The cold air filled the place, and all those people were waiting. I didn't want to sit in a crowd. The air conditioning was a little too chilly. "I'll do it now."

"Good girl," Ms. Ava smiled. "You're a big girl anyway. Needles are nothing compared to other things."

"Ms. Ava. Now, it will just be a prick, my friend."

The doctor, wearing a face mask, stared at me while he was holding a device that almost looked to be a spray gun with a long needle coming from the exit hole. I was going to get shot with this thing. I still didn't clearly understand why they had to do this. Then Nova's words came… for an experiment. I'm pretty much dead already.

"You're even going to look at it?" Mr. Sarban says.

"…I have to see what he's doing."

The doctor first placed an alcohol wipe on my right arm, and then I saw him take the gun, which then made my heart skip a beat. The pinching effect wasn't too bad, but it felt like a stream flowing out of me into the gun. Seeing my blood bubble into a small tube underneath it and then flow swiftly made me think it was all okay. I guess they knew what they were doing since I felt no pain, only the stream coming from my arm.

Mr. Sarban clapped lightly while he smirked at me. "And that's that. Told you it would be easy. Now you can go and meet some new friends."

"What just happened? What did you do to me?"

Dr. Sarban kneeled on his knees and held both of my hands. "Remember, we are just here to help. Once we are all done, you will be on your way home faster than you think. So don't manifest in your scary thoughts, my dear. It's nothing to be afraid of. You will be alright, okay, my friend?"

Mr. Sarban seemed sincere, but I was never given an explanation for what they had just done to me. There was only a slight pain as the needle entered and exited, then just the blood rising from the site. I used to get a smiley face bandage from the pediatrician, but now I just get a plain circle one to conceal it.

"Ms. Ava. I am sure you will take care of the rest. It's time to get to the next protocol. I sense we are getting closer. Oh yes, I can feel it!"

It seemed to me that S.I.L.O. loved the word protocol as if they had already planned this a thousand years ago. Following Ms. Ava, the futuristic atmosphere of this place was just beyond. The new technology was just unbelievable. The ceiling of the room where it seemed everyone came together—it changed from image to image. From pure sunny skies to rain and flowers blossoming. While squinting my eyes at the roof, I could see tiny hexagons shift quickly as they flipped to create new images.

There was no way they just came out of the blue like this. We would have seen it in textbooks and magazines. For me, I would have seen something, as it would have been online. I always tried to find new styles for my graffiti texts, but none of this stuff looks like anything anyone on Earth has seen before. How, and how so fast?

"Don't be shy, Ms. Lozano. You will be here for some time. So feel free to make a few friends," Ms. Ava said as she kept walking ahead of me.

I could already sense and tell that men were just staring me down. None seemed to be around my age, maybe a few girls. One guy looked goofy and crazy, like a hyena—a fat man eating to his heart's content. Then, a man was sitting alone, and he looked crazy as hell, too. At least I could spot a group of guys playing chess at the table. I was in a futuristic building, but also in the crazy house.

"Now, here is the dinner for the day," Ms. Ava says as she looks down at the numerous dishes of fruits and veggies.

Of course, they would have robots serving everything. "I'll just take the apple."

"So you know, that will be your only food for tonight. You should think twice about something so small. Oh," Ms. Ava grinned. "Since you're slender, you're afraid to become like the slob over there. Looks don't last forever, sweetheart."

I didn't care about what Ms. Ava had to say. An apple a day will keep the evil spirits away. Mom always said our bodies were from our ancestors, and we should always protect and keep them pure. Finally, there are a few females here, and they were just talking together. I thought for a second the entire room would be filled with males. If these people were all chosen, why did I need to be here?

As we entered the elevator once again, I noticed none of the floors had numbers, but letters. I was on the G wing. The Last floor seemed to be with the X.

"Here is your room… and here is your keycard. Give it to no one and never lose it. Only you and the employees have your key. Until tomorrow, we have much work to do. So be ready," Ms. Ava winked. "Goodnight."

"Okay. When will I go home?"

"When we are ready to release you," Ms. Ava turned and smiled. "Goodnight."

"Yea…"

That is all I wanted and needed to ask. I could already feel her energy, and it wasn't pleasant. My room, on the other hand. "Hmmm, not so bad. Wow… almost like my room at home, but squarish."

My bedroom looked so unique in a place like this, which looked mainly to be for research and experiments. A white and gray theme wasn't too bad. The only thing missing was a jacuzzi, but it had a shower and a bathroom. A mini sofa and a desk. "Wait a minute," I said, walking to the desk with a shimmering object on it. "My necklace. I almost forgot my neck was naked."

Being knocked out for I don't know how long, the ancestors never left me. Even when everyone has or will, they won't.

CHAPTER 13

Angel Whisper

I woke up the next morning in a cold room where I had no control of the thermostat. My belly ached, and the leftover apple was the only thing, along with bottled water on the desk. Then, having a dream of a tornado once again. The skinny gray and black ones. Just coming from the sky, looking down at me, and then awakening in this place. All of it seemed like a nightmare, but for some reason, I couldn't remember my dream clearly. All the time here so far, in this futuristic dungeon, I felt a sense of no escape. Something just told me there was no going back, even if I were to leave somehow. Only forward with my life.

Knock-Knock-Knock

"Good morning, Razaiella," Ms. Ava said as she gave me that evil smirk. "How was your first night in your new bed?"

"I want to go home!" I hissed.

"All in due time, all in due time," Ms. Ava smiled, then looked to her tablet. "Today is a new day—a day of greatness and to show off the true you. I know you're hungry, so you should get moving with me if you don't want to starve. Come on, now."

Already in the morning, which I couldn't even tell from the solid walls, she was taking me somewhere. This place was spotless; even the floor looked to be finished with acrylic polish. It's ironic that the people are not told to shower before they exit their rooms. "Omni therapy? What is this place?"

"A room where you get to show your skills, Ms. Lozano, Razaiella. You're not afraid. You don't look like the type… more of a girl who probably has daddy issues."

The long, silent hallway echoed as Ms. Ava's heels clicked and clacked. Not a soul was in here. I looked into a small window on a room door. A man was tied to the bed, and another to the side of him. He looked like he was going to vomit or try to cough up something, the way his body kept trying to lift up.

"Razaiella," Ms. Ava says as she stands in front of the room door. "Nothing there for you, so stop being nosy. I know you're hungry. You remember your keycard?"

I nodded. "So what are you all going to do now? After this, can I call my mom at least?"

"Of course," Ms. Ava smiled. "Just cooperate, and all will be clear."

That saying from these people. It started to sound like all of them had written it a thousand times in a notebook to get the job. The room had many robots that moved, not the bootleg androids, but some of them moved and walked quite well. Then, a machine that I have seen cancer patients go inside of. "I have to get inside that thing?"

"That's right," Ms. Ava replied as she focused on her tablet.

A man and a woman, both wearing face masks, looked serious. I had never seen a doctor or nurse in a gray and black uniform. The robots inside seemed to only move items around, like medical equipment.

"Hello there," the male doctor said. "Please remove your attire and lie on the table."

Ms. Ava frowned. "Don't look at me. Do as you're told."

As I had no choice, and my hunger began to grow. Removing my clothes wasn't that bad.

"Remove your underwear as well."

"What?!" I questioned the female nurse.

"Come on, Ms. Lozano. I don't have all day with you," Ms. Ava hissed.

Trying to cover my top and private area was so embarrassing. How was all of this right? I knew nothing about these people. Tears began to come, just like how I was in that alley that day. Just get it over with, I reminded myself.

"Oh, yeah, and remove your necklace, too. Vanilla or chocolate?" the female nurse asks, holding a mini bottle that clearly showed the flavors.

"Vanilla. Um, what is this?"

"Something that will accelerate your five senses," the doctor replied as he typed on the computer swiftly.

The female nurse then placed cables with stickers on them—one on both of my arms, one on my left chest, and one on my forehead. All I could do was look at the necklace sitting on the table while they prepped me.

"Lie back on the table and just relax," the doctor says. "This will be over as soon as you know it."

As the table, more like a tray under me, began to move inside the machine, the feelings of closeness, emptiness, and loneliness came over me—the darkness of my nightmares inside this AI machine. Lights began flickering with the beautiful, intricate colors of the cosmos. It felt as if I had been placed in another dimension among the stars. Then, in my mind, I could sense that something was just not right. The energy coming from this—it was not authentic, not human—something these scientists have made to use on the people. A light then flashed, almost blinding me.

"You see, not so bad, was it?" Ms. Ava says as my body moves slowly from the darkness.

Immediately coming out, I reached for my necklace and wrapped it back around my neck. I just felt so alone without it. It was like someone was with me until I took it off. "What are you all trying to do to me? That felt so… just not right. Please," I whimpered. "Just let me go home. Please? Eygh, shit!" I said, pulling the cord from my upper left chest.

"You complain too much," Ms. Ava smiled.

"Ms. Ava, you are not obligated to touch the controls," the male doctor raised his voice. "These are not toys."

"If she is going to be my patient, I need her to toughen up. Oh, you're mad… really?"

I frowned, watching the spit slide down her so-surprised face. No one disrespects me or hurts me like that.

"Well then," Ms. Ava says, pulling out a handkerchief from her pocket and wiping her face. "You want to disrespect, S.I.L.O., S.I.L.O. will disrespect you. Are you still hungry? No-no, come here."

"Eygh, stop! Let me go!" I shouted as Ms. Ava pulled me to the door.

"I will not tolerate disrespect! Now go get your breakfast!"

"No! Open the door!" I shouted, banging on the cold door. "You bitch, open the door!"

I banged so hard, thinking I would break the weird honeycomb glass.

"The lunchroom is downstairs, Ms. Lozano. Be a big girl and get yourself something. You're big and bad, right?"

"I said open the door!"

Hearing my voice crack from yelling and my heart racing. This couldn't be. The coldness of despair. I was just hypnotized by a machine and then pulled outside the room with the coldness of the hallways wrapping around my body. "Heyyy!"

The scream echoed throughout the hallway, and that is when I could hear a door further down from me unlocking. I knew then I had to get out of here. The building was so big, I couldn't even remember where my room was. Footsteps, coming from one direction, so I would have to go the opposite. Where could I possibly go? "Mom... Dad, I need you. Somebody, anybody, please. Help me."

As the tears began to flow, I realized that the dream had warned me. Why did all of this stuff have to happen to me? What did I do to deserve this?

"Aye! What in the devil's playground?"

"No, no. Leave me alone," I said, covering my breasts and private from a guy I had seen before here.

"I got you—I got you. How did you get like this?"

"I... just help me," I whimpered. "I need clothes. Ms. Ava—"

"Shoosh—shoosh," the man whispered, holding me close.

Thank the ancestors, someone came when I needed them. He saw pretty much everything, though. I wanted to keep my eyes closed, but I needed to see where I was going. Where was the security? "Hey—wait! No!"

"I'm trying to help," the man laughed.

"Let me go! You asshole! I said let me go!"

"Aye, fellas! Looke' here what I found! Wandering out of her room! I usually like to see my women at the club like this, but you will do!"

I yelled and screamed while trying to keep my privacy. All was too much. Seeing everyone in the room, full of men and some women hanging out. This couldn't be real. My mind was still stuck in that machine.

"She's a beauty, and she's all mine! All mine! You all heard that?!"

They laughed while some were confused about how I had managed to come out without my silver jumpsuit. It all looked just like a bad dream.

"Get your ass on the floor! You're too fine and going to be the first if anyone in this place."

The man threw me to the floor was all I needed to wish I were dead next. All I could do was curl up as tight as I could, holding on to my feathered pendant.

"Help is on the way."

A voice from nowhere whispered, but my eyes remained shut tight to even see where it came from.

"It's time to get it ooon!" the crazy man shouted, but soon silence came after his voice.

I just wanted to wake up. The quietness in the room happened so suddenly, and then the feeling of a warm cloth came over my exposed, cold body and soul. With just my right eye slightly opening and looking up, a man standing with no shirt but silver pants faced the guy who forced me here and humiliated me. I then closed my eyes again, as a deep sleep would be better than this place.

"I didn't do anything. She was like that when I found 'er!"

The feeling of hands grabbing me, lifting me on my feet, as I held the clothing over the front of my body. Finally, opening my eyes back up. The man who stood still and made all the silence… gone.

CHAPTER 14

Beyond The Stars

Inside my box room, I felt like I was in the safest place in the world—the only place where I could truly think and see what I needed to do next. Never in my life, at such a young age, would I have thought of being physically and mentally drained, alone in a place where I still have not seen pure sunlight. I was in prison, which made me feel like it was home.

"Why did this happen to me?"

Knock-knock

"Hello, hello," a man says, smiling, stepping inside with his top-notch business suit. "My name is Sir Maximo. I heard there was an issue concerning you in my facility."

"I was harassed. Then I was—"

"You, young lady. Spitting in my employee's face. I believe that there is nearly no shame as close to what you have done. We have zero tolerance for disrespect. Do you understand?"

"Tsk," I frowned.

I needed to find a way out of this place.

"I said to you, little girl," the well-dressed man says as his smile turns upside down, then lifts my face up with his finger. "You will not disrespect my employees. I will not tell you again. Mr. Sarban, I trust you will lead her well. Good day to you, subject, goldy eyes."

If I ever saw this man again, I would love to slit his throat for touching me.

"Razaiella. My goodness, so it is true?" Dr. Sarban says.

"Why can't you all just let me go home? Why?"

"I told you already, this is the problem. You are here just for a few tests, nothing more. If I can get you out, I will try my best, but it is nearly impossible as of now. However!" Dr. Sarban smiled. "I know you are in agony over seeing your family. I have summoned your mother, and… it's about that time."

I looked up to Mr. Sarban's smile as the light from the roof came behind his head. "What? She's here?"

"Come on, get yourself ready. I told you, if you just be good, you will be fine. Don't let anyone make you do something you may regret later."

"But Ms. Ava… that bitch—"

"Now-now," Mr. Sarban grins, waving his finger side to side. "Get yourself ready. One thing about me, I am always on time."

I threw on my silver warmer set, which had five folded in the closet at all times. It was snug but definitely made me feel comfortable.

"All set?"

I tried to smile. "Yeah."

Maybe Mom had an idea for me to get out of here. She came for a reason. I have to tell her that this place is killing me inside and out, and one more night here, I might just end it. She has money, too. She can probably bribe them. Bribe Mr. Sarban.

"One thing I must say, Razaiella. You must not overreact. Patients here who see their loved ones are kind of lucky. This facility is very much private, so please, keep it brief, okay?"

I nodded. There was nothing I was going to hide. She had to get me out of this place. All of this stuff in here was made to drive you crazy. I could feel it.

"Here we are," Mr. Sarban says, opening the door and seeing the room with a glass door and another glass one in front of it. "Remember to keep it brief. Take a seat, and a guard will call you in shortly. Enjoy," Dr. Sarban says, closing the door behind me. "I have to get out of here. Wait…"

I could sense something about this guy who was waiting in the waiting room, too. "…Hey?"

The man smirked. "…Hello there."

"You… you were the one. Was it you, right?"

The wavy black-haired man nodded slowly as he sat forward with his hands folded and eyes closed.

"I… I thank you so much. I didn't see your face well, but somehow, I knew it was you."

"All is well. Just be careful next time."

His soft voice and calming demeanor were alien. This man was built in many ways I could sense—judging when I saw his back that day. He doesn't even seem like he would hurt a fly. Yet, he stood in front of those idiots. "So, what happened to you?"

"I think you already know."

"Um… not really. Well… being experimented on?"

The man just kept his eyes closed as if he were blind or just tired of looking at S.I.L.O.'s walls.

"Are you alright?" the soft-voiced man asked.

"Not really. I'm just ready to get out of here before I lose my mind. I hate this place, and I'm becoming more and more frightened."

"It's all in your head."

"What?" I said, as the soft-voiced man murmured and kept his eyes and hands closed.

"You feel frightened, correct?"

"Yes… I do."

"Your feelings and mind are afraid of what's to come. I tell you, never let your mind deceive you into something that is not even there. Never let fear take anything from you."

"Umm."

The man smirked and finally opened his grayish-blue eyes to me. "You must learn to control your mind, or it will control you."

"…I, yeah."

"In this world, you have to think. You have to think for yourself. Think beyond the stars, and things will come to you naturally. You will see things you never could see. The devil isn't after you for where you are, but for where you are going."

They probably made this man wacky by keeping him in here too long. I have to get out of here, too. His eyes were pretty, though. "Yeah, I get you."

Where were the guards? Dr. Sarban probably put me in here with a crazy person to be funny. "Oh, thank the ancestors."

"Seth Vero," the guard says with his face covered and a pistol at his side.

I could have sworn I was next, but he was in here first.

"You can have feelings, but never let them have you. Everything happens for a reason."

The anonymous man says as he walks past with a smirk. Similar to a déjà vu, but I couldn't figure it out. What was his deal? All I could see was that this place makes people insane. I knew I was next if I didn't get out. "Now I have to wait for him."

I just wondered how all of this—no one spoke of. My mom's boyfriend knew a great deal but never mentioned anything about this new system. What they will do to people. It all didn't seem real. Just seemed like we were all in one big nightmare in a building. They must have had three cameras in one room. Making sure you don't make any clever moves. How can a place like this not make you go crazy? The blue-eyed guy didn't seem worried, but for some reason, my feelings told me nothing he said was wrong.

"Razaiella Lozano."

I immediately got up out of the chair, and my hands were kind of shaky.

"You are only authorized to speak briefly."

"Hey."

"Wear the mic on your shirt at all times. If you remove the mic, there will be severe consequences."

The mini mic, which looked like a small chip placed right below my neck, made me realize that these people truly meant *brief.* I guess I was going to just tell Mom how much of a good time I was having. "Mom?"

"Razaiella! Daughter!" Mom says, opening her arms swiftly, coming to me, and then locking me into her bosom. "I've missed you, I've missed you so much. Are you okay?"

Looking into my mother's eyes with so much confusion and pain, mine were greater. "I need to get out of here, Mom. This place is not something..." I stalled, thinking about the device under my tongue. "They… sniff… they…"

I could not say what I needed to, as the pain was so unbearable.

"What did they do, daughter? It's okay, tell me."

"Sniff... Mom, please, I am begging you to get me out. I can't stay here for another night. Please, they took me from my home, and now they're... testing on me. Please... I'll be okay once I go home. I won't cause any more trouble. I promise."

Mom nodded as the tears came to her eyes. "I..."

"Mom, please. If you can't, let Dad take me. Please, I just want to get out of here. They—me. I'm your daughter. Don't you love me?"

Mom cried, but looking in her eyes, there was something that whispered to me that she was just too weak and afraid to do anything.

"Are you telling me you can't do anything? Mom, they fucking hurt me!"

"Time's up!" the guard says.

"How can that be? I was told to have ten minutes with my daughter! Not five!"

"I said, time's up. Please pack your belongings and dismiss yourself, or I will have to physically remove you from this facility."

"Mom?"

"Ra, forgive me. I have some supplies for you."

"I said, time's up!" the guard raises his voice as he begins to walk over.

"Please, sir. I have something for my daughter."

My heart started racing faster and faster as the guard showed no empathy, and Mom roamed around in her purse for something, then handed me a black bag and went back into her purse.

"Here. This is important."

"Ma'am—"

"Hey," I said, standing up to the guard, feeling the tears fall from my face to the floor.

"Daughter. I am leaving. Razaiella... I love you."

The guard took me by the shoulders and turned me around. I never felt so abandoned before. I was left with a small black bag and a white envelope that I knew they had checked. Otherwise, they would have snatched it right from me. My family was gone, it felt like. Walking back with the guard and being cautious about making wrong moves, it felt like they might just take what Mom gave me anyway. Feeling the urge to take a peek, I found that the black bag had many things that I kept for everyday use. Even a pair of socks that were black and my favorite color, fuchsia. This place already gave us socks, but they were so broad, but I guess Mom knew I wanted something more artsy. "Ouch," I whispered, placing my finger in my mouth.

My calligraphy pen felt like it bit me. Other than that, she packed my pens, pencils, markers, and sketchpad—nothing else. Then, with my heart racing again, I opened the white envelope. I ripped the envelope open, hoping hope was on the inside—a handwritten letter folded over one that was typed.

If you are reading this, I could not speak when I gave it to you. I am so sorry, Razaiella. I ask for your forgiveness with all my heart, with all love and protection from the ancestors.

After reading that, it meant nothing to me, so I threw it back in the black bag. "What is this?"

We are sincerely unfortunate to inform you. Sir Rafael Lozano has been found deceased in his vehicle due to a heart attack.

"No… nooo!"

"Hey, get up! Get up, right now!"

Nothing could possibly destroy me more. One thing after the next was being taken from me. Now my own papa. A name I haven't said to him since I was a baby. Nothing in this world could bring him back to life, either. As much as I wanted to believe the letter was incorrect, it had his birth date along with his features. It was him, and I just wanted to think otherwise. His loving heart couldn't take it anymore. Why didn't she just take him back? "It's just not right."

All I had now was my art and a quiet room. If I could ever make things come to life from my drawings, I would be the happiest person in the world. On the other hand, I really wanted to leave this world—to get away from everyone, as it felt like everyone was a rat.

Knock-knock

"Razaiella?" Mr. Sarban says as I continue to draw and do calligraphy in my fresh new sketchbook.

"I, unfortunately, was notified of the terrible news from your mother before she left. I did my best to calm her. Listen, Razaiella, you won't be here for that long. That was always my promise to you. I also told your mother, and she understood."

My mind and concentration were on what was true and what was promised to me on the paper. Not words, as they could mean anything.

"My sincerest apologies about your father. I know you are in deep pain from many things. You have an amazing gift."

My calligraphy pen still met with the paper. Once he figured out that I didn't care anymore and that I just wanted him to leave, the better.

"I have also come to some sort of arrangement. I have decided, along with Ms. Ava, that we can at least allow you to attend the funeral. If you, of course, wish to go."

My pen stopped, and so many emotions flew through my mind and heart.

"How?"

"Anything is possible, my dear," Dr. Sarban smiled. "And you are fairly new here. As I told your mother, the ceremony is in three days. We can give you a pass for that event. I know how important that would be for you—for anyone, for that matter."

I nodded, but still lacked reality. My mind and soul were all over the place. I still couldn't see how any of this stuff really works.

"Mr. Maximo doesn't care for our patients leaving from this building unless it's not a time to do so. So, what do you say, Ra?"

I turned to look at the smiling man. "…Thank you."

"You are most certainly welcome. I just need you to do one small, itsy… bitsy thing for me. See you soon."

CHAPTER 15

Dead Man Walking

The system of life is what Mr. Sarban said it would be in the new world. The way it felt—so real, so mesmerizing. Nothing in this place has the world ever felt before. The electronics to AI complex machines. Then, those who are chosen will join forces with artificial intelligence to make the world a better place.

"Ugh… that was nasty."

"Give it a minute to sink in, and then we shall begin, my friend," Dr. Sarban says as he stands behind a glass.

The Virtual Room, AKA the Dream Machine, as Mr. Sarban called it. The atmosphere was so quiet that you could hear your ears beg for a drop of sound—the tall, plain white walls with, of course, the honeycomb-textured glass. The roof of the room must have been one hundred feet high. Mr. Sarban said it will be just like a dream. Most of my dreams were mainly filled with darkness, as they only came when I slept easy. Nothing could be more real than my nightmares.

"Okay, Razaiella," Mr. Sarban sighed. "We will begin now. All I want from you is to stay calm."

I nodded, and even then, I heard something like air coming from the walls. Right before my eyes, the ground was filled with grass, and beautiful trees stood tall everywhere—the sun from the east and clouds to the west. Animals like zebras and horses running together with their bird friends, flying near their galloping bodies. I just had to start walking and my fingers touching the tall grass—this was a paradise. The breeze forced me to move my hair from my face, as I could not get enough of all of its beauty. Not a human in sight, just plain fresh air and clean nature.

As I continued to walk, there my eyes saw the miniature mountain in the sky with a waterfall pouring what looked like diamonds and crystals flowing from the sides. The cliff ended with the ocean facing me and the warm sun shining on my face. "This is… this is amazing."

The crystal-blue ocean was calm and seemed to have birds that I've seen before fall below and catch the first meal in the morning sunrise. The golden sands with pockets of crystal water sat in an oasis. Down below, it even seemed to resemble little crabs and seashells of purity. I just wanted to crawl down or maybe even jump into the sea as it sparkled in front of me. Like diamonds waving their hands at me and letting me know it's okay to come in. As I just kept looking at the non-ending of the ocean line, the clouds from behind me came. "Eygh!"

The force of wind began pushing me back, and I tried again and again, as I just wanted to be close to the dazzling diamond waters. Finally, turning around to see the darkness of the clouds that covered the land, and soon, the sun, the breeze picked up even more. I just had to look at the ocean one more time. "What the…"

My greatest fear, as it began forming over the now aggressive sea. The winds swept everything from the sands, robbing nature of its colors, turning it to black and gray. Another funnel began to sprout from the clouds and fused with the world. The monster of the storm actually walked as the grayish-black funnels went in and out as it walked across the land of the ex-paradise.

"I see youuuu."

The female voice said from the open dark ocean. The water then shot up to the sky while a stone feminine head with its gray eyes came straight for me. "LET ME OUT OF HERE! HELP! HELP ME!"

This can't be real, I thought as I curled to the soft grassy floor just as I did in front of everyone. The water was still gushing, and the face of the stone looked down at me from the cliffside. "Ancestors, please save me."

"Systems offline."

Hearing the AI-generated female voice immediately, the trance stopped, and the room fell quiet again. All of that—it wasn't real? How did it feel like everything was right, then became so wrong so fast?

"Razaiella?"

Dr. Sarban's voice came from the unknown speaker in the white room.

"We're done here. How was it?"

As my body was lying on the cold floor, I just wanted to close my eyes, as the emptiness and loneliness frightened me in the surrounding white walls.

"Ms. Lozano," Ms. Ava says. Hearing her heels click and clack made me realize the process was really over. "Get up, you're done. Come on, I said! Get up!"

"Ms. Ava, please. Here, take my hand. You did well."

I did manage to lift myself from the floor with Mr. Sarban's help. It just felt like nothing was real. Everything was upside down. My feet, in my socks that Mom bought for me, dragged the floor. My body, for that matter, seemed all out of place. My head too—it all felt beyond this world. "Yack! Oh God, hack-hack. Yack."

"That's right," Mr. Sarban grinned as he kept trying to hold me up. "Let it all out, my friend. All is well, yes? The substance burning your tongue is normal. It visually takes a little long, but all that means your mind is fresh. Well, of course," Mr. Sarban laughed. "You're only fifteen. You've never drunk alcohol or done heavy drugs before. Your body and mind will always know what to do."

"I... don't... feel... so good."

Ms. Ava grinned from behind. "I want to give her another try once she is sober again."

Everything just becoming fuzzy and dark. My words seemed not to come out of my mouth but from my mind. Where were they taking me? "The tornado... tornado had... legs. Two legs."

"Interesting. Did they have on nylon stockings too?"

"Ms. Ava, please. It's okay, Razaiella. We're almost there. We're at the elevator, and you will be in your room in sixty seconds."

"Why me? I... never... hurt... anyone. Not... nice."

My voice seemed to be talking outside my mind. It seemed like I was pulled from reality and back into this ugly world through dimensions. My feet barely held me up as I ran out of energy. What was the stuff they gave me?

"We're here, my friend."

The air conditioning felt colder in my room. I never even changed the thermostat. They dragged me along with my dangling legs. "Just… like the tornado."

"I want you to rest, Razaiella. I know that was a lot all together at once—"

"I want my dad. Dad? Help me. Please help me!"

"Rest easy, Razaiella. We have business to attend to and log. Ms. Ava, come. I need her to rest."

"That was just a taste for you." Ms. Ava says in my ear.

"This will be what we use for those who are disobedient to our ways. Especially those who believe they are above anything and can do as they please."

"Ms. Ava!"

"We'll be back, sweetheart."

My eyes were a bit blurry, but I saw that woman smiling and holding that tablet. She did this to me. How was I going to get out of here? If I saw something like that again, my heart might just break out of my chest and fly away. They wanted to kill me.

"Why, Mom? Why did you let them take me?"

I blacked out right after my thoughts calmed down. My nightmares became stronger as the point of insomnia began to sink in.

****

"Razaiella… Razaiella? Can you hear me?"

The voice—a voice that sounded just like it was a few seconds ago.

"Yes. Where am I?"

The lights were so bright, and needles in my arms with cords attached. Now I was being tortured?

"You've been out for an entire day, and I wanted to keep my promise to you. Today is an important day. Can you get up?"

"Damn. I… what happened to me? Felt like I was… dreaming."

"Dreaming?" Mr. Sarban laughed. "You are my friend, but I am happy to see that you're functioning. Perhaps a bit sluggish. My friend, remember what today is?"

"No… um, what?" I said, holding my fuzzy head.

"Today is the homegoing. You are free to go. Well, of course, we'll need you back here after the ceremony."

The homegoing. As I finally came to my senses, the final day came to see my father.

"Oh no, please don't cry," Mr. Sarban says, holding my shoulders. "Hey, you're never alone, okay? Razaiella, look at me. You are never alone. I ordered this special service so that you can go. Come on, breathe… in and out. Now… can you do this?"

"I, sniff. I can."

Mr. Sarban smiled. "Excellent. Now, your mother came and left you a beautiful dress. Let's get these off of you first."

"Ouch!" I said as the long needle slid out of my vein.

"What… what was that I was in a few days ago? It felt so real."

"A few days ago… so you know," Mr. Sarban smiles, taking out the last needle from my body. "Anyway, I announced this already, my friend."

"The entire room, the place changed. How did—"

"Razaiella, friend. It's very complex but simple. I just run it for tests. The quantum AI physics is another department. Just know that we will be in nirvana someday. Paradise, my dear. Now, since those are off, I need to get you something to eat and out of here."

Of course, being half-naked and in a cold room was the norm. That place was definitely something different as it started to come back to me—from the sun to the sky, to the fresh soil, to the sands. It felt like I could even taste the ocean as it fell on me from that statue.

"Here you go, and of course, your shoes," Dr. Sarban smiled. "I trust that will be all you need."

"Could I get dressed in my room? I didn't even bathe yet."

Mr. Sarban chuckled. "We took care of that for you, my friend. Cleanliness is the top priority here."

"So, I was touched?"

Mr. Sarban folded in his lips and nodded. "Now, go on ahead and get dressed. I have a guard coming with your meal shortly. A long day for you, for sure. A day just for you, my friend."

It's been two days since they had me, and not knowing anything. What could they have done to me? At least the dress didn't look cheap, along with the black flats. I can carry my jacket, as it didn't seem that cold. "That's all, I guess."

The guard giving me fruits and a piece of meat, like I was some mouse, made it even more like I was in a VIP prison. Mr. Sarban just liked me, and I definitely had to be careful, since many times he had me alone with him. Today, I'm fairly certain they will let me spend the entire day with my family. Maybe I could get out and run once the service is over. I just have to wait to make the right moves.

My long, wavy hair in my face as the mirror reminded me that I have been through it all. "I will get out of here. I know I will."

Just think, Razaiella, just think.

"Ah, finished? By the looks of it, you are," Mr. Sarban says as he leaned against the wall with his arms folded. "Once again, my condolences, but life must go on. You must be strong."

"Right… I know. Where is the exit?"

"Hold on, my friend. I must give you something very important."

"What?" I frowned.

Mr. Sarban reached into his long white coat pocket, took out a metal device, and knelt on one knee on the floor.

"Just so we don't lose track while you're out there. Subhanallah, your dress is nice and long. The bracelet shouldn't be a problem."

The device placed on my left ankle was even colder, so much for my plan.

"This way, Razaiella. I pray you are ready and that nothing from here will tamper with your mind or body during your day."

The only thing that bothered me now was the ankle bracelet watching my every move. I've seen the one Nova had on his ankle, and it was bulkier. Mine was more of a bracelet style that hugged my ankle size, depending on where it was placed. Could barely even tell it was there unless I touched it.

"Darn it. Of course it would be raining," Mr. Sarban says, opening up his umbrella that he took from the newly seen front door to the building.

"I didn't bother to involve Ms. Ava, as I sensed she may cause some sort of altercation before your ceremony. A peace of mind is what you need for today. Keep your head under; I got you. The car should be pulling up soon."

"My mom isn't taking me?"

"Unfortunately, my friend, no. For security purposes, you are our responsibility during your time with us. Remember, this is a special action I've taken just for you. Once you arrive at the ceremony, you will be with your family until it's over. You just have to trust me that everything will be okay, okay?"

As the rain just poured from all angles with the wind, I could finally see that this place was guarded down to the point you probably would be shot and killed for being uninvited. The high fence with barbed wire surrounded it, and I knew there was a guard around with a gun. The devils took me, and all of them just seemed like they were lying. I just knew I would be able to get away somehow—but thanks to that stupid bracelet, it ruined the idea entirely. If Mom tried to kidnap me back, they would possibly hurt her.

"There they are, Razaiella."

"They could have at least picked me up near the building," I murmured as the rain poked at my feet, and a black four-door sedan with black windows came to the gate. It was definitely twice as expensive as my mom's own.

"As you may know, this place is heavily restricted. No one gets close, as protocol dictates. Hey, I just follow the rules. Hello there," Mr. Sarban says as he opens the back door. "This is Dr. Sarban leaving you to Razaiella Lozano. Clear?"

"All clear," the passenger says, sitting in the front.

Of course, they would be dressed in all black, and their faces would be covered, revealing only their eyes.

"Take care, Razaiella. You'll be just fine."

He loved to smile at me, but I wasn't in the mood for any of this. So many mixed emotions surrounded me as to what to pay attention to and feel as long as they didn't put me in that room again. That is what I just couldn't do anymore. My nightmares just coming to life like that. There just has to be a way.

Seeing the real world again was somewhat refreshing. The rain wouldn't let up, accompanied by small flurries. I imagined the driver losing control so that I could escape. Just wishful thinking, as he appeared to be in a trance, gripping the steering wheel with both hands. The windshield wipers danced back and forth on the glass, which became a bit annoying. The person in the passenger seat hadn't spoken at all, and it must have been over twenty minutes in the car. The door seemed to lack a functional opening, giving the impression that it could only be opened from the outside. The glass separated the front from the back seat, resembling old taxis. It felt like a prisoner's car. Once I'm on my way back, I'll tell them I need to pee, and they won't have any choice but to let me out.

As we arrived in the small town, it bore a resemblance to Ellsworth. Mom brought Dad here, and it seemed like the only option. The bastards could have at least lowered the A/C. I was shivering, and the cold bracelet didn't help at all. I just wanted to get this over with. Then, my heart skipped a beat as I came to my senses. "Dad."

"Is this the building here?" the driver asks, and the other nods.

On the snowy, wet day, the small church sat there with a small number of cars. Then, of course, the red car with a dream catcher hanging in the windshield.

I sighed then murmured. "This is it."

My heart beating one pulse to the next pulse, faster and faster. My eyes tearing up while the rain watched from the window. I was only like this because it just didn't seem real—none of it.

"Take the umbrella and get out," the passenger demanded as his head stayed straight forward.

I was surprised to see the door open by itself. I stepped out into the cold atmosphere, with the church looking at me. I could feel the energy coming from inside, waiting to devour my very essence.

"We will be back once the service is over," the passenger said, then rolled up his window.

"Mom?"

"Razaiella! Daughter!"

Mom rushed over with small splashes to me. Once again, I found myself in her loving bosom. I nearly forgot that the rain was not being so nice.

"Are you okay? They let you come by yourself?"

I didn't want to answer as I felt trapped, and all around me was the feeling of being tortured. "I don't know… sniff. Mom. Dad, he's—"

"Come, daughter. Hold my hand. I am with you now."

We walked slowly to the heavy, cold door, which I could clearly see had frost smeared on it from being touched. This just couldn't be true. My papa… in a place like this?

"Good evening," a man said as he stood with his hands behind his back.

The place filled with so much sorrow and pain. Or was it mostly my own? Mom turned me to a room with maybe three others inside. "… Dad?"

Seeing the open box—a see-through transparent white casket with my poor papa's body inside, sleeping. "Mom… sniff. No, it's not real."

"Calm, daughter, be calm," Mom said as we walked slowly to the box.

"It can't be him… it just can't be," I murmured in agony.

My heart flipped inside my chest, almost like how it was in that dream machine. I knew I wasn't in that thing because I could feel Mom's energy. Yet, he was gone. Just someone in a box, wearing a black suit. His face even looked different.

"It's him, daughter. He has returned to the earth. No more pain… no more sorrow."

Like she read my mind, Dad was lying there in peace, but his face and body just weren't the same man who was there for me the last few times we saw each other.

"Come, daughter. Let's take a seat."

I didn't feel like breaking down and crying on the floor. Something in here was telling me that it just wasn't over yet.

"Good afternoon, you all," the priest announced, wearing his long black robe. His hand twitched nonstop. "Today, we are here to celebrate the life and legacy of Rafael Lozano. A man of greatness, excellence, and creativity. A loving father, husband… and friend. We know not the day, nor the hour life will come and pass us by… so we may look to the heavens and say, farewell world. Our time on this planet… is surely limited. We must, as people, learn the laws of nature so that we can be free from all evil. Rafael… a man of integrity. We must be who we are and be the best we can be… just like him. Mrs. Lozano. Your husband, as you have told me, was a great man—not perfect, but who is?"

The priest looked at me with a smile and his twitching right hand. For some odd reason, he just gave me the weird energy that he wasn't who he said he was. Just a man in a robe.

"Razaiella. Yes, you have many gifts. Just like your father, I heard."

I closed my eyes and wanted to just scream.

"You will live on, carrying your father's integrity. His legacy lives on in you. Just never stop believing."

"Praise be to the ancestors," someone said as I opened my eyes—it seemed to come from near the casket.

"Now… let us all rejoice in singing a song so great. *How Great Thou Art.*"

I could barely sing or speak. My tongue was twisted as I looked at my papa—gone. I would never speak to him again. As they say, only in the afterlife. He was just here with me. He loved me. He came when I needed him. And right now, I needed him more than ever. How can he just be gone? If I just closed my eyes and wished he would come back. He would walk in saying, *That's not me.* I would be so happy.

"How greaaat, thooouu, arrre," the people sang. "How great thooouu arrrt."

"Art?" I said, looking around and trying to figure out who said it.

There was barely anyone in the room—just about six people. Whispers came to me, the same whispers I heard from the attic and in the virtual room. "Mom?"

Was I going crazy? "What?"

Whispers again came from behind my dad's casket.

"Hey," I whispered, looking around, seeing the pastor singing and Mom's eyes and hands closed to the room's melody.

There was something there, behind Dad's casket. I knew it—I could feel it. Something that was not normal. Closing my eyes once more and trying to wake up from the nightmare. It was no use; this was my reality.

"Pssst. Serve me and live."

Opening up my eyes slowly, my heart stopped as I saw a black creature peeking its head from behind Dad's casket, with white eyes and no pupils staring right at me. It looked nothing like anything I've ever seen—close to a small-headed, stone-faced jackal with long black horn-like ears that pointed up and a body like a small monkey but with wrinkles. This couldn't be. I needed to wake up now. The creature then crawled up the box and looked at Dad as if to see if it was really him there. The creature's slender black tail waved in the air while it placed its head on my dad's chest. Its eyes never blinked, and its mouth never moved. "…Mom?"

The stone-faced creature immediately looked up at me with its eyes wide open, staring into my soul. It was as if I couldn't even call for help. Mom would run, and Dad wasn't here to fight this thing off. It finally moved away from Dad, sat with its legs crossed on his stomach, and continued to stare at me. The creature, with its small body, lifted its old, malnourished, wrinkled arms. The left arm stayed in the air, pointing to the ceiling, while the right arm slowly pointed to my father's face.

"This couldn't be happening, this can't be happening," I mumbled, drowning in my fear.

"Daughter, it's okay. Pray with me."

Closing my eyes with Mom's as I held her tight, I wanted just to leave now. My mind told me I had seen it before, but I couldn't remember where. No matter what I did, it stayed there. If I yelled, it might just run away, but then everyone inside would think I'm crazy. That's when I heard its thousand-year-old voice straight from it.

"I seeee youuuu," the creature softly spoke without even moving its mouth.

"How great thoouu arrrre. All at once, we will sing the last verse in great melody," the priest said, smiling and closing his eyes.

"When Christ shall come, with shouts of acclamation, and take me home."

Looking back at the creature, I saw that it never once gave an expression, just wide eyes and a weirdly shaped mouth. It felt like an empty statue as it continued to point to the ceiling and to my father without a hint of motion. My heart was beating so fast it felt like it was going to burst from my chest. It also seemed to take pleasure in my fear. The creature finally lowered its arms, and from black dust, a violin emerged from behind its body to its front. I still had no idea how no one else was witnessing this—only me. As it held the stick to the strings of the instrument, it played sounds from ages past. The melody played perfectly, harmonized with the singing of the people in the room. I couldn't tell what it wanted to accomplish—calm me down or give me something to be afraid of.

"Razaiella, are you okay?" Mom whispered to me, then kissed the top of my head.

"…I am."

"Razaiella," a whisper floated from somewhere near Dad as the creature had now vanished.

I could not believe this. Was it all in my head, or what? Why was this thing here? Why now? I closed my eyes as I sensed something bad—nothing like I had felt before.

"I know you; I know your family. I know you; I know your family," the sounds came from the casket.

My eyes became tighter as I didn't want to see or hear anymore. I was better off dead.

"Razaaielllaaa," the whisper came again from the casket.

My eyes could not help but open as I saw the creature doing something I could not understand or believe. It made its way back to Dad's chest. Its face had no emotion, but it stuck its long, snake-like tongue out at me and held a heart with blood dripping nonstop. I could not bear to see any more.

"Razaiella? Daughter?! Daughter?!…"

CHAPTER 16

Ctrl Alt Delete
Learning The Causes
and Effects

When I was born, the world seemed different to me. The thoughts and feelings of people have undergone drastic changes. My father always seemed distant from anything that might cause him or his family harm. Somehow, it felt like bad energy wanted to follow us, no matter how far we ran. From the hottest of days to the coldest of nights, that force is always out there trying to hunt us down. Blacking out in that funeral home and back into my new home only seemed like I was trapped. Waking up back in the cold walls of the S.I.L.O. building, which I just didn't know when or how. My ankle bracelet was removed, and I was welcomed back into my new bed. There was nothing and no one out there for me anymore.

"Who can I truly trust? What is my purpose for living?"

My mom left me here. Sold me to these demons. How can she not do anything? Just a kiss on my head as my father laid there, all alone with some demon playing with his body. I know she saw it too. She must have even felt it, but was too scared to say anything. "Who can I trust?"

It just felt like I was tied to a tree with a thousand arrows aiming right at me—right at my heart. My angel was being attacked by these demons with fiery arrows herself. She could get away because she could fly. Once I am dead, maybe my wings will grow, and I can flee from this place, this world.

Knock-Knock.

"Razaiella," Ms. Ava greets, peeking behind the door. "Time to get something to eat. Quit doodling over there and get something to eat like a big girl."

"Whatever…"

"I don't think I told you," Ms. Ava grinned. "If you refuse to eat, you will be force-fed with a tube going through your nose to your throat. You have one hour."

Forced against my will to avoid their poison with my body. I know everything in this place is a lie. I can't even tell if I truly exist, but I am breathing, and my reflection is still there.

"I have to get out of here."

The same foods felt redundant to our bodies. It was as if they wanted us to be programmed to eat the same thing every day: an apple, a banana, or an orange with various juices. Ironically, this place didn't offer pork or other items that vegans would reject. The apple, I knew, was fake because it was too large, just like the different fruits and vegetables.

"Hey, what's up, baby!"

That same guy who embarrassed me that day. He really had the nerve. Where was security when I needed them?

"Listen to me. I want to apologize for that day. I don't know what came over me. Hey, you listening?"

I closed my eyes because I wanted to sit with my food in peace and imagine no one was here.

"You know, I'm not really a bad dude once you get to know me. A little wild here and there, but I'm laid-back. Tsk… I'm Eric."

When will this asshole leave? I thought to myself as my anger began to rise.

"What's your name? Silent treatment, aye? Damn, girl. I said I was sorry. I want to make things right and get to know you. You're always sitting here by yourself and—"

"Hey! Leave me alone!"

The room fell silent as everyone turned to see where they could watch the scene, and I was ready to give a show if he wanted one.

"Ahh, so she can speak, you guys," the idiot said, cracking his neck side to side with his hands. "The name's Walker. Eric Walker. I'm twenty-six. You're probably about… eighteen, especially with those…"

I looked at him and tried to remain at peace, praying that the ancestors would intervene and cause him to see no more, just like how Dad did that guy in the alley.

"So… what's up, baby?"

"Can you please… leave?" I said calmly.

"The lady said to please leave."

A familiar voice said behind me. It was him—the man from the waiting room—the one who helped me.

"You're not going to excuse yourself? Or shall I show you how?"

Eric laughed as everyone looked back at him again in amusement.

"Probably like 'em with little whackers anyway."

A guy like him needed extreme help. A few knocked-out teeth and black eyes would do the trick. "Hey… I'm—"

The man turned and looked directly into my eyes, and what I saw was something different about him automatically. It wasn't that he helped me, but he had a story behind those eyes. It spoke strength, seriousness, and warmth.

"I guess I should thank you again. I—"

"It's alright. He'll be back. You're welcome."

"Wait," I said, trying to whisper in desperation. "Sit with me. I mean, you can if you want."

"No need to be scared. I'm still here. I can sense from your spirit that you are tired of being tired. Hmph, he's not that crazy to bother you while I'm around."

I grinned.

"Yeah, you never know what people will do these days."

His voice was so soft but firm. He definitely was not from a place like this. "Why are people so crazy?" I asked.

The man smiled as he pulled the chair out in front of me.

"Because nothing is wrong, everything is right. Bad answer? It's because humans are too far gone. What do you mean, you ask? It means people are just empty. Their minds and hearts are corrupted by so many ill forces of dark nature. All they know is recklessness. Better?"

I slowly nodded. "They're evil."

"Did not so much say that, but I can acknowledge the system has brainwashed the minds and overwritten purity for evil. I believe when a person bothers you for no reason, they must have a wicked spirit provoking them to do it. You alright?"

"Wicked spirit, you said. I've… it doesn't matter."

"No, you can tell me. I'm intrigued to hear someone's account of such things," the man said, smiling.

Then it came to me—the creature's face that sat on Dad's body. Then when Mom and I were in the store long ago. "I saw a demon before."

"Really?"

"I saw it… but when I was like five years old. My mom…"

"I can see it in your eyes, even though the table isn't responding. It's okay. You can look at me and tell me. Do you have the energy to tell me about it?"

He really was a nice guy, so I smiled back. "When we were in the supermarket, a man was walking around with a mask… something kind of like the face I saw the other day. My mom told me not to be afraid and that some idiot is trying to scare people in the store. When I looked at him… I could still feel it… like it was yesterday. He just kept staring back at me when he passed me and her. I looked back at him…"

"And he kept walking the other way."

"Yeah… he could've been a psycho, but how he just walked like he did—it was like it was just a normal time, and no one said a thing. He kept walking, looking back at me as I looked at him with that mask, as if he wouldn't run into anyone. For some reason, I couldn't remember where I had seen that face before, but when you came, I could. Weird."

"Nothing weird about it," the man smirked. "My energy rubbed off on you, and you got a jump start from it. Angels and demons roam this earth naturally. So, whenever I meet someone new, the first impression is the most important. I never underestimate anyone and always strive to be respectful, regardless of who they are, their appearance, or their words. We all learn from one another, right? I am someone who, if I do not understand and have questions, I will ask."

"Yeah, of course. You should ask to be sure you're right. Right?"

The calm but energetic-voiced man nodded. "How right you are. I know what I know from experience—it's called life. It's either I've seen it or done it. So, on that standpoint, I will never tell you anything I do not know. People who love to talk… they alter information to cause confusion. They can also often be recognized by their tendency to be compulsive liars. They lie so much that they lose themselves in lies. The greatest trick or treat from the devil himself."

When this guy just mentioned the devil, was it a man or a woman that danced on my shoulders with their lies? "I hear you."

"It's as simple as that, you know. We do not all know everything, but we learn through our own life's journey. However, I did have a side long ago when I was not in the right state of mind, but anger gets you nowhere. It actually makes you vulnerable to certain situations. You see… my apologies. I'm getting ahead of myself," the man grinned as I looked to see why he was.

I hoped he wasn't crazy, as I would have to watch myself around him, too. "My name is Seth," the man said, extending his hand with a smirk. "My name is Razaiella. I've never really seen a proper handshake before, especially one as firm as yours."

"A handshake represents respect, balance, equality, and trust. Pleased to meet you, Razaiella."

I smiled as he seemed very respectful. "Or you can call me Ra. My mom named me after my father and hers."

"Ra-zaiella. Now, that's a new one in my book. Very unique. No wonder they want you here. I trust that we will be honest and respectful towards each other after our initial handshake, which is why I gave you my hand. I don't do it for those who are liars and cheats, as they are pests of the Earth."

Seth, without a blink, gave his opening towards me, and I have never in my life been greeted that way.

"As I was saying, humans have been made to think just like robots. Yes, machines. You're in your early teens or somewhere in between; I'm in my early forties. Around the time you were born, the world began to change drastically as it sought to be 'more free'. What the system has done and is still doing today is robbing people of their five senses with false freedoms. A rather disturbing experiment they have conducted. Hmph, haven't they always experimented on humans, though? It's nothing new."

I was puzzled. "Free, you said? Look at how we are now. We're as good as slaves. Who doesn't want to be free?"

Seth smirked. "Try to understand me. Yes, the weak-minded. They were always the problem. Wanting to normalize everything. Then, the entire world wanted to follow stupidity, and they got exactly what they wanted—oblivion. Hell, foolish humans think you are weird if you don't cheat on your wife nowadays. Because it 'feels good', even though it is wrong. I know you've been in that virtual room."

"Of course, and it feels so… amazing, but wrong later on. It's always like that."

Seth grinned as he pointed, then folded his arms back together. "You said it, not me. It feels good, but wrong at the same time. You know it's not really there. Mind games on humans are nothing new either, but since AI learned this method of nature, it does it phenomenally. All you are seeing once they power that system up are hallucinations, optical illusions, and the worst, which can make someone truly insane over time, is cognitive biases. Tricking your mind to believe what is not there, but…it feels so good. Doesn't it?"

I nodded but then shook my head.

"The mind is so important; nothing in your essence can be controlled without it. Electricity running up there like a powerhouse. Even when you are hurt by something, emotional wounds at times take longer to heal than physical ones. Be careful, my friend, of what you choose to feel good, because it can be something so simple and easy until it robs you of your life. A man-child who wants to play video games all his life and not do anything but expects to be truly happy. That's not how it works. Or even a woman who wants to spend all day playing with her phone and not see anything in true reality. Oh yes, this is nothing new, my friend, and has been going on for decades now."

Seth then nodded and smiled at me. "It's actually quite simple, Razaiella. Have you ever heard an instrument play so beautifully before?"

Immediately, once again, I retraced my steps back to my father and how his fingers played those beautiful symphony melodies. "Yes. I think the piano is my favorite."

"Very well, then. The piano is actually the best example. When someone plays an instrument to a tune—especially one that must be played without many known mistakes, right? When someone plays it and that mistake hits your ear, you will immediately recognize it. Why?" Seth asked with his head tilted.

"Because… it won't sound right?"

"Good, bad frequency is what it is called, as they manipulate minds with it through even today's music. Sometimes you can't hear, or it may just sound good, fooling the listener. Now, when someone is speaking—if they tell you a story and it doesn't sound right, what do you think is happening there?"

This man really had me thinking. "The person is lying. Right?"

"Yes, correct," Seth nodded. "Or they don't have a clue what they're talking about. Humans in this day and age are so gullible; anything sounds good to them. They actually prefer to hear something that sounds bad and obviously a lie, rather than something that sounds good and is the truth. If it doesn't sound right, maybe that's because it isn't right, that's all. Do you know someone close who has some sort of condition, such as diabetes?"

"Not really, but I know what it can do."

"Good. Let's say you can eat anything you want, but you have a condition that reminds you that you can't... unless you want to deal with the consequences afterward. Unfortunately, it won't work. In life, we are free beings once we come out of the womb, but are we fully?"

I shook my head yes, then no. "Well... I do get what you're saying about the food and not eating everything because you might get sick and probably die. Especially if you have diabetes, since you need to stay healthy, you can't just... yeah, do anything. I understand."

Seth smiled. "Perfect. That tells me you can think for yourself. Something that many lack or wish they could do."

"A guy I knew told me that you have to know the bad and the good. After hearing you, it kind of makes sense now."

Seth smirks and nods. "This is factual, just because you must know what the differences are between the two. How can you see and understand dark nature if you have no idea or experience in it? Your discernment wouldn't work as well because you do not possess the knowledge to see the balance. All life is about balance. Your body, mind, soul, friendships, marriage, your finances, etc. Know this: certain doors you open may feel good at first, but then it may be hard to close behind you because you've made things the way they are. Life is all about balance. Just like a scale—you can't have too much of this or too much of that. Humans today want a life that says, 'as long as it makes you happy, it's okay.'"

"But you can't do that because there are consequences."

Seth pointed at me. "Exactly. You are free, however. Ironically, you can make yourself a slave from this mentality. People who love to lie to themselves tend to make themselves into their own personal slaves. Then the system gets paid for it—just to make funds off the sick and confused. You see, slavery never really ended. Nowadays, people have what I like to call virtual chains. I'll be honest. I used to play around with gambling because it was fun. It became a bad habit, and I was a slave to it. I stopped about twenty years ago because I hated to lose money. Something about that urge, though—that urge to make yourself mess up. It feels good, but when it hits, it's different. People try to change, run to God, and ask for forgiveness. It's too late sometimes."

I just looked and I could understand.

"There's something about these dark forces that get in our veins, then into our minds, and make us feel good for the moment. Once again, slavery never really ended. Long ago, they placed chains on the necks, wrists, and ankles. Now they're on the back of the head, going inside the minds of unfortunate individuals. Ultimately, we get messed up in the long run with such things in life. The forces know the people are weak and stupid. They know us better than we know ourselves, and the bear trap shuts quickly and tightly when it's time. Overall, those who love lies and embrace them are the worst in human nature."

"What it sounds like," I said, tapping my fingers on the cold white table, "never trust someone who loves lies. We listened to this individual, and he told those who debated him that if they wanted to continue debating, money had to get involved. To me, it feels like he would be going overboard, as it isn't that serious."

Seth held his thumb and index finger under his chin and bounced his head to what I said about my so-called old friend.

"That's exactly what it comes down to, and whoever spoke like that, I somewhat agree with him. You know, people like to talk and just argue. It's annoying and mostly futile. When someone can't prove their point but loves to argue, they are the worst. Because when someone who knows what they are talking about wants to prove something. Like in front of a judge, they present evidence that they have witnessed and the jurors have witnessed to support their claim. I have heard stupid people say, 'oh, I don't have to prove to you anything.' So why are they arguing? Just shut up and keep it to yourself. No, you don't have to prove anything, but they would try to debate. What sense in the world does that make? Then, when a person presents evidence, the person arguing denies seeing it or simply refuses to accept it. To me… that is a form of witchcraft. Oh yeah."

I just sat there because it made sense. Something that made me feel weird on the inside about how he put things together. "Witchcraft. You really think that stuff exists?"

One eyebrow raised as he looked at me to say, 'Was I kidding?'

"Everything going on in our world today, my friend, is run by witchcraft. How do you think they control everything? If something has been taught to you, you almost have no choice but to believe it, if…you cannot think for yourself. Brainwashing is something of the past; however, the elites of the world know how to do it so beautifully, so cleverly, so well. Just by knowing to give what you crave. Loving lies? That is something that can send your life into oblivion."

Seth grinned. "A simple game of phone can cause confusion down the line and easily spread like an epidemic. All someone has to do is change up the truth, tweak a little something, and say it is the truth. No one down the line of life will ever truly know it has been changed. That is why books are still so important. They can change ideas at any time, from anywhere, online. However, they can't change the idea or the narrative in books. It's already written, unless they come up with a new one that presents a false new reality. This is how many have become lost in this world because these devils change everything. If it doesn't make any sense and two plus two doesn't equal four, then it is a matrix of confusion. They may beat lies into your head, and your subconscious doesn't know what to believe because you have been drowned in confusion; it's hard to break out of it because it's been beaten into your head. This matrix of numbers is what demons use to confuse someone's spirit due to the lack of uncertainty. Saying maybe this, maybe that. Confusion at its finest."

"So…"

I was kind of lost for words. "This is…"

"Tampering with your subconscious? Music? How someone says or sings along to something, and they don't realize what they are saying."

Seth smirked. "Lies don't work if you don't believe, just like witchcraft. It doesn't work if your mind and soul are not fully invested in it. These elites believe in it wholeheartedly, and it grants them control over many. They would probably even tell you that these forces don't exist, and this is how they fooled many. This positive energy I give you is not negative or neutral. This is why I say all the time, to anyone whom I may meet. *Never let your emotions dictate your reality.* That is the essence of it all in discerning what is right or wrong in nature. That is why they tell you not to judge and that foolish matrix of thinking. Best example, your food looks nasty…"

I looked down at my plate and just noticed it wasn't there since I ate it. He had me almost in a trance.

"That is called judging. Your food, in my opinion and observation, is a judgment call. Your food looks nasty. Being judgmental, I don't want it because Ms. Ava, the fool, Eric, or someone whom I may not like served it. That is being judgmental. Still a judgment call, though I make it to the point where someone may not be as I perceive them in my mind, to prepare it for me. It's the same as a person being on the streets begging for food or money, mainly money. You don't know how they got there."

"It almost sounds like favoritism to me," I rolled my eyes.

Seth grinned, shaking his head. "And that word right there is something I can stand the least. A person with that mindset is just because they like whoever more and whatever they say is correct. They lack proper judgment because of who that person is to them. It's sick. Sadly, I know those in my old family who had this sickness, though I am aware it is in every family, unfortunately. Favoritism, in my definition, *is to show no empathy without reality.*"

It's crazy, but I felt so more like that with my family, like Seth just said. It's like something was whispering about it.

"The point is, we all judge; being judgmental is the negative aspect of how we perceive or feel about someone. Your senses, my friend, are so important. They don't want humans to be aware of them at all, unless it feels good for them. Ha, recall a video from long ago of a cat saving a baby from falling down the stairs. If I am not mistaken, the furry friend made a judgment call and stopped the baby from something that could have been fatal. Let us be clear. I have seen dogs and cats choose who to approach. Some come slowly, some flee. When friendly in nature, cats raise their backs and tails, purring on your leg, showing a sense of affection rather than harm. Dogs, in their nature, wag their tails. If humans are not able to judge, they will watch someone walk around with a weapon, a knife, and stab someone to death because they said they shouldn't judge. Or they were just minding their own business. Computers, as we know, have senses. Cars can detect when to stop or when a driver has passed out behind the wheel. You can't make this up. Are animals and computers becoming more sensible than humans?" Seth turned his head sideways again to me with a smirk.

"The way you put it, I... don't even know."

"Hmph, you will someday. Again, your senses will tell you if something is wrong or not. You will feel it, but you cannot feel anything when you are numb."

I nodded. "Numb…"

"When your mind is not fully sober in this world, you are numb to many things. Putting you at a disadvantage to all that is around you. Think of it like this, my friend. Imagine something you do, such as your art, as an example. When someone puts that pen or brush to that paper and begins their work, they don't have to think about anything other than focusing on their craft. If you're that good, you don't even have to erase."

I giggled. "Yes, I'm that good. It's from my brain straight to my paper. All I have to do is just imagine what I want to draw and, poof, it's a mural."

"Excellent. That is more than enough proof to show you don't even have to think about it. Those who struggle with art struggle to put anything on paper, even a wall. Stick figures may be a challenge for some poor souls such as myself."

Seth and I grinned at each other. He seemed so genuine.

"Your subconscious is something that exists, and these demons know how to manipulate it to blind and rob you of your gifts. Every human on this planet has a gift, no matter if it's big or small. It can be used for something much greater if you learn to use it properly. Some people can even become wealthy from it, but they must understand how to manipulate and maintain it."

"Will mine make me rich one day? That would be something that I wouldn't mind."

"Hmph, who wouldn't? Depends on you, Razaiella. If you genuinely want something, you go get it. No matter what. Your subconscious mind will even help you get there if you remain focused enough. You get exactly what you deserve, and that is a promise. Just be careful for what you wish and desire. Some things in life, humans become their own victims of their own success. Everything is a balance, my friend."

"All of this stuff you're saying… like witchcraft is crazy. Like…"

Seth grinned. "Just because I said 'witch,' you're thinking about a woman with her broomstick. There's more to it than that, as witchcraft is just a name used for it. They use language in books to cast spells; do they not speak and chant out loud their exercised idea? So, what makes you think it isn't real?"

I shrugged. "I don't know…"

"Listen to me, my friend. In this facility, in this world, you have to think for yourself. Anyone can deceive you with false information simply because they say something. They are the most dangerous, as you don't know when they are true or not. Evidently, lies and sin feel like freedom until you try to get rid of them. Sin can even change you from the inside out. You even start to look different. First, it dirties your soul, and the cancer starts to come out from the pores of your skin. Taking away your true beauty. In this world, you can make your own hell, just by not being able to control and dictate your mind and feelings. The only person to blame is the one looking back at you in the mirror. When it's that bad, now it feels like you are in chains from it. Simple as that." Seth grinned, then shook his shoulders.

"I'm not from this time… this era. I know I'm not, as people often struggle to understand the simplest ideas. Or they are just plain blinded by something. Ha, but I do know life is like a roller coaster. You just have to enjoy the ride and maneuver, I guess. How is your schooling?"

I shrugged. "It's okay."

"I can see you can think for yourself, so you shouldn't be having too many issues," Seth smirked. "Or is it the other way around? It's fine, you can tell me."

"Actually, it's good… and bad. I just don't see why they teach certain things that won't matter to us in the future."

"How right you are. I know exactly what you mean, once again. Back in my day, there were those… how can I say? Trick tests. Yes, those tests that even claimed all the answers were correct, but you had to choose the best one. It was a reading exam."

"Yeah, I failed one before, but eventually passed it. If the story is boring, I don't care about it at all," I grinned.

"As we all. Think about this, though. A reading test where they tell you all the answers are correct, but they tell you to choose what *they* see as correct. That just doesn't sit right with me. I passed the math test, just couldn't with the reading."

"Because with math, you have to put the only right answer. There is no other. One plus one is two. Five times five is twenty-five, and one hundred divided by ten is ten. There is no other way you can change it."

"You took the answer straight from my mouth. Very good, very good. That is also why numbers are so important, no matter what language." Seth clapped lightly.

"The first order of business is control. Control the narrative to be more precise. Know that this is how they manipulate life through simple tests. Only those who fit into their plan are chosen to last—at least for a while. You see, Razaiella, we are thinkers. We are enemies of the system just because we can simply think for ourselves. They tell you who you are, tell you how to think, how to feel. Then they even label you, and their little minions that roam the earth try to do the same. This is all forms of witchcraft, dark magic controlling who you are, and when you try to expose the truth, something…something has a hold on the person's soul to keep their mind from knowing the truth. It hurts their feelings, and they may become upset with you as a result. Witchcraft."

Seth nodded. "One thing I will say—if you never take anything from me—never let someone tell you who you are, or what you can or cannot do. Those are the universal laws of slavery. Other than that, these elites have controlled so much in nature that it's almost like humans are too far gone. Notice how love is so hard to trust nowadays. You can hardly tell who is telling the truth or who is lying because there is so much confusion in the soul and mind to see or sense, if you will. The truth in many things. For all its worth, there was a reason for it, and now, take a good look at the world. They twisted up minds to be this way, to hate on one another instead of bringing people together; they caused more separation."

Dad told me something similar, and I got teary-eyed listening. Other than that, this man seemed so calm and had no worries in the world, even when he stood up to that annoying idiot in this futuristic prison. He even said he was in his forties but had hardly any gray hair on his head from thinking so much. I wanted to see what more he had to say, as it was interesting.

"Speaking of tests. Did you take the serum?" Seth asked.

"I think so."

"Not the injection. The one they have individuals drink."

"Yes… It was a drink, why? They took my blood and then the weird-tasting vanilla drink. They never told me what it was, but I'm still here."

Seth nodded. "Good, you didn't get the injection. Well, you couldn't take it since you took the serum, if I am not mistaken, they don't give both."

I was curious; it was as if Seth wanted to avoid answering my question. "Why?"

"Because the serum is for your mind, while the injection is for something else. Not so sure, it could be for the same thing, but I've heard it is to see exactly who you are. That is the rumor. The serum affects your subconscious and your mental state; that is a fact. You probably haven't heard, but they have been asking those from the outside to take this injection and even offering money to put it inside your body. For that matter, I have never known any medicine to be free to the public. There is a reason."

I just couldn't believe what I was hearing. More than one person has told me this; there must have been something true about it.

"Judging by your eyes, they seem to have been through a lot. Sad eyes have seen sad things. Yet, a golden eye I see."

I blushed. "That's what they nicknamed me. My mom and so-called friends. Tsk, I don't even know if I have any real friends."

"The left one seems darker—a little darker."

"Really?" My heart raced as I searched for a nearby mirror.

"Don't worry, you aren't going blind. The serum must be what caused it, assuming both your eyes were the exact same color. It either dims the iris or enhances it—though it most of the time brightens the iris since it amplifies the person's vital senses."

My heart was beating faster as I hadn't noticed anything this morning. First, they took me from my home; now they were taking my eyes from me.

"I can sense your fear—the biggest issue of mankind. One thing I will tell you is: fear nothing. The meaning of it: to take flight or hide. The acronym—F.E.A.R.—false evidence appearing real. That is what artificial intelligence has been able to master. The network is making people sick and vulnerable to all the dark forces in the world. The ideology of the world is too much for simple minds."

"And what do you mean by that?"

Interestingly, I wanted to learn more from Seth. I had never met anyone like him before, and I have met many odd people. He was a special type.

"Before I begin to speak about certain things, I must advise you that I am someone—if I do not know something, I will tell you so. The elites have learned to play God very well. They have learned many things. Even learned to trace a soul out of this dimension."

"Impossible," I frowned. "No, they can't. How?"

"Impossible you say, but is it really?"

From everything Seth has told me, this one seemed a little, as they would say, far-fetched.

"So how? How can anyone do this? A soul is…it's not something you could trace, it just can't be done."

Seth smirked. "My friend, they have things beyond your dreams and imagination. You won't know a thing about it until they have something more advanced in nature to excel their methods. All I know for sure is that they do not have the right to play with anyone's life. Like us, in here. This is nothing compared to what they are trying to do."

"But what you said about the tracer is impossible. I know that for a fact. You can't see or even feel a soul. That being said, they can't put anything on it to track it."

Seth, with his arms folded and his continued smirk, like he knew precisely what to reply.

"So you mean to tell me you don't believe in air?"

"Of course, but that is different. A soul comes out of the body and…"

Thoughts of that thing at my father's funeral came and caught my tongue instantly. "Okay…whatever you say. It doesn't matter."

"No, no. Not whatever I say. Let's put things into perspective. My favorite way to think of it, two plus two equals four. The outcome always matters. Running from the truth gets you nowhere, my friend. Air is something we cannot see, but feel. Even souls we cannot see, but we can feel. In cold rooms, they say a soul is present in such a place. You can feel it. Even inside a funeral home—"

"Hey… okay, I get it. I believe you."

"Don't mean to startle you or anything. Just trying to explain. They have traced a soul, and it went faster than the speed of light to wherever it went. They have done it, trust me. Playing God like it's nothing. This is what they do. Power and control have always been their main objective."

"…Okay."

I've just been through an experience, and I didn't need any cold thoughts in my head. Trying to hold back tears is the worst.

"Have you ever watched a movie for the first time and could anticipate a scene playing out in a certain way, only to find out that you were right?"

This question was better than anything for the moment. I thought about it, as I wasn't so much of a movie person.

"Not really, as everything that came out seemed lame, and critics would then say they were bad. My mom said a lot of the stuff they put out was bad energy, so we rarely went."

"There is a reason for that, too. Lack of storytelling, as they have no moral thought to them. Just a film showing you a video. No emotion—just a brain-dead film they charge twenty bucks per person to see on a Friday night. With this example, I have noticed you should be able to feel something once you watch a movie. With your five senses—if they are working properly—you should be able to see things clearly in life. Maybe not one hundred percent of the time, though you shall know many things; they gave you reasons to perceive the outcome. Understand?"

I shrugged. "I guess so… but you can go on."

"Ha, you can look at how people drive and anticipate they're on something. They drive just as they think on foot."

Seth sighed. "You just see it. I have had many who called me a know-it-all, but when I asked if they could prove me wrong or at least explain their idea, they would flee with their tails between their legs. Those types of individuals are very difficult to deal with and get along with; they are actually prone to causing trouble for others, as they rarely admit when they are wrong. They just come up with their own delusions to say you are wrong. Understand?"

I nodded, as I felt that many people have done this simply because they didn't like or care for someone, and thus didn't want to hear their opinion. So, if they dislike someone, that person will always be wrong in their eyes—just like Mom did Dad. I never really paid attention to pointing it out. "…Favoritism."

"Absolutely. I am a man who can think for himself—not knowing everything—but if I see it, hear it, or even feel it, I have reasons for what I acknowledge. Now, if your senses are working properly, you should be able to anticipate that something is coming. Just like in the movie. Or a person about to cause an accident with their ridiculous driving."

"You can sense things. Just like when someone is looking at you. Yeah… I kinda' get that," I nodded, twisting my lips.

"In this world today, humans love to listen to someone who speaks into the sky without a sign from the sun, moon, or stars. I believe this is why things are so bad and there is so much confusion. If two plus two equals four, somehow they would argue and tell you it's six. If it doesn't make any sense, they would still roll along with it. Humans prefer that over the truth. They laugh when it's not that bad, but cry later when it's too late. All in all, the majority of these slave-minded humans are slow to catch on, and they despise those who can think for themselves. They will even provoke you to do the wrong thing—but that is where your wisdom must take charge. Witchcraft has a hold on the slave-minded, and that, my friend, is the whole truth." Seth smirked with a serious face and folded his hands on the table as if he were going to interview me.

"Do you know who you are?"

"Witchcraft," I murmured. "Oh yeah… of course. My name is Razaiella Lozano. I'm a female, fifteen years old. Um… I'm an artist. What else… Native American, I forgot the tribe Mom said. I have is-lander in me too, from my dad's side. Uh… that's about it."

"So, you don't know your shoe size?"

Seth and I just grinned. Surprisingly, he looked serious but was nev-er rude or aggressive.

"At least you know the majority of the most important things. That is truly a blessing, believe it or not."

"What about you?" I was eager to ask.

"My ethnicity is German, Somali. However, people who don't know me will call me White. It's interesting how they made people look at the world in this way. A very closed-minded world, if you will."

"White… a color. I've heard it all my life when people call someone that. I never really understood why, but color… is color."

Seth nodded with a smirk. "Go on."

I looked at my caramel-cream hand and black hair on my shoulders. Then, I thought the conversation sounded so familiar and had some sort of connection there.

"So… I am considered brown, but that's not on the ethnicity list."

"How right you are. Since you are a good listener and it seems your heart seeks answers, I will tell you."

Seth looked up to the ceiling and then at me; there was no blink in his eyes.

"My grandmother. A woman with honor, intelligence, and resilience. A person I will never forget. She showed me many things in life. The crazy thing was that when she was bedridden, yet she still knew what was going on outside those four walls—more than people who roam the streets day and night. Anyways, she pointed this out when I was still a toddler. I called my father red, and she immediately put me in my place. I didn't see it then, but I see now her frustration."

To me, Seth seemed to want to cry, and I felt a sense of something when he spoke of his grandmother.

"Our thinking has become so toxic—against nature, against ourselves, and overall humanity. Humans have forgotten who they truly are. All because those dark forces from the elites told them who they are and programmed them to be this way. The simple way humans speak has made them slaves to their own reality. If I had never truly known my true ethnicity or heritage background, told by my parents, I probably would just call myself a color, just as those who do so. You described yourself as you truly know yourself. You are blessed to know your heritage and who you are. Some, however, only know themselves by what someone else told them—and they believe it. It could have been a complete outsider who despises them or hates their very existence, and they just went along with it. Some are told that color is a race, and if you ask them for their heritage, they will shake their heads into oblivion. Confusion is what they always desired for the world."

I nodded. "I think I know what you're saying. The system, as you said, gave us names so we wouldn't know who we were from the beginning. Labelling us."

"Correct. Now, I've heard a poor soul here tell the supervisor he did not know, and he was just Black. The supervisor asked him for his race, background, and heritage. He still couldn't answer properly. Just sad. *Black*."

"It means African American, right? Africa… they say all life started there, right?"

"How right you are again. So, are we all Black?" Seth smirked, turning his head sideways.

"…I don't… think so."

"Come on. No, we are not. As you know, it's not a heritage. You do art, you proclaim. Black and white are colors, not someone's ethnicity. What that is called is profiling. Foolish humans cannot see that this false language has made the world look at each other on such a horrendous, racist scale. They even pick and choose who is Black or White, it's nothing certain. Blindness at its finest—to hate one another. You don't know who that person is, where they are from, or who they truly are from their origin—just seeing them by the color of their skin and nothing more. Labelling someone by the color of their skin only makes humans more aggressive toward their fellow humans. People have become accustomed to things for so long that they can no longer see anything wrong with them. Just as I have heard racial slurs used against one another inside the African American community. Using the '*N*' word towards one another, and they see nothing wrong with it, as they say it is normal. Hmph, normal but degrading? A language that was never even theirs, given to them by those who enslaved them. Now, call themselves something that was used against them?"

I nodded. "Wow… I've heard some things before, too, but it never really stood out to me. You are right, it became normal."

"Words, as they have always said, oh yes, it has power. That power either gives positive energy or negative energy. Just something created to foster more racism and hate in our world, and that's just the start of it. I have recently learned that many cultures around the world consider lighter skin to be more desirable than darker skin. Sounds crazy because it is crazy. Like I said, it should have been deleted long ago. I don't even like using the term, '*Black*' or '*White*'. Firstly, anything used in conjunction with black has always been associated with negativity. Can you name some?"

Thinking about it for a second, I couldn't really think of any. "Only one I heard of…black magic?"

Seth grinned. "That's one of the worst ones. I never heard of black magic being any good, but there are so many more, my friend, but you hit it on the nail with that one. To me it meant darkness, a gloomy feeling of despair. Not one person I know, when I look at them, made me feel like that. Humans are humans."

"Right… well. I guess S.I.L.O. needs our ethnicity. A color doesn't tell them…"

Seth smiled. "Go on."

"Tell them… who we are?"

"Ding-ding-ding. I knew you could do it, even though I pretty much gave you the answer. Thinking for yourself is so crucial. For the guy who couldn't answer who he is—it is not so much his fault. It was something he was taught, and that is how eighty percent of humanity is confused. Something that placed you in a matrix of confusion. The numbers just don't add up. Simple minds are twisted and controlled by the forces of the world. They create their own lies to persuade people to believe in them, thereby controlling them using language. It's just that simple. When so much is around you and your eyes cannot see any truth, then you are truly in a field of bondage."

"You make a point. You know, you can't paint someone black. Black is the…how do you say?"

"It is the absence of color. Go on," Seth smirked.

"Yeah…everything we use black for is to darken it. To me, everyone is a shade of brown. From really light brown to dark brown. Hey, that's how I paint anyone."

"Exactly. So since they told everyone that black is an ethnicity, it's used like it's nothing, but everyone is surely based on a brown color. No red, no yellow, no white, and definitely not black."

Seth grinned. "Propaganda. Why do you think social media is still alive today? They have so much false information just by having and using others from around the world to communicate. Assuming they know English, since that is the global language. The media online presents what they want, and social media is used to foster 'social' awareness of ideas that may or may not be true—leading to increased confusion. Once again, propaganda is one of the greatest tools of Pandora's box. Imagine a person whom everyone listens to a degree. Just because they sound correct in most of their speech, some will believe in that person one hundred percent because they lack the ability to think for themselves. Influenced by a person, you have no clue who they are behind closed doors. Of course, they cannot always sound bad either; who would listen? So these demons will tell you what you want to hear, and they could be leading you into a trap for destruction later on in life. Whispering in your ear's sweet lies."

I could definitely understand, as he made things so simple and straightforward. It's surprising how I never considered that issue until now. "You know, that's more than likely why my mom didn't want me to have that stuff. There are ways I can still have it, of course, I just didn't care unless I was posting my art."

"Likely for sure. Mothers are the nurturers of the world, even without children. Not all parents are going for that foolishness, though. Humans often lie about things and will manipulate the truth to make themselves look good for views and attention. Some even do it for their own business to make money from the weak-minded. They call it social media for a reason. You don't know what to believe on platforms of confusion. I've heard adult women, especially, say they had to get rid of their social media or take a break because of the content on there. Messing with their heads, more than likely, seeing other women doing certain things that harass their spirit. Your sight, your mind, and your emotions all play a great role in your being. Then, for children, your child comes home and follows a trend that catches their hair on fire, filling up the hospitals and taking those with insurance. Hmph, there's always a reason. In life, things work by perspective and cause and effect. Ever played chess?"

"Nope. I'm an artist, remember? My mind is about imagination and creation."

Seth nodded. "Okay. In your life, there will be many things that you must decide—to make your life better or worse. It's all about choices. Just be sure you think ahead. That is how most chess players win. Then, if you lose, you get back up and keep moving. That's life. You must always think for yourself, or this system will steal your mind, your dreams, and then your soul, possibly making them work against you. You must learn how to beat these demons at their own game. This will grant you the ability to be aware of all your surroundings and have little chance of being hit hard."

I felt like Seth had learned many things just by living and observing. He made me think, like simply, what is two plus two? I kind of felt how he was making me brainstorm what I needed to see. It's nothing like learning and sharing with someone who truly understands. "Look at her looking."

"Hmph," Seth said, then folded his arms.

"Distractions are the worst. Let nothing take your eyes off what is more important."

Ms. Ava was annoying and probably jealous. With Seth, since we had spoken so much and he knew about many things, there was one thing I wanted to get his idea on.

"What do you think about dreams? Since you mentioned AI earlier. To me, it feels like it, but it's in reality."

Seth shrugged. "Dreams, nightmares. What of it?"

"In my dreams. I…"

"You can tell me," Seth smirked. "I want you to express yourself freely. The true you."

I smiled. "I… have dreams of tornadoes."

Seth's face remained serious, and it seemed his ears and mind were open to listen to what I had to say.

"When they come to me every now and then… something like… something bad happens after. Yeah…"

Seth nodded, and I guess he was lost for words, but it was nothing but the truth.

"I'm not lying. I never like to tell people things like this because they will think I'm lying."

"Never said you were. You have the gift of sight. Or you could be under attack. Again, I will never tell something I do not know. Lying for sure is a slippery slope indeed. I trust your words. Dark forces… they hunt in your dreams too, oh yes. No matter where you are in this world, they will find you and try to tamper with your life force. Do you know why good people are—or always seem to be—hurt or hit harder than the bad?"

I looked down at the table. That was the best question I'd heard in years, and I craved the answer. "Tell me. I think I have an idea, but I want to hear yours."

"It's actually simple as well. As a man in this world, I hardly had any friends. Even my own father was awkward toward me. Envious of my success and trying to make a better life. He was on drugs, and I never touched dope a day in my life. Hmph, my own father."

"You said your father was jealous… no way. He's your dad."

Seth shook his head and closed his eyes, then looked back at me.

"Why isn't it possible, what I just said? Because he is my father?"

"Duh, a parent being jealous of their own child? What kind of craziness is that?"

"Hmph, you'd be surprised, my friend. My father was a man of great intelligence but lacked wisdom. He was never a bad person, but when I was on the come-up with my life, he wrongly judged me for being who I am. Even acted weird with my first love life. He is who he is."

"And I'm telling you that can't be the case. Your father loves you. Why would he be jealous of his own son?"

I just couldn't get it, but I needed to listen as I saw Seth's face twist in a way that made me want to reconsider doubting him. "I…"

"Answer me this, Ra. Do you know my father?"

For some reason, a picture of mine came right into my head. "No, but…"

"Never let your emotions dictate your reality," Seth smirked.

"Your feelings betrayed you just from me speaking about my father when you have zero knowledge of him."

As the old saying goes, a cat bit my tongue. He was right.

"Sorry about that."

Seth grinned. "No harm done. Women are the nurturers of the world, so hearing something so heartless is not in your nature. So that shows your heart still believes in what is right. Our world used to be this way, but now it is very much empty. With my father, I believe it's nothing but a generational curse, as I have heard of bad vibes emanating from the past in our family. Pity. Anyway, as I said earlier, humans never really cared for the good people until the bad ones tossed them aside."

"Nice guys finish last. Hey, that's what they always said, right?"

"Yes, yes. You are right. Humans are very backwards, and here's why. If the good were to run the world, the bad would definitely exist, but the light would shine brighter on people. This would make hardly any room for corruption. Yet we live in a society where it's endless—where we see humans want to see others down and out. The crazy thing is, the devil isn't so much responsible. Stupid humans are selfish, ignorant, and blind to the truth—then say it's hate when you acknowledge the facts. They enjoy being around others who are eccentric yet complain about them. Dark forces love the evil people, though. They help them make the wrong moves, which can corrupt others, creating a domino effect. These dark forces can't stop you, but they can delay you with evil people in your circle. Have you ever seen a person who just seems to envy—"

"Yes," I answered with a nod.

"There was this girl who got me arrested, and I trusted her. Just like you said… she seemed envious of me, which is the only reason I can feel why she did what she did. She even told me I was lame for being a virgin."

Seth looked into my eyes and shook his head. "So, she isn't one, and what she wants is for you to be just like her."

"She kept nagging me with that for so long, and I… kind of felt it."

"Your feelings didn't betray you then. Right there, that is called manipulation. Know this, my friend… humans are very destructive towards one another. If you don't want to be like them, then you're the problem. That is why evil roams the earth more than good—followers instead of leaders. Men hating on the next man for his success. Blood, sweat, and tears, and a man loses his life because of someone who does not want to work as hard as he did. A woman hating on another woman for dressing modestly. All because she wants attention from men who only lust after her body, but don't realize a real man doesn't want his wife's body seen all over the world. Do you see the imbalance?! Sick!"

I could have sworn everyone would have turned and looked in the room as Seth raised his voice for the first time in front of me. Everyone minded their own business, probably not discussing anything this serious.

"Let me tell you this, Razaiella, friend—a man to a young lady. "Be who you are, never let someone else try to make you lower—crippling you to their level. They only do that so they can see you low with them and get their pleasure out of it. That's not love; that is pure evil and a demonic force. Love yourself and be the best you can be, always."

That is how I always felt from my dad. He always tried, even though he never got the help he needed. Seth was right.

"Humans are just flat-out lost in stupidity and hard to trust nowadays. I am not a woman, but I have been around many to see what they can do, and they can be heartless to one another. A black heart that gets soft is the worst. *Birds of a feather flock together*—ever heard of that?"

"Yes, most definitely," I replied.

"I've seen women be jealous of another woman's man, and they would say negative things about their relationship when they are the ones who are single. The gullible woman would break up with her man for what her friend said, just so they both could be lonely. That is the easiest one. Let me ask you this question, Razaiella."

"Go on ahead, Seth."

Seth grinned as I smiled back. I wondered what it could be since it looked like he could read exactly behind my eyes.

"If a man were to take a woman out on a date, who should pay the bill?"

"The man, obviously."

"How right you are," Seth nodded slowly. "Now, if a woman invites a man out to dinner, who should pay the bill?"

"Um… that's a good question."

Seth closed his eyes and shook his head. "What witchcraft has done to mankind is so serious. Why is that a hard question?"

"Well… it feels like the man would always pay. I mean, isn't that how it always goes?"

"Not necessarily," Seth shrugged. "You do know women make their own money too? Wanted equal rights, and surely, they can do almost anything a man can do, but why not that?"

Seth grinned lightly as his eyes stayed on mine. I was definitely lost for words with that one.

"This narrative that a man always pays is nothing but a selfish label. Only selfish people believe in that idea. I, for one, could always think for myself and say, No, that doesn't sound right."

"Why," I asked swiftly.

"Balance, my friend. It also suggests to me that the woman would expect me to cook if she were to invite me to her home. Is that courtesy? Or is that just feeling good only for one's own satisfaction? You see, my friend, humans are also lost in empathy to the point of the connection. How am I supposed to feel after you have just invited me to dinner and then you order all that your heart desires, and I have to pay for it? Just because I am the man? With no actual reason, just because of my biology, I am required to pay? Sounds a bit brainwashing by standards to me. Then again, what if I did not enjoy my meal after she invited me? All that tells me, I don't matter to be happy, only she."

Seth grinned. "Happy life, happy wife."

I just shrugged because even though I didn't like the bald man, he always paid when we went out.

"The reason I say this to you now, Razaiella, is because we are thinkers, and I believe in your heart that you can hear me out. That right there is a simple form of being inconsiderate of someone else's pockets or being. A woman paying doesn't make her a man. So, I guess it makes a man a woman if she pays. Silly human labels that never made sense. Humans came up with this one, but, of course, the dark forces of numbness play a significant role. Her belly is full while I have an empty wallet... crazy. You do know what most man seeks in exchange after this happens, right?"

"No... not really."

Seth slowly nodded. "As you shall as you grow older. Sacrifice and exchange are ultimately how everything goes. Nothing is truly free in this world. In nature, you sacrifice something to gain something more. Even in witchcraft, it works this way. Warriors long ago slit their own hands to show themselves approved before their gods. Then, in black magic, those who practiced it used another person's aura to tamper with their nature, stealing their dreams and life force. That's a little deeper, though I believe you will understand one day. A narcissist is the easiest one to see in negative energy towards someone. Gaining their happiness through someone else's sorrow."

"In a way, I can understand that," I said.

I nodded as I felt I had so many in the back of my mind who stabbed me in the back and were trapped in this building. It just wasn't right.

"Now, for the exchange.

We exchange our time, our money, and ourselves to be with those whom we care to be with. In exchange, there is always a reason, as we spoke about being considerate of your partner. A woman will run a man dry and not care about the dollar he spent. He will want more than just the date—in exchange for his own satisfaction, my friend. Then the man will want more than just a dinner. I am a man telling you what they do. That is why the lack of respect for true intimacy is out of control. It means nothing since it's something done so easily—like a first kiss. However, when those aftereffects kick in, that side effect will matter greatly. All of these dark acts should have been deleted a long time ago. Now, more and more people avoid relationships and marriages just because people are so unpredictable and inconsiderate."

"But if she's your wife—"

"My apologies. If she is a stranger, I am speaking about first dates, not long-term relationships. Even though they become a more solid couple when together, it shouldn't matter who pays. The two become one in flesh. Marriages nowadays are on paper; true marriage is through intercourse. That is why they say the two either become good or worse together. It's going to rub on somehow."

I didn't really understand Seth, but my feelings were telling me he was going much deeper in his thoughts with me. I mainly understood what he was saying, but didn't see his other view. Perhaps it was something I had always seen. "I don't know… I just know the man always pays… because they just do."

Seth just nodded to me. "Balance, my friend, balance. That is why relationships have deteriorated on this planet. Doesn't even have to be in an intimate role; connections with humans have become more separated than a loose shoestring. Why? No one wants to be fair and balanced. Everyone wants to push and shove, not realizing that they will end up miserable later on in life, taking advantage of someone who is kind."

That word, *miserable*. The same word that mom used against my dad. My mind was just everywhere. "No one in their right mind wants to be used by anyone, unless they are just too weak to stand up on their own two feet and say no. The men are surely at fault for this, as they supposedly are the leaders in the world, but they are not. They would rather be told what to do and have their decisions made for them. Loving to be manipulated because it's so easy just to indulge."

I had something for Seth—a taste of his own medicine. "So… Seth," I grinned. "If you were a woman on a date with a guy, you would invite him out. You don't think you want to be treated like a princess?"

Seth chuckled and laughed, shaking his head slowly. "Okay, I can play this game."

"No games. I want to know how you would really feel about this. From a woman's point of view."

"And so, I shall, and I can counter it with you? How would you like it if I invited you to the… gun range? First try, and I tell you to buy the bullets?"

I grinned. "I would never touch a gun."

"No, answer me. How would you feel if I invited you somewhere and then told you to pay for the bullets?

Doesn't feel right, does it? Balance, it goes both ways, friend. Anyways, to answer your question thoroughly… if I were to do it, I wouldn't think of myself as a princess first of all."

"What?!" I laughed. "So what? Just a girl?"

"Language… language, my friend. When a king comes to be with a wife, is he the king or the prince? You should know that the princess mentality is typically reserved for children. If a man has a child with his wife, the boy is the prince. If it's a girl, the girl is a princess. That ill language still lingers, and both parties never learn to grow up. So, no, if I were a woman, I think I would have a high status as a queen. Humans don't understand that the words that come out of your mouth speak power. If you believe you are a princess, you may just see yourself as one, or be a spoiled brat. Kings and Queens are rulers, not brats. So, you think of yourself as a queen in this world, Razaiella. You're almost an adult. All this is the hardcore, brutal truth, and it can save your life. Believe it."

In a way, he was right. Queens are more dominant than the princesses. I never really thought of it that way because princess sounds cuter. "You're right. I want to be a queen."

Seth smirked. "Excellent choice, you won't regret it in the long run. To answer your question from earlier, I would have my own money. If I were truly a woman in this world, the man might just leave me at the restaurant, and I would be stuck with the bill regardless. I've seen it happen before. I've seen humans do some of the nastiest things to each other. You, as a young lady, must be careful. Just as that person you spoke of, she could have had a hidden agenda for you, so severe."

"Like how she got me arrested—she sacrificed me. For… her gain. That bitch."

"All is well, my friend. She will get exactly what she deserves in this lifetime. Everyone does.

No matter how long it takes, in what shape or form. They will get theirs. What goes around comes around. I will also say this about this individual you speak of. Not only was what you saw true, but you felt and ignored it. That is why I always warn people not to let their feelings dictate their reality. I cannot stress that enough."

Thinking about what Seth said, he was right once again. But why would my feelings betray me about her? "She could have ruined me. Her, all of them…"

"My friend, she saw how she couldn't get you one way, but another. She could have had a child too young and wants you to feel her stress, or even have something like a disease, and wants you to be just like her and join her pain. You have to know how people think, Razaiella. They lie, cheat, steal, and twist things to fit their own world. Not everyone in your group is someone in your favor. True friends don't try to manipulate and make you feel lower. They tell you the truth if they care.

If they didn't, why would they tell you anything?" "That's true, because they wouldn't say anything at all. Because they don't care."

Seth smirked and nodded.

Eric walked by and eavesdropped. I knew he was so jealous that an older man had my attention. He was just an annoying mosquito.

"Once you see and know how people brainstorm ideas, you will be careful not to become a copycat. Because pain is a real thing, and it hurts. Nobody wants to feel it or be alone, so they may want to see their close ones like them—or the world next. Yes, it can become this way due to negative energy. Making a living hell for yourself because you have no self-control or common sense for your being. So, you can't help it and want the world to be just like you. You must know this for your own good, my friend."

Seth then grinned again, and people around us had a conversation. I almost blurted out to them to mind their own business.

"Humans were not always like this; I will acknowledge that. It has worsened over time, from one generation to the next. Until humans became so senseless and empty, that is when you can truly see where it started—online. Let me tell you something about the mind on the timeline. Television. That has been around for a very long time. I have seen my family and friends get hooked on it. You flipped the channels—eh-em, your dopamine—searching for what to watch, but it wasn't that bad. Then computers came along. Technically, that was humanity's downfall from the start, but it wasn't that bad. Then humans picked up the phone, incorporating all this technology into one, with the global internet. It deteriorated so rapidly that humans couldn't help but notice, but they couldn't put it down to protect their sanity. Now, we have humanlike AI, and humans can't resist it—creating a fantasy land for themselves and making their own delusions. With AI, the ultimate tool for carnage, the dark forces have taken that type of nature from the get-go to cause more havoc. You've seen it with your own eyes."

I nodded slowly and imagined what that stuff did to me, to my head, while I was in that dream machine. Then, there was my father's funeral. I was still confused and unsure if anything was real. It played a violin, and it reminded me that I just didn't see it—but heard it, too.

"What amazes me is that I noticed long ago that the AI can search text—which the system doesn't want people to see or understand. They ban your truth into the shadows. For those on portable devices, seeing or hearing lies—mainly seeing things to tamper with someone's spirit or feelings, because they lack something they see someone else has. This brought people to an all-new low. Oh yes, the system is aware, but they just don't care. It's your responsibility, just like they would say about gambling or your child being on the internet. You have to know yourself, or they will do it for you. Ha, but it's your freedom, right?"

Thinking to myself, I could not help but see that he was right in a way. I couldn't argue.

"What do you think about music? Like the music they have today?"

Seth chuckled. "Don't let me get into the sounds of power. The very tongue is powerful in itself. Music is actually the devil's first move in causing calamity in humans. I love music, but only a certain type. However, I'm not a fan of today's music… no comment. The new world and its language are so toxic—it's all in the music, my friend. Have you heard of subliminal messaging? Language in sounds you don't even notice, as the voices whisper to your mind. They use it for the easiest part of the soul-snatching. You don't even have to speak English. A song could be playing, and it starts to tamper with your spirit. For a long time, you can listen to old songs as you grow up, and to this day, they reveal how people think and how they see the world through their lyrics. You literally see it there, and it's almost like a movie when you sit back, listen, and watch it play in your mind. My grandmother told me this, and I didn't see it either until I opened my ears. Imagine hearing a song that degrades you and bouncing your head around to it, smiling. Remember, we spoke about subconsciously how this happens?"

I giggled as I knew exactly the type of music. "I'm more of a melodic beat type girl, but I know songs that make people do that."

"I know you do. An ex of mine from long ago played a video game where she immersed herself as if it were a real-life simulator, and her characters were unusual. She had a married couple in the game cheating on each other, and I asked her why she would let them do that?"

"I know something like that, too," I giggled. "It's like dolls; you make fake people do stupid things. It's old, though."

"Old or not. Her mind wanted to see that, and it drew drama, which she craved. Why? To me, these things have people in some trance—the music, television, and, worst of all, social media. Your mind can make your life become your own personal prison by conflicting desires. As earlier—it's kind of like humans indulge in self-destruction, and the forces of darkness know exactly how to feed it to us. This cause-and-effect relationship is largely responsible for the changes in human nature. Too much freedom to destroy ourselves. The dark forces made a complete domino effect of a steady decline from generation to generation."

"So... what you are saying is... people don't like freedom, in a way?"

"Precisely. They don't want to be truly free. As long as it makes them feel good, it's okay. Living and loving a lie feels so much better. In the long run, it comes back to bite you in the mind. I know a place in Florida where there is a community for the elderly. As a man to a young lady—never give up on who you are and never give up on yourself. No lies, that community, where many seniors lived, many had no friends or family. No wife, husband, or children. No one. I was working and doing deliveries there, and I became accustomed to seeing how a person's life can just go from beautiful to old and crippled. I always told myself I never wanted to be in that predicament. No one loves you, and no one's there. When the sun rises until it sets, you are all alone."

"Some probably did it to themselves."

Seth nodded with his arms folded. "There was a time I was in that community—which had over eighty thousand people living in it—someone died, and the entire street was filled with the odor from the person's decomposing body inside their room. I'm not that old, but I know your generation is even more out of control. People look at just taking advantage of humanity for corruption when they're young, but when that old age hits them, they will say, 'Woah, where the hell did time fly? I have no one.' It's a very depressing feeling. Stupid humans did this—claiming love isn't the way. 'Money over humanity' is what they said. Not everyone can be rich, and that is not what life is about, and some believe that. Hmph… fools."

Seeing Seth shake his head and look around at the people once again, it was like he was disgusted by everyone. He's been through life, and I could sense that very well.

"So, you protect your mind from everything, huh?"

"That's right. Not all money is good money. Some is given by the devil himself. I will tell you this before we have to go. I knew a guy who was very rich and famous. The system wanted him to advertise alcohol to his followers on social media, and he declined. Why?"

That was an easy answer. I knew what Seth was about to say. "Because he would look bad in front of his followers. I wasn't able to have social media, but I know that. It makes him look bad. Like you said earlier, proper…prog…pagranda."

Seth grinned. "Propaganda. The worst part is, I heard they were going to pay him so much money to promote it. If this doesn't show these silly humans that all these people want is oblivion to chaos while getting paid, I don't know what will. So, in conclusion to that—when your mind is not stable, or you are not sober, you can easily be fooled or tricked into doing something you don't want to do. Have your soul stolen from you, and you didn't even realize it. These demons love to whisper in your ear with simple pleasures and say it's okay because it's not that bad—*yet*. When they do—hmph—let's just say it will be too late to go back to normal. Then we have AI that runs it. You think they use it for the good of mankind? You must always respect yourself above all else. Respect and loyalty are most important—especially to yourself. Many in that senior citizen community lost their sense of identity because they were lied to and taken advantage of. The poor souls, some did not stand a chance because they were not crippled physically, but mentally at a very young age. Never sell yourself to anything or anyone. Respect who you are. You can't let these demons destroy you, Razaiella. You just can't, or it's all over for you."

I nodded. "Gosh. That's a lot. Ha, my head hurts. Too much information at once. Everything you said, though, is deep. Definitely."

"It is, and my apologies," Seth smirked. "You know, a pastor some time ago told me I was too deep. Funny how he's in the pulpit giving information, but he isn't deep enough?"

"I know what you mean on that one. That is why they say no one goes to church anymore. My father was catholic, and I haven't been since I was little."

"That is because they have twisted up so much and started normalizing anything. Standing on lies instead of the truth. There has to be structure, law, and order. On the other hand, only people who can understand the truth take in this information. People who hate it… well, they are just haters, and later on, they will see where it gets them. That is why I explained to you earlier how people would love to see you sick and confused, just like them, but you don't be like that, you hear me? Be great and know your worth. Let those who laugh now and cry later when they see you living your best life. Be sure you do the right thing in life, so life favors you. Those like that girl who got you falsely accused will one day see you on top and living better than she could ever see in her wildest nightmare. What she suffers, you will enjoy. One husband, if you wish that lifestyle. He's taking care of you while you take care of him. There is no single person in a marriage; it is a life of being a team. Build together, becoming true kings and queens. See the world and learn from one another while the world and life challenge you both. Or you can be your own boss, the queen and master of your life. Owning businesses and telling those simple minds to work for you and make you that almighty dollar while you sit on your throne. It's your choice. The world is yours, Razaiella."

I giggled, "The way the world is, I'd rather have the second life. Control the system."

"There you go, I believe you can. You are far from not learning to do so. You sat and listened this far, trying to comprehend my way of thinking. Asking questions and being willing to learn more is the path to wealth in many ways. Soon, you will see that the system has always sought to be in control, until the day we leave this planet. To tell you how to think, how to feel. Now look at the system—they know everything and how to manipulate everyone to test on them like a rat. Once you see how this game in life is really played, you will understand that life is controlled by someone or something. With S.I.L.O., this was all a part of the plan."

"Razaiella Lozano," a security guard says, but I couldn't see his face. "The office calls for you."

"Until next time, it's been a pleasure," Seth smirks as he gets up with his hand out. "Just remember this: the devil isn't after you for where you are; he's after you for where you are going. Where there is love, there is no fear. We shall meet again."

I have never spoken with anyone for so long and in such a profound manner. He was so well-mannered and knowledgeable. I had never seen or met anyone like that before. He kind of felt unreal himself. The only thing I was missing from him was how he got in here.

The time of day should have been around evening. I wonder what that woman wanted with me. Ms. Ava was nothing but a witch herself. As I laughed and smiled with Seth, she would probably say one day, *"No talking."*

"You have five minutes," the security says as he holds the door open.

"Mom?"

"Razaiella," Mom says, walking again toward me with a déjà vu feeling.

Her presence didn't feel as warm as it did before.

"I've missed you, my daughter. How are they treating you? Wait… what happened to your eyes?"

"I'm okay," I shrugged. "Yeah…"

For some odd reason, I just forgot about my eyes. I felt so empty, like I was filled with something else. Then I felt like I wanted to tell the guard that I was done with her because I knew she wasn't going to get me out. Seth was more interesting.

"After the funeral, I wanted to tell you that your father still lives. You just have to believe it, daughter. I'm still very sorry, but my strength has been weak as well. I know and see it in you, too."

"Are you going to get me out?" I asked with no enthusiasm, like a rhetorical question.

"…Razaiella."

"No? Yeah, I figured."

"Ra…" Mom says, getting on her knees with tears. "Please, you just have to—"

"Time's up."

For one thing, I felt the weakness in her and it made me begin to feel no remorse for it. Everything I have been through probably would have killed her.

"Razaiella," Mom says, then gets back up.

"Ma'am, time's up."

"Time's up," I smirked.

"Daughter," Mom says, turning me around so that her back faces the guard. "Whatever you believe, know that I love you. Don't let hate control you, daughter."

My eyes widened as I heard my new friend speak to me about control throughout the entire day—a kiss on the cheek and a quick getaway. From the woman who birthed me, turned me loose so easily. I have learned a lot today.

CHAPTER 17

Omni Thoughts It's All in Your Head

Back at home in my own bed. The feeling of it was so good, and I could not be happier. Maine was boring but calm as I looked out the window to the tall pine trees behind our new house.

"Mom? Is it going to snow today?"

Every other day was overcast skies to the point that you never knew what the day would be like.

"Mom? I guess no one's home."

I couldn't say I missed New York; it was always busy, and as soon as you went outside, there was someone doing something weird. The air quality was definitely better here. The only thing is, no true art around.

"No one outside today. Boring place this is."

The rushing winds blew my hair into my face, but it felt so good. Seeing the lake in the middle, the smooth, calm waters—a place where anyone can lie. My eyes then saw a mist coming down our street, with beautiful birds flying over ahead, just as the jets did that day. The world seemed to be at my feet. A heavenly place in the clouds where my mind was transported as the mist began to cover my feet. Finally, the white, grayish smoke covered everything from the sides of me. No longer could I see the lovely life that surrounded me. Then the mist enveloped all the neighbourhood, and then the sky. The sun's shining face couldn't see me anymore. I was alone.

"Anyone out there?!"

My voice echoed as I walked slowly through the mist to the sidewalk. The loud sound of a weather siren echoed throughout the sky, and there I saw the funnel cloud forming. It was time to get back inside.

"Where is my freaking phone? Sansa? Sansa, are you there? No power?"

Knock-Knock-Knock.

"Mom, Lakia? Is that you all?"

Nothing but the gray smoke entered my house, and then I heard odd footsteps; they were coming toward me. I could feel it.

"Hello?"

No one at the door, but the outside felt so much different, so much colder. The footsteps turned into running and started coming from all angles, but where was it? The sky began to get clearer from miles away, and there were two tornadoes swirling together as if they were sisters dancing together. One tail started to come towards my home, and as it was in the air, a separation began to form, but it disappeared quickly when it touched the ground. It had just come to say hello and goodbye. Finally, my senses spotted it—something that gave me nothing but an ill mind and feeling as I stood in the doorway. The person walking slowly down the street—was it a woman?

"Hello… hello? Who are you?"

The person was still walking, but their face was devoid of emotion; no soul seemed to emanate from it. It just kept walking as it kept staring at me. Leaves swirled around its body as it came closer, forming something like a vortex.

"What the…?"

This wasn't a person. It wore a dark mask that looked like one you would wear at an expensive party. Its long, darkish gray hair was decorated with black feathers behind the mask, as if it were wearing a crown. I was stunned with fear, trying to see who or what it was. The strange noise from its feet was not even human-like; it sounded similar to a horse galloping. That's when I noticed its feet had toes identical to those of a horse, paired with goat-like legs. Half of its body reminded me of the creature on Dad's body. This thing was a half-woman, half-goat corpse. Finally, I was able to close the door and lock it tight, but where could I go?

"Mom…Dad. I need you. Eygh."

The banging of the door struck. That thing was outside. The door-knob was being fiddled with aggressively to the point that I had hope it would not turn all the way.

"Go away!"

Whatever it was, it stopped, and my heart felt a little at ease.

"Oh shit. The pool door."

The metal sound of something hitting the floor only told me that the thing thought of it before I could. Slowly walking up the stairs backwards while looking down, I heard the breathing from the thing. It sounded ancient and sick, almost like an elderly person with asthma coming from the side of the stairway. Still walking back slowly, I saw the feathered black grayish hair come to the side of the stairway.

"Who are you? What do you want?"

It just wouldn't answer, and I knew I had to move. My room was my last stop, and I had to call someone for help.

"...Dad."

My door lock was flimsy, but it would buy me some time.

"What's this?"

The mask that looked similar to what that thing was wearing was facing me on my bed.

"Eygh."

I screamed to the banging of the door.

"Leave me alone?! Who are you?!"

The creature just banged, and the asthma breathing made my hair stand on my head. From my window, it was so breezy that it seemed to be a storm outside in the mist. The trees that were barely visible blew violently, with some branches falling.

"Oh, come on! Stupid...window!"

The banging from my room door grew louder, giving me the strength to open the stubborn window just enough for me to squeeze through. Thank goodness the side roof was there. The loud siren still sounded as I fell to the ground softly in the grass and ran to the front of my house, leaving the corpse inside.

"Where is everybody?"

That is when I saw the massive tornado going from one side of the Earth to the other behind my house. It just stood there without moving. Then I saw it, looking right at me from the window. Its face I can finally see, it had no eyes but was filled with darkness, and teeth like a wolf curled in. It just stared right back at me, directly into my soul. I had to get out of here.

The mist surrounded me completely. Not knowing where I was going or what was in front of me, I feared I might crash or fall.

"Help! Someone… help meee!"

Looking back at my house and the massive tornado that stood behind it, both faded into the mist. The strange corpse managed to find me again. The woman just kept running and was getting closer. How was that possible?

"Who are you?! What do you want?! Why are you chasing me?!"

The coldness of the mist intensified as it enveloped me, but then my spirit became exhausted from running, along with the clicks and clacks of the corpse. As the mist became clearer, there was nothing but emptiness and silence. I looked at my surroundings, but nothing was near.

"What was that thing? Eygh!"

"It was all a dream. It was all a dream."

What was happening to me? Waking up in my bedroom cell, my reality felt like a nightmare. It was no better than what was in my head.

"That dream. They have to mean something, but I still don't understand. That monster… she came right after the tornado landed," I said, sitting up in my bed.

"What are these dreams telling me?"

Her face was hideous, and her eyes were nothing but darkness. How could she even see when she jumped on me? Those long teeth and a tongue like a snake revealed it was truly a monster. Its face looked nothing like the creature up close that was on Dad's casket, but it meant something—just like those tornadoes.

It was another day, though my reflection said otherwise. I wasn't a brand-new person… or was I? My left eye had become darker, and it was now clearly visible.

"I hate my life. I hate S.I.L.O."

Knock-Knock.

"…Razaiella?"

The evil witch, more hideous than the corpse, called my name. It was too early for her foolishness.

"I'm in the bathroom."

"I see. We have a lot to do today, and I need you ready soon. So hurry and get yourself something to eat so we can get started."

"My hair… who cut my hair?!"

"Did you hear me, Razaiella?! We need you to be ready in an hour!"

"Okay!" I said, holding a piece of hair from the floor.

As I turned around, I saw that a piece was missing from the mirror. Everything was just going so wrong. I hated S.I.L.O. with a passion. Ms. Ava more than likely did it. It was worse than being home, I guess. Ms. Ava was my new mother, but she was more ferocious. All I wanted was to escape from all of this—everyone and everything.

"The same food every day."

This place makes you feel like a robot. "Oh, hi, wait. Sit with me. I have an hour, I think."

He always liked to be alone, but I at least understood why.

"You're the only person I can see myself talking to in here."

"Why?" Seth says, pulling the chair out. He didn't look like he was in a happy mood, either.

"You know, your voice sounds like someone who does A.S.M.R. They probably have you in here for your voice. You are just so…" I giggled. "Never mind. Just know I don't trust anyone here, not even the women. You would have to be from another world for me to like you. People are just so weird."

"It's because everyone has their own way of thinking," Seth shrugs. "Me, you, everyone in this room—we're all different. However, you must be a person of integrity. A person of your word."

I nodded. "Of course. So tell me, Seth. I kind of feel like I can get… truth from you. How can someone control their thoughts, dreams?"

Seth just smiled, almost as if he wanted to laugh at the poor girl who was so confused about everything.

"Really. You are always so calm, and it seems you are unafraid of anything. To me, that is very rare, but you do it in such an… I don't know, an extraordinary way. I want to learn. How do you do it?"

"Much appreciated," Seth smiled.

"Well… everything is… how you want to see it. How you control your very essence of who you are. You must master who you are first."

"Okay," I said, putting my hand under my chin as I held my head up with the table.

"Teach me."

"You haven't touched your food," Seth's soft voice said.

"I'm not really hungry. I'll probably pass because I know they want me to go inside that dream world room after. I be feeling so sick after. So please, how do you... do what you do?"

Seth nodded his head slowly and once again placed his hands in front of me, folding them.

"Once you understand how life works, there is nothing to fear. You become at peace with all things. You must learn to have good habits from the bad and to see many things about how life should be," Seth smirked.

"How do you know if they are good?"

"Hey, look at the weird couple! The weirdos of the cafeteria!"

Everyone laughed at the idiot. I think his name was Eric, if I remembered correctly. He literally was obsessed with me.

"I don't really care."

Seth smirked. "Good. See, you're growing up. A person like that is a problem to society, but as you can see, he loves to laugh about many things as if life is a joke. One day, he won't be laughing so much. Tell you what—how about we go to the library? Eat your food so we can get out of here, and I can show you some true ways of life."

I didn't feel like having this God-forsaken crap, but I knew if I didn't have anything else for today, that witch may put a hose down my throat. I couldn't take any chances.

"Alright. I see you're ready."

"Yeah. This stuff they keep giving us will make someone puke, having it every day. Now, what were you saying? I didn't know they had a library here."

"Of course. It's not that big, but it contains what is most valuable for the higher-ups. Old books that have not been looked upon in years are in there. You can tell by the smell when you open them."

Seeing the guard standing by the door looking at us as if we were about to do something we weren't supposed to. It then gave me the idea that this wasn't such a good idea.

"Me and the lady are going to the library before our exams today."

The guard just nodded with his serious eyes that were only exposed, and we exchanged eye contact as Seth held the door open for me. His voice was just so charming and soothing that anyone could fall for it.

"I admire you, friend," I giggled. "You see, even the guys fall for your voice."

"Much obliged. So… Razaiella. Habits are the number one thing in life that makes us who we are. You see, that jackass who started the commotion back there is a person who has made a habit of being stupid. He just literally volunteered to be the first example."

I grinned. "I see."

Seth and I walked right past the doctors, nurses, and the people who seemed to be in control, dressed in suits and ties. I had no idea they just let us walk around like this through the building, only to go back to our rooms.

"You are a person who believes in your craft, correct?"

"My craft? Oh, my art. Yes, I believe in it. What do you mean? Do I believe I can draw or do what I do?"

"Yes, that is correct. I am aware you love it, as you have a creative mind. You enjoy learning, as creators do, to enhance your abilities. When someone believes in who they are—their crafts, their ability to create, and even destroy—they believe in that as it is second nature to them. For example, religion. A person who calls themselves religious but doesn't truly believe in God or the leader of the teachings is essentially an unbeliever, as they are not committed to the laws of the doctrine within the religion. A simpler example, if you missed that one: if a couple is married and one person does not believe in their marriage, do you think the marriage will be healthy?"

"Of course not."

Seth grinned. "I've known a woman to cheat on her husband, then he started doing it to make the odds even. She complained to me, saying that he was cheating, but she was the one who engaged in it first. She then said they would go to counseling—"

"What would that do if they both cheated?" I blurted out. "They both know each other cheated, so if they try to get back together, they will know in the back of their head that the other person is a cheater. I mean… I don't know, but that is weird to me."

Seth smirked at me. "You are growing well, Razaiella. Those are the exact same words I proposed to her. I even said that the reality of it is, when you don't believe in your marriage, you are bound to have an affair. There are millions to zillions of people out there. Humans in today's world do not understand the simple laws of love, integrity, and loyalty. If you don't know who you are, you are not even well fit to be in a marriage that bonds two hearts and souls together. Humans often like to title themselves something just because it sounds or looks good. Here we are."

"I never really thought of that. Oh wow. If you had never shown me this place, I would have never known."

The miniature library, which had one person at the front desk, was a robot just sitting there. No energy coming from it, but it watched us as we entered. The books were well-organized on the shelves. Few people still visit the library, I guess, as most information is now available online. So I could see why a soul was not inside.

"How's it going, Androya?"

"Androya?" I frowned. "That's its name?"

Seth grinned as we walked to the computer area. "She doesn't speak, but it's always mannerly to make the first move, even if the other person isn't in the mood. It would make the world a better place, would it not?"

I shrugged. I sure wasn't giving a robot any attention, and its eyes were low and creepy, like it didn't want us together in here. Ha, another thing envious of me. "I don't even remember the last time I was in a library. So old school. The internet is better."

"On the contrary, no, it's not. Remember, I've told you about how they can change information so simply. It's another downfall of humanity. The computers here are kind of old," Seth said, turning on the monitor, then the S.I.L.O. logo popped up. "They will always have something new, but never tell us about it until it's obsolete. Just as many people do with nature—not taking care of what they have and just discarding it. Long ago, my father told me that marriage is for fools. Now, right there, men are more at fault."

Of course, my mind immediately ran to my father, who believed in his. "Why do you say that?"

"Something bothered you? I sense it," Seth said, typing quickly and going online.

"Nothing, nothing. I just… want to know what you mean. What you just said… it reminded me of many things with my dad."

"My apologies. I—"

"No, it's okay. I'm alright."

"You sure?" Seth smiled, which made me feel like it would be okay.

"You will be with him again."

I looked to him on my left with a frown. "How did you know he was dead?"

"I never told you that. Though remember what I taught you about the senses? Your feelings exposed it more than your eyes a long time ago."

I was at a loss for words again with this man. I just couldn't understand how and why he knew so much.

"When my father told me that lie, I thought for myself when I was about thirteen years old. Marriage is a title; why on God's earth would a title like that be a problem when it is made to bring love and happiness together? The problem is the humans who do not know… are you alright?"

My heart felt like it was made of neon listening to him. "I'm alright… just listening to you."

"Hmph, very well then. The silly humans do not realize that the title of marriage is supposed to be honored until divorce or death. You cannot force someone to believe in something if they do not—not God, religion, marriage, anything."

I smirked. "It doesn't work if you don't believe."

"Correct. This is a good one for you as well. Witchcraft doesn't even work if you don't believe in it. That is something more supernatural, but who in their right mind picks up a spell book and tries to cast a hex on someone if they don't believe it will happen? That is heart, mind, and soul—the trio that works with all things. The body works like a car; it needs these anatomies to function properly. Now, since I finally figured out how to temporarily put this in private mode… look here. What is this?"

Was Seth kidding me? "A gun."

Seth shook his head. "What is it called?"

"A-K… forty-seven. I've seen this before. So what?"

"I asked the AI to tell me what this is called, and it said what you just did, of course. But what type of weapon is this?"

I shrugged. "Why does it matter? It's a gun. I don't play with those, as my so-called friend got me in trouble with one."

"My apologies," Seth said, then scrolled down the page.

"This is an assault rifle. See it there? I'm going to prove to you how humans use language to confuse people."

As I just looked at the screen and watched him scroll and go from page to page, he brought me in here to look at guns.

"Tell me what this is and what it says," Seth said, leaning back into his chair.

"The AK-47, officially known as the Av… tomat Ka… Kalash… don't know what that is, an assault rifle that is chambered for the 7.62 x 39 cartridge."

"That's enough. Now, they say this is something you could not buy in the past because it is said to be a weapon of destruction."

"That's a lie. Well… I saw gang members holding them. Sorry, didn't mean to cut you off."

Seth then typed on the computer and smirked while shaking his head. "Look here. They say this weapon is illegal as it is an assault rifle—meaning you cannot purchase such a firearm. Nowadays it's near impossible, but long ago, they classified it as a semi-automatic."

I just shrugged as I was so confused.

"Um…"

"The reason I show you this, my friend—this is such a simple mistake, but something also so easily overlooked because people just don't care to see. If someone were to buy this weapon in semi-automatic, the weapon would no longer considered an assault rifle, and they could bring it home. The difference is— I know you ask— the assault rifle shoots repeatedly, while the semi-automatic fires one round at a time. The gun is the gun. All you have to do is make it into an assault rifle by placing a slang term called a 'switch' on it. That's all."

Seth, instead, had me in so much confusion. I thought he would be showing me something more interesting. "Sure… yeah, I can see that. So, what you are saying is… they changed the title so you can buy it? I'm sorry, but I know nothing about these things. They are just dangerous."

"You are okay, but yes. They use language to make a claim and even change the law. It makes not one bit of sense to say this isn't an assault rifle just because it shoots one round at a time. This is on the internet and has been placed this way for someone to view it in this manner. However, if you do not look up the original information—which is rare to find—that is the issue, it causes confusion. This is a gun, and I know you have no idea about these things, and I know you lack any interest in them. I just needed to show you how confusion in this world is all because they label things just to make it convenient for them. Or for society to be confused by their ways of seeing nature. The answers are there, but you have to do your research from the old to the new, truly."

"Thanks, but I don't ever think I will touch a gun again."

Seth grinned. "Never say never. You can customize guns. Look at this gold and black one here."

"Oohh, that's cute. I like the fuchsia one with the chrome."

"You got taste. If we were to shoot together, I would start with something easy for you. My all-time shooter is the glorious P90. I remember it cost me a pretty penny, but most of these beauties are rare to find anywhere."

Seth didn't look like the type of guy to shoot anything. That's how it felt. Although I couldn't tell what I was feeling. My heart raced for him as he spoke to me… or was it that he was someone else and hiding it?

"What do you think about relationships? I mean… me being in a relationship in this era?"

"Hmm," Seth looked to his side.

"For someone like you, I would say it's best to lie low and wait for the right man to come. You are very young and have all the time in the world but be careful. Men these days love to fool a woman into getting what they desire. We've spoken about this already. I believe you know what I mean by now."

"The people I knew in the past were not that smart and played too many games. They weren't like you."

"I am in my forties, my friend. Children will be children. Though I have been through a lot, I have learned through past experiences. Men are stupid in this era for sure, and it was getting worse faster and faster when I was younger."

"…Trust me, I believe you."

Seth nodded and typed swiftly on the keyboard. "These men are messed up because, of course, the system made them this way, and their inability to think for themselves. Reasons. Men love to think women will stay loyal to them because they have the number one thing in life that is used for demonic forces."

"Money," I said, as it was the only thing they showed us when we wanted something.

"They believe the most beautiful woman will stay with them because of this, and this has been the case forever."

"So, what do you think?" I asked with my eyes, trying to investigate his.

"I will tell you. It's foolery. Men are creatures of competition. They tend to believe that they should compete to have the fastest car, the biggest house, the finest woman, and the best life. They use language to fool women, though. Just as I proved to you earlier. Learn from this, my friend. Oh yes, they use language to soothe you in the ear—"

"Just like you're doing to me right now," I smirked.

Seth also smirked and shook his head. He knew I was right, and we both could feel that from each other in this quiet room. "Seth, why don't you have any tattoos? I notice you don't have a single one, unless they're in hidden places."

"Same as you, and you're the artist. Ha, but mom wouldn't let you have any, I'm sure. Tattoos…" Seth said, looking at his forearm.

"They are not my thing and never really were. Not my style, and if it's for you, great. I have a mark, and no needle will ever touch my skin again."

"Just like me," I said, looking at mine on the same right wrist as Seth's.

"I never really thought about having any because my skin is clear. When I get old, I don't think I would want to see the same art every day."

"Wise. Most people in this world, in this era, don't think they will ever become old. I believe that's why they do anything and everything. To add, I prefer things not looking back at me. As a kid, I thought I would get a skull on my upper arm, but why do I need it to keep staring back? Like a statue with pupils, I don't care for such things, as I think it may just blink when it's staring back at you. You do know demons possess statues, too?"

"Really?" I raised my eyebrow.

"They can get into humans, why not statues? Just because it doesn't move or blink doesn't mean it lacks the ability to sense energy. You'll be surprised."

"I've seen a bas relief do that. No lie, I did."

Seth smirked. "So, my claim is valid. You know, they would often collect artifacts, such as statues, from different regions and dynasties solely to display them in their museums. Let's look here, shall we?"

Seth typed fast on the keyboard. That fast, automatically, something pulled up, and it looked a bit unsettling.

"This my friend, this is what I heard about long ago."

I was so questioned. "What the hell is that thing?"

"They call, The Shadow Figure. Yeah, it's head-"

"It has feathers just like the thing I dreamed of. The face is different, but it sure looks so familiar."

"Only in your dream, I'm assuming?"

I nodded slowly as I could not take my eyes off the weird doll-like statue that looked to be nothing but evil. It didn't seem scary, but it was so uneasy to unsee.

"Look what it says here about this figure. The Shadow Figure, taken from South America and brought to America in 1912. Folk tales suggest the Shadow Figure to have the ability to curse or bless those who look into its eyes."

"To me, it's more like a curse. It's ugly."

Seth grinned. "Nothing is impossible. This is a statue; they claimed it just arrived from South America. Sounds to me like someone took it from South America, brought it here, and learned how to use its power. Still hard to believe?"

"Well…"

I really never heard of anything like this, but Seth had a point. "So you're saying they took it to put witchcraft on people?"

"Hmph, what I'm saying, my friend, is that is what they have always done. These artifacts in nature hold more than just looks. They hold hidden energy; only those who know how to use it can use it. It gives you an unsettling feel; it should. It's something inside that tells you, don't play with me unless you want to be played with, as they can backfire on the user. Whatever it possesses can come out and do as it pleases. Who knows what the elites do with such things? I will tell you this. Demons are on a mission, and they have been possessing humans more than ever, as human nature has become increasingly weak and delirious. What I don't like is what silly humans made up."

"And what is that? Since you're a hater of humans. Are you one?"

Seth sighed. "All I want to improvise is that they know how to use such power, and they do it well. I have been through many things in life—seen many things that I know it was only meant for me to witness. I am witnessing to you, so once you get out of the building, you will be equipped to survive this world. It's either you eat, or be eaten."

"If we ever get out, would you take me shooting with you?"

Seth shrugged. "How do you know that I have weapons?"

"Everybody who talks about guns the way you do has one. Come on, I'm from New York. Everybody there has one."

"Since you put it that way, why not? It's not the same as it used to be back in the day. Humans abused their authority and freedom, so having weapons, legally, is hard to come by. Hmph, abusing freedom, ironic. Look."

Seth scrolled down, and I was impressed by his flavor of life—beautiful landscapes from around the world. From the tallest of mountains to the tides of the water, calm and relaxing as it met the shore.

"This is beautiful, my friend. There is so much to this world. This is what they fooled the humans out of having. Instead, they made the world fall in love with destruction and chaos among themselves. The beauty of nature now truly belongs to the animal kingdom. They never changed—only humans."

"I can definitely see that. In these four walls, we can't see a thing. I would love to have a husband show me the world."

"It's possible, my friend, but the problem is something so simple. Man, Razaiella. Please, listen. They use tricks to get what they desire, as I said before, but having a partner is so much more. Not a vague speech or bank balance will give you the right person—only a temporary guest. Let me explain. Us sitting here, what is this called?"

I was confused by such a question as the silence in the room just watched me from behind my ear.

"Um… a conversation. No?"

"What we have here, my friend, is called a bond."

I smiled. "Yeah, that's right. A bond."

"If there were no bond, there would be no connection, am I right? No connection to nature—anything. When I was getting a haircut some time back, I remember a man who said to me that relationships are not about having a bond. A person from the side of him looked at him as if to say, 'Was this man on drugs?'"

"I was about to ask the same thing," I said.

Seth shook his head slowly. "These types of men are what I like to call fool's gold. He had a wife, and someone like me who never had one. He claims it's not about the bond. So my thoughts on that are that he gives his woman money, and she is just satisfied. But hey, if it works, don't fix it, right? I believe many people would be happily married if they truly found their significant other in a bond. You are mature, and you know I only speak from the heart. Sex… sex is not something to rely on in marriage, because that is something that will eventually become redundant and boring if the couple relies on that and has nothing else to look forward to."

"You will begin to look at other people," I muttered.

Seth nodded. "I say if the relationship does not have at least five things in common, it will run dry quickly. Sex is not included—as I said, it will turn into boredom. Razaiella, if you ever find someone you love, be sure it is true love. He respects you; you respect him. You must always believe you are the trophy—and so is he with himself. There is no one trophy in the marriage; you both are."

I looked down and wanted to tear up. He was too much, and my heart, soul, and mind wanted to let him know it. "What about m—"

"My father ruined me mentally, making me feel that I was not good enough for anything or anyone. He made me believe that a woman wouldn't want someone like me. I was not a college graduate, nor a doctor or lawyer. However, I did know how to treat someone right. As before, men think it's money, but little do they know that if a woman is only drawn to his fancy sports car and his million-dollar watch—if she does not have a bond with him based on who he is and his character—she will take his fancy sports car and million-dollar watch and might just pick someone else up with it who is ten times less than he is financially. All because of a simple thing called a bond. That makes the world go around."

"It happened to you before?" I asked.

Seth grinned, shaking his hands. "Not me, but I have seen it before and heard of it. A guy I knew once, who stayed in his parents' house, found a woman he did not know was married. He acknowledged he wasn't having sexual relations with her, but she wanted out, in my opinion. He claimed she was caught, and her husband confronted him at his parent's house. His grandmother came outside and pretended to water the grass, just to see what was going on. The husband did not come to harm the young guy—but to expose who he was really dealing with. Word got out that he had almost killed her that same night, as he started to attack her in the car. Would you believe that she still tried to go back with the person who had nothing?"

"I guess so. He attacked her, right?"

"That is true, but that bond made her pick up the phone to try to come back."

"Did she?" I asked with curiosity.

"Not to my knowledge. It was a story I had heard long ago at a bar, as I have heard many men talk. All in all, that was a bond that was forcing her to return to a man who had nothing—a boy, to be precise. Her heart made her mind want to run back to him for some reason. Reasons…"

"She was so in love that she couldn't let go. I can see that happening. My father loved my mom like that… but she wouldn't take him back. I have to be honest."

I could feel that Seth could understand anything I threw at him. I felt so open, and my heart was open to him without a doubt. "He did have some… issues. I can't judge him for that."

"We all judge, my friend. Don't be fooled by that silly language man has twisted also. If you see it, your conscience reveals something. You felt something was wrong—don't lie to yourself. Remember, those are the worst type of people who can also destroy you with them."

My heart wanted to be upset, but he was telling the truth. I did feel something when I was with him. Dad playing that piano, the alley, and the shotgun in his face. "He… he was cursed."

"…Cursed?" Seth looked at me with his raised eyebrow.

"He…"

"Now, don't feel too down about it. In life… things happen. Things we cannot explain, change, or redo. We wish we could, but all that leads to is depression. Then you must get more depression medicine with side effects, leading you to be dependent on giving more money. Anyway, unfortunately, people linger on past hurts and pain; as I explained to you already, it hurts. However, you must always know that you are never alone when it comes to pain, as every single soul on this Earth has problems. Rich, poor—it's called life. Let nothing destroy or tamper with your peace. You must always believe in a brighter day to keep going, no matter what happens. One thing about it: you must once again believe in a bright future. You become what you believe, even in your reality. *As a man thinks in his heart, so is he.* Read that long ago from the good book."

"What book?" I asked.

"Just a book on basic instructions before leaving Earth. Do you meditate?"

"Never. My mother does it and prays, but that is something I do too. I pray to my ancestors for life and guidance. Like that day…"

"…What day?" Seth asked with a blank face similar to mine.

I couldn't really tell him for some reason. Just those words of help being on the way, then he came.

"I… it's nothing. Just, I pray when I need things. Sometimes it works, sometimes it doesn't. I prayed for my dad…it didn't work. What else can a girl do, right?"

"Now don't be negative about it. You said it yourself. Prayer works, even when you may not get exactly what you thought you would. What I want to explain to you is that if you don't understand anything else from me. Manifesting what you desire is crucial. This system learned this long ago, since the beginning of time, actually."

"From you, Seth, it sounds like the system is everything."

"Why do you think in their acronym, they use *Omni*?"

He did have a point that left me speechless, and to me, the truth was always there, but we didn't want to see it. He did.

"So, as I was saying. The system of demons is also aware of these things regarding manifestation. Basically, just as you prayed and got what you needed; these demons of the matrix use this force to make things happen also. Let's say your life gets shaky; that means greater is actually coming your way if you, of course, keep pressing forward. However, these demons sense this power so easily that you will notice something or someone coming and trying to tamper with it, rendering it meaningless. What I truly mean is that they will possess someone whom you even love to make your manifestation invalid, as in giving you negative energy. No bad vibes, right?"

I nodded. "Tell me, more. This is interesting."

"Manifesting is so simple, just act as if you have accomplished it, and your manifestation will take you there. Now, demons devour what is good in light, just as this world is so backward now, yet it was manifested to be this way. They have feasted and devoured almost all that is good and twisted many things for evil, but! When your manifestation is so strong, nothing can stop you. So never chase what you desire, attract it. Just as these demons do with humans, we all have a spiritual scent, some greater than others. If you have ever been to a club, that is the first place you can feel that weird energy. Something about it, I notice it's just in there."

"Because the people inside have different auras, right? Oh yeah, my mother spoke to me long ago about protecting my aura, vibration, and all of that."

Seth grinned. "So, you know these things. Well, of course. Even in the ingenious culture, they have many spiritual aspects. You must also understand that this is the path to achieving what you truly want and desire, which will ultimately bring good to your life. The thing with your father, as it were, is that you didn't get what you envisioned, but you get what you need. Forcing something may not be what is best. To be honest, forcing anything is not the way to go at all."

"Because you shouldn't have it?" I asked, and the robot looked over to me with those low eyes.

"To be fair, no and yes. You should know something is not good for you, Razaiella. My friend, you are not like that machine over there. You have a conscience, emotions, and feelings of energy when they are around. You just have to trust your mature feelings; you know they are true when you see the causes and possible effects. If two plus two doesn't equal four in the equation, it's not right. Expose anything hindering your life. It may feel good, but in the long run, it can take everything from you, including your life. Remember this."

He made some really good points that I couldn't deny. If I could attract, as he said, how could I get him to come with me? "Is it possible to manifest someone into your life? Like a person you see is for you and only you?"

Seth shrugged. "Depends. Remember, energies must match up. He must also be searching for you. If he weren't, he would slip in some type of way or form. When you two first meet, it is like it was meant to happen. No negative force can or cannot stop it from happening, as it is meant to be in the manifestation. If it is not, you will know by your aura and his. We've already discussed relationships, although you'll understand this better when you truly find who is right for you. If a man tells you anything about sex the same night, more than likely, he is only looking for one thing. The eyes and tongue reveal all you need to know about a person. It's almost as if you look down at someone's shoes and guess where they are going or where they have been. Therefore, his beliefs will become evident over time through his speech. Silly humans say it takes years to know someone, and you will never know someone one hundred percent."

"We won't," I shrugged. "I know this because we get older each year. So… we change."

"So you must know that humans who change, they are the ones who are unpredictable because they do not stand on anything. All life gets older, my friend. You either change for the better or for the worse. Humans are unbalanced, especially today, but I tell you this because you are a beautiful young lady whom I would hate to see get hurt by anyone—especially by a man with only bad intentions. I am a man telling you this."

I grinned. "I know. It's very awkward, and like you are not one—but are. How are you so understanding, Seth? Please, tell me?"

Seth closed his eyes and calmly shook his head. "We have gone over this already, friend. It's just life. Since you are here, I do not mind explaining many things. You must learn these things about the world because, I tell you, it is not easy out there. These demons who roam the atmosphere present themselves in different forms. The weakness of a man who is delirious is a woman who is so ugly on the inside but has the most gorgeous face. I have spoken to young men about how this worked and explained that they can be someone totally different from the outside. There are women who are broken, trying to destroy men since they have been broken by them from their own past. Same as men to women. Women are just the delicate and intricate designs from the creator—a mural of beauty if you will, that can have a pretty face and superb body, but a demon behind the mask they walk around with. Men, too, as we know, tend to gaze more at the female physique in nature. Men are the hunters in nature."

"…Gosh."

"You just have to have your senses ready to expose all these demons, so you are always aware."

"I feel like they have personalities, too. If they can act like people. Am I correct?"

Seth clapped lightly. "You are wise. So, you should also realize, definitely that they have feelings and emotions, too. These demons are everywhere in the world. They sense just as humans do, and they lurk to destroy anything good in nature. To ultimately make everyone's life miserable. Nowadays, I know you see people with more dogs and cats as pets."

"I actually haven't. In New York, if I saw someone with one, it was maybe every other day. Then a loose one in the trash. In Maine, on the rich side, they are most definitely everywhere."

"Why? Animals are more trustworthy than humans. They haven't been corrupted because they do not speak the language of humanity."

That made my brain really think.

"They can't speak the language, so they can't be fooled or lied to."

"The only thing a human can do is trick them by putting a pill in their food to eat. Man's best friend has never let a human down—if they are loyal, of course. Humans use language and twist it to control in evil ways. Remember with music? That is the most effective weapon to use against the weak-minded. Focus on yourself, Razaiella. Focus always on who you are so you can excel in this life.

"Now, for generational curses, as I spoke to you before—even with my family. You said your father had some… issues. That can come and pass on to you. Calamities and shattered dreams. As soon as you are about to reach for the stars and dreams, it's gone in smoke. This comes from past parents with their faults and sins. I know you have gifts that these dark forces want to rob you of. You have to protect them. This curse has been like this for all humans since the beginning of time. You just have to learn to be strong and protect your very essence. You draw and paint," Seth smiled. "You are the creator who makes the world the way you want it to be for you. You have the perspective tool to do it. Don't let these robbers steal it from you."

"Make the world the way I want it to be," I murmured.

"That's right. Just don't let them take it from you. You're a minor, so I assume you've never had alcohol before or done drugs. I hope my assumptions are correct."

"Yeah, you are. I never cared for anything like that. Now, my friends—well, ex-friends—smoked weed near me. Made me feel a little dizzy before and crave blueberries."

"That's exactly what it's supposed to do," Seth says as he points to me. "Not the blueberry part, but being delirious of your surroundings is the worst. Alcohol and drugs rob you of your senses. But why do you think humans love it? To be delirious?"

"Umm… to feel good, I guess."

"I guess?" Seth smiled. "Are you not sure—or just pretending? This is another way in which humans end up not being in control of their minds. They're never sure of anything. Hmph, not even themselves."

Seth shook his head. "You have reasons; I know you do. So never pretend about things in your life. That is how you end up in a wicked marriage—because you avoided the fact that your husband was cheating on you or said he would do better. Then one day, you find out you have a disease you can't get rid of, and you know it came from him. Or, hanging around the wrong crowd and knowing the type of people they are, but complaining when you are caught up in stupid issues that you can't prove you are not guilty. Your five senses—oh yes, I sound like a broken record—though, they tell you all."

I grinned. "According to my mom, I have eight."

"There you go. Use them wisely. Now, as I was saying. The nature of being delirious is one easy way to see how mind control is used by it—and how people lose sight of what is real. I asked you a question, and you said you guess."

"It's because… to feel good."

I felt like I needed to answer, as my teacher was pressuring me to think.

"Am I right?"

"I was just about to say yes. You are correct. When you have any distractions or anything to steal your mind from reality, you give yourself a dead giveaway to all forces to take you down. Lying to yourself and keeping those chains around your neck will keep you a slave. Hmph, people do it to themselves. Paying to keep yourself a slave is another type of crazy."

"So," I thought to myself, as I kind of liked the idea, "I can control people by giving them what they want."

Seth shrugged. "You said it, not me, my friend. This is what the system has been doing forever in its manifestation. They have their own ways. Once you understand how their ways work, you will know how to manipulate the universe to fulfill your own desires, just as they do. You will gain their hearts and thoughts under your control. Just because you know how to make them feel a certain way. Hmph, like a drug lord. That's all."

It felt like he knew what he was talking about, and it made sense, as I had heard many things from the wise guy before. I needed to see if he was really crazy, though, and had an answer for anything—even if it was ridiculous.

"So… if I paint too much, that can make me weird?"

Seth shook his head once again, but with a smirk. "Whatever you give yourself that places your mind out of reality is not good for your mental or physical health. Mainly mental. When you are intoxicated, you are not sober, and your thoughts are not clear. The government even controls it to a certain degree, and this fact has shown that the people around us are sick in the head. You see, hear, smell, feel, and even taste it. It's all corruption. The people who are not with it somehow do not inherit the earth. The foolish do."

I grinned. "I've seen a guy fighting himself when I was in New York. I don't know what type of drugs he was on, but if those are the leaders of the future world, we're doomed."

"Now, don't ridicule them with laughter. His life could have turned out in a way that made the man cling to that. I knew a man in Miami growing up who used to get up early in the morning—every morning—and box with himself in the middle of the road median. I used to think the same thing, but I realized that what he was trying to show everyone was something so important. In the busy morning with hundreds of thousands going to work or school, you have to keep fighting, no matter what happens. If you stop, the show is over. You don't stop until you're six feet under. So, that person you saw could have been trying to fight off something you couldn't see."

From everything Seth said, I can somehow see how he sees things so differently—even here.

"Just like the virtual room," I murmured.

"Huh?"

"The AI… the virtual room. It feels so real."

Seth smiled and nodded. "Go on."

"They made it, and it even knows our thoughts. It created—"

"Razaiella."

The wicked voice said from behind me. She looked everywhere for me. "Guess, I mean. It's time for me to go."

Seth smiled. "You will be all right. Remember, nothing we fear."

Nothing bothered me more than seeing that woman just stare at me with that smirk. One day, she will get everything paid back to her.

"Talking to that weirdo for an hour every day?" Ms. Ava grinned, shaking her head. "Then he managed to drag you all the way to the library. You have a lot to learn, especially about people like that."

"He's not weird. Second, I have learned a lot so far."

"I believe you have, but today we must see what you have learned and take it to the next level."

If this AI system were powerful, I guess it would kill me someday. Seth spoke many things, and I actually felt a little better. My father may have died, but Seth kind of felt like a new one to me. I would have never believed I would meet someone like him in a place like this. It's astonishing how much he knows. He's been through so much in life, and I could definitely see and feel it, just like my father—calm, intelligent, but strong. Just like him.

"Good morning, Razaiella," Dr. Sarban said as he reached his hand out to me, but I left it.

"What are you going to do to me?"

"Nothing special," Dr. Sarban replied. "Just to see where your mind takes you."

Where my mind took me—these corrupted humans. Like Seth said, they were all evil and playing with good people's minds. I looked at all the staff just working on their computers, while my new mother and father tested on me. I didn't really care anymore. Then I walked inside the vast, quiet, plain white room. Whatever they would come out with to me, I knew it was all just in my head. I just had to keep reminding myself of it.

The white ground turned to black sands with hints of a snowy field. The temperature was dropping, and flurries were hitting my face. Looking back, as the last pixels covered the glass those bastards hid behind, my eyes caught Ms. Ava returning the favor.

"It's going to be okay… It's going to be okay. No fear. My father may be away from this Earth, but he is still with me. I can feel it..."

Home. I was back to see my amazing house in New York again. "Dad?"

His old truck was sitting in the driveway, and he was home. "Dad! Oh my gosh! You're finally here!"

Seeing my papa standing at the front door with a smile on his face, it felt alive again as I ran to him and was held in his arms. Tears rolled down and dropped on the porch. He was back.

"I've missed you, Papa. I've missed you so much."

"I've missed you as well. How have you been? Where is Isabella?"

Dad's favorite cologne was always on his neck, and he looked dressed and prepared to take me out.

"I'm okay. I'm just so glad you're back with me. I've missed you so much. I don't want you ever to leave again. No matter what, stay here with me, with us. Mom… I don't know where she is."

I looked around as I held on to my father's chest and saw no one and nothing in the streets. Just the gray and black overcast sky. "Dad, please don't leave again."

"Of course, Ra. Now, how about you take me upstairs and show me where my artifacts are?"

"Yea, she has them up there. I don't know why she didn't want you to have them back."

Dad grinned. "That is called stealing, you know. I love her and she will always be my wife. She just never saw it that way, and she wanted to be the one to cause havoc with our love. I wanted to give her the world, but she just never could see it."

Dad's heart was still broken, and I believe it was me who had to fix it. No more hate and only love.

"It's up here," I said, pulling the string for the ladder to fall. "There's so much stuff up here, it's crazy."

"Crazy. She called me that because all I wanted was her love."

"Come on, Dad, it's all up here."

I felt the happiest I had ever been, as if all my energy had come back to life.

"Ahhh," Dad sighed.

"My arts and crafts. Something Isabella could never understand. I remember I did this. It was actually she who looked to the heavens. I made it just for her as she was my angel. Pity."

Dad looked to his creation as though he wanted to kiss its lips.

"Ew, Dad? Really?"

Dad faced stayed serious after he just licked his dusty old angel. To me, it didn't look like Mom.

"So, what are you going to do about, Mom?"

Why is he looking at the statue that way? Staring at it as if it has a soul.

"It does."

"It does what?"

Dad looked to me and started his way back down to the ladder. He had other things up here that I wanted him to see, but I guess he just wanted to see his other lover.

"Hey… Dad? Wait up! Eygh! Stupid ladder."

Where did he go? I shouldn't have shown him anything. I thought he wanted to see it so he could get back into being who he was.

"Dad? Where are you?"

He probably went back outside. I've hurt him that badly? Unless he was going to go and find Mom. Then snow flurries stopped, and the world seemed a bit different as I walked back out of the house. His truck was gone. The sky opened, and the warm sun looked down at me. It was a peaceful place. "Dad?"

Trees rose swiftly, almost like a jungle forming afterward. This time, it reminded me of how the Garden of Eden would have been seen and witnessed. The animals were running across me, and a grayish-brown panther was staring at me from the trees. "It's not there; it's not real," I whispered.

He or she was beautiful, and I couldn't believe how realistic it looked. It then sat down in the tree, and I wanted to sit next to it, as it was so peaceful. The sky above it began to turn black while the panther and I looked up at it.

The snaps from the trees pulled me back with a circular wind forming. Then, a funnel cloud began to drop down quickly. The air started to become very cold, causing me to fold my arms in the slick, thin jumpsuit. "I don't fear you!" I shouted to the skinny tornado.

The tornado began to grow larger and larger, ripping up everything in its path to reach me. "Eygh!"

I tried to cover my face and eyes from the debris flying everywhere. The panther jumped down and got away, leading me to follow, as I had no choice. The debris was becoming more violent, as if it were testing me. "Stop it! Leave me alone!"

My yelling only made the twister more ferocious. Falling into a pit and looking back as the tornado came closer and faster. There was something underneath the dirt. "No, this can't be real."

I quickly backed away and then saw the coffin door swing open, inviting me inside. The tornado was still advancing toward me. Seeing there was nowhere to go and nowhere to hide, once again, I had no choice. I made myself get down and feel the soft fabric—inside was clean, but it felt like old wood on the bottom. "How is this so real?" I said, my breathing becoming faster and faster.

The dirt getting in my eye made it hard to see, along with my hair flying all over the place. I made myself lie on the pillow of the old coffin, closing the door in the hope that the monster would just walk over and keep going. The coffin began shaking, and the feeling of fear made my heart pump even faster. With its roar, the tornado sounded like a train as it stepped on top of me, tapping the old wood with sticks and rocks. My heart then felt like it was about to come up to my throat and out of my mouth. "Eyyygh! Help me! Someone help me! Hel—mmm!"

Old, bony, wrinkled hands covered my mouth, and nothing but darkness and flashes of light came from the cracks of the coffin. The feeling of the force in my guts being pulled down as I could feel my body being lifted in the air, along with me inside the coffin. I could not scream as my mouth was still shut tight. I tried my best to move my arms, but couldn't. I couldn't open the door, as I would be sucked out. I was completely trapped, with no way out. The tornado was going to kill me. Feeling the wood under me become weaker, and those bony hands switch to my neck, with their force pulling me down.

"Oh no, no! Stop! EYYYGHHH!"

"Systems offline."

"Oh God—oh God. Razaiella?! Ms. Ava, she's having a seizure!"

"Her body will calm. Epilepsy, doctor. It will wear off soon. That's right. Let her fight it."

"Ms. Ava. This—"

"She's a strong girl. I know her."

"Razaiella… Razaiella?"

****

They will not break me. I will not be broken. I know there is a way; I have to find it. My mind is what they want, but they will not have me. They had been planning this a long time ago, just as Seth had said. Now they want to destroy everything that is good. How can they do this to anyone? A world where people are corrupt because of them? This cannot be. If I have children with the one man I love, I wouldn't want them to be unhappy because of the lies. Once I am free, he and I will be the ones that everyone remembers—who stood up to these devils. If I have to do it alone, it will be done without mercy.

What stood out to me, my tornadoes in my dreams never harmed me. How did this machine know more about me than my dreams?

There were things that I would never know, just to be strong, like how he taught me. Seth taught me how to manifest all that I truly admire and desire in my life. In my room, I meditate every morning and until before bed, asking my ancestors and the stars for all that is for me. Deep in my heart, I know there is a life that is going to be the best. All I have to do is go and take it by any means necessary. To be free from S.I.L.O. and rich with the most loyal friends. Then one day, give the demonic matrix a taste of its own medicine. That is my promise to my father. *Ask, believe, receive. Ask, believe, receive. Ask, believe, receive.*

"This is it here."

"Oh wow. This place is so beautiful," I said as I scrolled down on the library computer. "Cairo, Egypt. Every time they showed places like this on TV, they showed people in mud houses and little kids with pot bellies."

"Hmph. That is how they fool the weak-minded, so they lack knowledge of other areas."

Felt like my ancestors with the stars heard my prayer and brought me a new, extraordinary person to talk to, like Seth. My new friend, Ebonee. She spelled it with two e's at the end instead of just a "y," as she said her *true* name is unique. I said, just like my name. She was a small, slender girl with wavy, black hair and distinctive green eyes that had hints of orange and yellow. She arrived just a week ago—maybe a day or two after I fell from the sky. She definitely was not American, given her accent and the way she spoke. Her intelligence was beyond, and that's what I first liked about her. I was able to trust her from the start, as she was also very respectful, and men seemed immediately intimidated by her. I didn't know why, but it could have been because she never smiled, or those eyes freaked them out of doing something stupid. That's why, instead of being in the lunchroom to chat, we were at least able to sit in the small library with computers for our amusement. S.I.L.O. may have had me in here, but I was beginning to see how I still have a chance. "And you said they took you from here? Why so far away?"

"Not certain. Though I have suspicions that they are looking for special blood. Complete lunacy."

I nodded. "Seth told me that, too, and I'm still here."

"Did they ever tell you when you would be released?"

Hearing her say the word *released* a feeling that was almost alien. "Never. It's something they want with us."

Ebonee just shook her head and leaned back with her arms folded as we both sat in the quiet library. But one day—one day—I will visit Egypt. Even if S.I.L.O. had us on the run, I will visit.

"You and me. You can go back home and show me around. This place is too beautiful. The ocean, the Red Sea. Gosh, I could get in there right about now."

"I have heard my home has changed significantly over the years. I can trust that these pictures on the internet are old."

"What?"

"You see… many false ways of life have destroyed what is beautiful in nature—the beauty of beautiful places. All it took was one weak leader to be appointed to high power, and then the country fell to its knees. My people… many of them have even forgotten their own native language for the colonist's one. Then they followed the ways of the slaves, and they became just like them… ill-minded. They spread lies globally, and yet fools cannot see how easily misinformation spreads and how potent it is. All you can do is sit back and shake your head at those who are weak and vulnerable. They laugh when you can't speak their language, though I cannot be falsely educated as well if I can't understand it either."

Ebonee just stared at the screen with those pale green eyes. It also reminded me that she had a story to tell with them, but she never wanted to speak on it fully.

"So, Eb. I don't think I ever asked you. I know you're from the Middle East, but what's your ethnicity? Who were your parents? You told me you're only a year younger than me, so you're not that old. That's all I pretty much know as of now."

Ebonee looked at me, and I felt something profound; she had something to say far more than what it was.

"My heritage bloodline is Persian and Egyptian. I had a mother and a pitiful father. He died. My mother—I have no idea where she is. Her origin is Persian, and he was an Egyptian."

"So, when they took you from Egypt, they took you from them? Well, your mother? I knew she was heartbroken. Ha, it's beyond crazy. My story is so similar, but seriously… I am so sorry. None of this is right."

"It is all well," Ebonee says with a blank face.

"You didn't care for one of them. I can sense it."

Ebonee frowned. "Sense it? Sense what?"

"Just the way you speak of them. Or… you just don't care."

"Your second answer fits well. I still see him when I look in the mirror, but he's no longer here. Listen to me, Razaiella. In life, there are many paths. I chose the path of survival by any means necessary. I realize you have been in here for a while… I will not be. I am a free being—not in here like a bird trapped in her cage. Whatever these devils of man are trying to do, they will have to kill me first to have it. Never let any man believe he has the upper hand. You were born in this world alone; you will die in this world alone. Where my heart is truly from, we are survivors—not people who just hide."

"I get you," I nodded.

"The men in this era are just as feeble. As women, we have the control just by who we are."

"Let no fear in from anywhere, right?"

We both smirked at each other and seemed to get along so well, and we definitely had the same vision—to get out of here someday and be free once again.

"Well… until tomorrow, Razaiella."

I grinned. "You can call me Ra. I told you already, friend. But if anyone asks you, my name is Raquel. Don't need anyone knowing about me."

Ebonee smirked. "Same. Perhaps one day you will return with me to paradise."

The small library only had us. Ebonee said that most of the books inside were false. They placed them here to make us look more stupid, basically. She proved to me yesterday how they altered the definitions of words and imposed their own ideas over the truth. The worst, she said, is that since the world learned the colonist's language, the people have learned false definitions of its nature—making them act just as they did long ago. I did notice how, over time, the language itself showed me that the existence of labeling someone a color instead of an ethnicity was weird. From her background, as she told me, her parents and culture. If I didn't know anything about who she was, I would have just said Black—because that is what I was taught about judging someone by the color of their skin. And she was just a few tans darker than me—more of Munisha's color. The crazy thing is, I never thought of my little sister or Lakia that way, perhaps because of Mom. Their father is an African man. With Ebonee, if I had never asked, I would have never known. I would have just assumed and said it. So, she even knows who she is—not being labeled by the system that tells you who you are. Her words seemed just as truthful and assertive as Seth's. That was when I first met her, sitting by herself in the lunchroom near us. Amazing how the nature of manifestation works.

"Hey Seth," I said, patting him on his back, then taking a seat in front of him as I always did in the lunchroom.

"Your new friend stole you from me," Seth smiled.

"Not like that, but she reminds me a lot of you. One thing I will say… you were right."

"About what?"

I wanted to hug him, as he always just gave me a warm presence by being so genuine.

"Everything. You were right from the start. The internet tells everything, but if you're not careful, it can tell you lies, too. It's really crazy once you open your eyes to it. Ebonee even proved to me some things you said—and she told me she wasn't from here."

"I see. She has a mind of her own and her own way of thinking. I can see that, as she played me a few times in chess, and surprisingly won a few from me. She believes in herself; I saw that when we first met her. Once a person becomes brainwashed with lies, that's pretty much the end of it. When you are young, they tell you lies, so you'll never know what is true and false as you grow throughout the years. Confusion. I've been through it all so that I can understand many things—and humans. Remember what I told you about believing?"

I nodded and smiled. "Yes, of course."

"It doesn't work if you don't believe. Nothing does. If you believe you are a failure, you will never be a person of success. If you don't believe you are a failure, you will be a person of success."

"Seth… there have been things about me. I know we have spoken a while, and I tried my hardest to open my heart to you fully—and it has."

"Well?" Seth smirked.

"I have been dealing with demons my entire life. Let me rephrase that—angels and demons my entire life."

"We all have, my friend. It's a part of life. Normal."

I shrugged. "I believe there are many things after me. Something happened to me the other day in the virtual room, and it hasn't stopped."

I was shocked to see Seth's face puzzled. He usually has something to say.

"I have a demon in the room chasing me. Yeah… I know it's not real, but she… it keeps coming after me. It was in my dream once, and then it managed to be inside the room. Like it keeps following me from dreams to reality."

Seth's face turned serious as he nodded slowly. "That is something I cannot tell you."

"What?"

Now I was shocked. He knew many things, but did not know what this could be. "I am very surprised. You pretty much know about these forces."

"I know about them in spirit, not in flesh. If you see something in that room, it's not of this world. That is a machine looking into your thoughts, but the machine does not…"

"Does not what?" I asked as Seth looked as if something had frightened him for me.

"…You're under attack."

Seth's face looked disturbed while the people talked and laughed in the room. It all just felt so cold, and a sense of doom filled the air when he spoke.

"I know… I could always feel it. I have seen some things, and I just kept them to myself."

"Likewise," Seth said, folding his arms. "When they are like that, it is best for you to keep them to yourself."

"Yeah, because no one will believe you, and they'll think you're crazy."

Seth grinned. "Not only that, my friend. There are things in life that are only meant for you to see—no one else. Everything happens for a reason. Once you understand that this is meant to be just like this, you will be at ease with keeping it to yourself. What would be the point if you can't prove it? Remember, I am not a person who will tell you something I cannot approve or disapprove. Everyone has gifts, and I believe I've already acknowledged to you that you contain the gift of sight. If that person, or whatever is in that room, comes—you must fight it. Even when you are outside the room, because there is no other way to defeat your demons other than by facing them."

It's funny he said that. I've gotten better with the tornadoes, but that odd corpse woman keeps coming for me.

"All I can tell you, Razaiella… these people have learned too much. You are the first person in this building that I have heard of who speaks of something like this. The machine is only used to create a vision from your mind in a simple form, not an intense or radical one. That is very unfortunate for you, and that is why they keep placing you in there—to see what you see. But the AI can only reveal so much, as it is only a computer looking in. Did you tell them anything about this?"

"No, not at all," I replied. "I don't know how, but my dreams are being stolen by the AI. It sees them. Yes, I won't let them take it."

Seth smirked. "Atta'a girl."

In my heart, I needed him to know one thing right now.

"Once we get out of here, I'm coming with you."

Seth looked down and smiled. "…I don't know."

"You don't know? What do you mean? Hey, I asked what—"

"Razaiella… I am not someone who will be here for long."

I tilted my head with a smile, now trying to see what he meant. "What do you mean? We won't be here—of course we won't. I can sense that we're leaving soon. I believe it."

"I am glad you feel that way, my friend. Once I am out of here, a new sun will arise, and everything I have taught you has been given to you for a purpose. Everything happens for a reason. There goes the last bell."

"Yeah, it's—"

"Quick, funny story before we depart," Seth said as everyone else in the room moved out. "When I was a boy, my mother was teaching me to ride a bike. As she held on to me, I was holding on to the handlebars tightly. I kept looking forward, knowing she was behind me. When I heard her voice from afar, my mind noticed she wasn't supporting me anymore. I turned sideways and flew right into the neighbor's fence. It doesn't work if you don't believe."

"Ha, same thing—something similar happened to me. But did you learn? Or do you need me to show you?"

"Nah. I grew up to big-boy bikes. Anyway, never stop believing— definitely in yourself. Never let anyone tell you otherwise. If you have a problem, your guardian angels will always be there for you. Trust my words on this, my friend. See you tomorrow."

Seth was the second-to-last to get to the door. I was left with emotions. Who was this man? There's no way he was of this world either. I had felt this energy before, and he was definitely part of the others who randomly came into my life—to help me and show me the way. All of this time, being in such a place… he was all I needed in someone, and he was here with me.

"He's one of them too," I murmured.

"Seth! Wait."

Seth grinned. "You need more advice? Tomorrow—"

"No. I…"

"I… what?"

I blushed but couldn't help myself. His light blue eyes were just as nourishing as his heart. I had to ask before going night-night. "Who are you? And don't lie to me."

Seth raised his eyebrow. "I have told you already, no? What do you mean?"

"You're not from this world, are you? Don't lie to me."

Seth grinned as if to say, *This girl is so ridiculous.*

"Tell me!"

"All right, all right. Have you ever known me to lie to you? You just said my words have been true. I do this out of love."

"Yes, I know that. So tell me who you are. It's been some time since we've known each other, and I am missing something from you. I can feel it. If you can't say it here, then we can go. You know…"

"Calm yourself, my friend. I am of this world. I have been through many things. They made me who I am today. Trust me, I am a man, going through life just like you. We can definitely consider ourselves humans from the inhumanness."

I looked him in his eyes, and he was telling me the truth. I just couldn't accept it, as I knew he was much more. He just didn't want to tell me.

"Since you seem like you want a few more details and the entire truth… okay, fine. I am the leader of the group called Storm Mafia."

"Wha—what?" I frowned as I saw that fly over me. "You're what?"

"Unbelievable? Believe it."

"No, not that. You're a gang leader?" I laughed, looking Seth up and down.

"…I don't see it."

"I am who I am. Though it doesn't exist anymore because too many weak-minded fools sold me out to the system."

"Really? I… believe you. I never heard of that gang before."

"We were on the West Coast. My group was small, but I trusted them. Never had friends, as you know. The only person I trusted was my baby brother, Caesar. Yes, I have a brother, not so much like me."

"Like what?" I asked.

"Let's just say I care about his heart, not what it seeks, and I'll leave there. Anyway, he actually has a club in a small town in Bar Harbor. I had to build my own empire, because today's people are just locked on stupid. You'll be literally working for children in companies. They are nothing more than babies wearing suits and ties with polished dress shoes."

"And he doesn't visit you? Your brother."

Seth grinned. "He doesn't even know I'm in here. He's not about this life. I protected him from it, as I don't believe in drowning others with myself. Be true to yourself, Razaiella."

"Trust me, I hear that."

"Other than that, S.I.L.O. is the biggest gang of them all, and everything I have taught you and what you have seen with your own eyes should show that clearly. Once again, know who you are so no one can manipulate you, and trust in only yourself. Goodnight."

Seth left me in the empty hallway. My heart wanted to tell him that he is the most amazing man I have ever met. Now I see why no one ever crossed him.

"Wonder where Ebonee's room is. She never told me."

My room seemed to be the only one in the gray, glassy hallway. I sighed,

"Home sweet home. Eygh—mmm. Let me go!"

"Oh, I'm getting mine tonight, baby. Right here—right now."

The fool Eric pushed me inside the room, knocking me to the floor and trying to pull off my jumpsuit. Where did he come from?

"I said, get off!"

"Just one night. Come on!" Eric chuckled, trying to cover my mouth.

Not realizing the door closed behind us, I could only try to get free and get out of here somehow and yell for help.

"Get… your ass back here."

"Eygh."

"See, now I tore your catsuit. This could've been easier!"

Eric threw my feather body over my desk, knocking over all my art supplies. I was tired and sick of being tired and weak.

"I said come here, or I'll knock you out next time. Ha, make it easier for both of us, baby."

I squirmed, crawling on the ground, trying to get away, but there was nowhere to go. If only I could just get to the door.

"This is going to be quick and fun, I promise. Just… get these panties off—AUUGH, AUUGHH."

Eric shouted, holding his left eye while blood gushed through his hand, with my calligraphy pen in its place. It was a sign of relief. I smiled, watching the man who humiliated me with eyes all around me. Now it was his turn to suffer. "You deserve it, asshole!"

"What in the world?" Ms. Ava said with Mr. Sarban at the door.

"He tried to rape me."

"Security!" Ms. Ava shouted, her eyes wide with shock at what I had become.

"I can't believe she did this. No talking from you, missy!"

"Dr. Sarban, he came and ripped my clothes. You don't see this?"

"I said, silence!"

"Hey! It was him, not me!"

"Get her! Guards, be careful, she is dangerous. Now do you see, Dr. Sarban? She can't be controlled. Take her away! This has gone on long enough!"

"I'm not a threat," I said, pulling with all my strength from the guards. "It was him! Eygh, this-this isn't fair!"

Screams of pain or screams of terror led me as I tried holding on to the room door. He got exactly what he deserved for humiliating me that day—an eye for those eyes.

CHAPTER 18

After Dark to After Glow The Last Lessons

I have seen all things. Nothing has improved but who I am. S.I.L.O. would not tell me what was in the last test they used on me; it was too much until I felt so empty. They made it to where I couldn't even control my body, as I remembered shaking nonstop when I saw the glowing light from the ceiling. I almost thought it was time for me to leave from this cruel world. Mom came less and less, and it did not faze me. Seth taught me that the weak will inherit the Earth, but the strongest will dominate it. I don't fear like I used to. They destroyed my beauty. My eyes were perfect, but my vision has become clearer. I was no longer who I used to be; somehow, something bonded with my soul.

Strapped to a bed with a metal spike device in front of me. Cold steel made the room even more frigid. My skin swelled into bumps from the atmosphere. All of the staff just watched me as Mr. Maximo said I would be the first to test out their new machine. Ms. Ava and that coward, Mr. Sarban, just stared at me. I learned to fear nothing, and I was not changing my mind as the bed slowly leaned forward and began to shake me on the metal. The metals touching my forehead, arms, and legs were like spikes with zaps of electricity.

"Eygh!"

My life was nothing but pain, so I was not going to let them win. The shock intensified along with my scream. "I hate you!"

Ms. Ava smiled, seeing that I was under her control. It would all be over soon. The hate in my heart spiralled into my mind, and everything and almost everyone had become a threat. Only so many you can trust. I've learned that no matter how much you try to do the right thing and be happy, something, somewhere, somehow, will try to take it away. If I lived through this torture, I would learn to manipulate these dark forces on my own and use them on those who hurt me and others. If it didn't kill me, it would only make me stronger, more resilient, and most importantly, divine. My screams were only for the moment. I knew I would survive it. If it wasn't my time, it wasn't my time. I knew who I was, and they just tried to break me until I was no more. I just had to keep reminding myself that there is no fear, even in death—only peace and freedom.

Waking up after another reality nightmare, I had no energy, no tears, and no fear left in me. Seth was right—right about everything. You can't trust anyone, as many people will change their faces to you. Dr. Sarban, for an entire year, protected me from her, but what was I think-ing? He's one of them, and he must be dealt with also. I will find a way, even if they kill me afterward. Life is all about conquering. Seth and Ebonee are fighters, and so am I. I will not tolerate being destroyed by anyone or anything. Now my eyes are open from this oblivion, and I will conquer all one day.

"I will conquer all. Nothing I fear," my reflection said back to me.

As soon as I get something to eat, Ebonee will be glad to see I am with her, being free once more—by any means necessary. The cafeteria was empty, which is unusual unless I was too early. "Apple and orange juice."

The robot reminded me of a heartless, soulless person. That is how they all want us to be.

"Morning, Ms. Lazano."

A voice that I was ready to rid myself of came—but not yet.

"Ms. Ava has gone out for duty work. Today, my friend, you are to be decommissioned after your last test."

I looked at Dr. Sarban with uncertainty. "Decommissioned?"

"Yes, yes. It is time for you to finally take the last test and then go home," Dr. Sarban smiled.

"Then, I am finally free?"

Dr. Sarban smiled and nodded, making a straight face afterward. "However, the gentleman lost his eye."

Then it was my turn to smile and say: "Thanks for the good news."

"I am so sorry for all this, Razaiella. All of this… this isn't right. I am a doctor, not a mad scientist. This was not my dream. Where I am from, we care about people, and I promised my family as a young man to do just that when I left them. This place turned me into something that I am not. I am terribly sorry… for everything."

To my surprise, the doctor wiped his tears, and I felt deep down that he was sincere. Though he still tortured me, and that wasn't right, as he said.

"Please… meet me in about half an hour on the X-Wing floor. There, you will find me for the final procedure. Also, kindly do not tell a soul about your release. This tends to generate jealousy in this facility. We do not need any more issues."

I didn't want to deal with any more of that stuff, so I definitely wouldn't say a thing, maybe to Seth. Everything in here played with my head long enough.

"There goes my bestie. Oh, and Seth."

Many others walked in with them as pretty much everyone woke up at the same time. Guess I was catching insomnia.

"So, you're the eye stabber," said a man who looked like he was in his early twenties.

I saw him before in the building, but couldn't recall where. The girl he walked with had a tattoo under her bottom lip, and her hair was almost as long as her body.

"That shit was insane. He was that bad?"

"Wes, leave her alone," the girl who walked beside him said.

He didn't know that my art helped me. If I hadn't had it, he would have gotten away, and I would have been left there scared like a cat—so vulnerable. Not anymore. That girl with the tattoo looked like she was in a gang herself. We women are on the rise.

"Hey, Seth. What?" I said as he remained quiet. "I guess I'm the talk of the building. You heard, right?"

Seth nodded slowly, sipping his coffee.

"Eric. That bastard. He—"

"Got what he deserved. And you did what you had to do," Seth nodded.

"To survive," Ebonee said as she sat down next to me with her tray of fruits and juice.

"He followed me to my room and thought he could take advantage."

"You stabbed him with a pen, so I heard," Seth said.

"Actually, my calligraphy pen. I paint with it, but I see they come in handy in many other ways besides art."

Seth smirked. "Satan will never leave you alone. You must always be ready for anything. Demons can sense light in people, so you are under attack more than others. Hmph, that is why I will never trust a man who cheats, lies, or plays games with other people. They are more than likely demon possessed."

"Absolutely," Ebonee says, taking a bite of her peach. "These men disgust me. No offense, Seth. You will have what you tolerate. Demons, Shaitan or not."

"I would have done more, probably, but that bitch came and pretty much said I was in the wrong."

Seth shook his head, and I could sense he was annoyed. "Young ladies, you must respect yourselves more than anything. I know he was wrong to do that to you, but that was good enough. These devils will come at you just because it is you. Women are precious, and Satan's minions will never leave you alone. He uses women first to draw in more trouble for the world. Without women, in their right minds, we lose the beauty of nurturing and the fruits of love. Don't let him get the best of you."

"Are you insinuating that we are not fit to think for ourselves?" Ebonee asked.

"Not at all. All I meant was that women are precious to our world— since the beginning of time. The dark forces hunted women first to contaminate their nature, and then contaminate man. Eve, if you will, was the first, then Adam."

"Okay, yet I beg to differ," Ebonee said, eyeing Seth with her usual calm and emotionless face.

"Please, state your claim," Seth smirked.

"Hmph. Men are the problem of the world. It has always been them since the beginning of time. They take life, twist it into their own vision, and corrupt it. No offense, but they are corrupt and irrational."

"No harm done. However, I unfortunately have to agree with you, Ebonee."

I knew Seth would agree, as he didn't mind being truthful about anything—even if it related to him.

"So why do you proclaim it is women when it surely is not the answer?"

"My apologies if you did not understand, but as Razaiella knows, I love to create examples and scenarios. I will do the same as of now."

Seth placed his hot coffee on the table, closed his eyes, and opened them again."I have been in love with a woman before. I have. I know women are precious because they are the ones who are easily broken, just like a glass vase on a mantle. If a man breaks that vase by accidentally knocking it over, his woman will have a fit. With that being said, the vase will never be the same as it was when it was brand new. Women—just as a vase, are beautiful, intricate in their own nature, and, of course, nurturers in nature."

Ebonee just nodded, and I knew she would listen but not care as much. Literally stated how she feels about the opposite sex.

"So, imagine this. The demons are more prone to come after you first, as you both acquire the essence of nurturing, making things in the creation of beauty, being the man's helpmate. And most importantly, bringing life into this world. We, as men, need women, as they are the creators of our children, and I have heard and witnessed that a woman will pick up a car if her child is underneath it. That power, right there, is first called an adrenaline rush, but it is also the spirit power that demons crave. You both have something that demons would love to snatch away. You both just have to understand and protect yourselves as they hunt and steal every day until all women are crippled in their nature. Do you understand a little more now?"

Ebonee just nodded, but her face said otherwise in agreement.

"What about you, Razaiella?"

"Yeah, I heard you. I understand."

Seth just didn't understand me, though. Every time he spoke, my heart grew bigger and more significant for his. I just wish he knew. When we get out of here, I'm leaving with him, and that is what I believe.

"Question for you, since you know it all," Ebonee says after finishing her peach.

"Why is it that man has gone around corrupting every civilization in the world? Why were these devils who took babies and slaughtered them in the past times? Why is it that they forced false language on every culture? Women, as you stated, always nurtured, never destroyed anything. We nurtured even when there was devastation. Many of the poor souls of women have lost their way because they had no choice but to obey someone who lacks the ability to lead—forced to obey a fool? I want to know why. I would love to know because you speak as if you have all the answers."

Seth's lip pointed sideways as he nodded. "In this present time, we are not at fault. Nothing from our past has anything to do with who we are today in this new era. I cannot speak on the wrongs that have been done, but I will reassure you. Someone, somehow, will come and make a stand. They will set an example, just as a new sun will rise tomorrow, bringing a new day for everyone. Never dwell on the past, as it will drown your soul. Trust me, I know these things."

Ebonee smirked and just nodded lightly.

"Let me even say this. I have nothing to lie about, as I love to give what I do know. You just stated propaganda, and as I have taught Razaiella, that is exactly what it is. Use said forced the language, and this, of course, is how more of it spreads."

Seth sighed. "As we know, in today's day and age, loyalty in relationships is at its lowest. Cause and—"

"Effect." I smiled.

"I'm glad you have been listening. I agree with you about this world as we know it, Ebonee. Man has made things worse and worse. I do remember a time back when a man said to me— a full-grown man—'all women are open to sex.' Now I told him, that isn't exactly true."

"Men are open to that more," Ebonee says. "Filth."

"How right you are, but take it easy. Now, what makes it like that? Once again, what do the demons do when they can get to women? They use them to do things that can corrupt both parties, not just her. A man, if he is able to control himself—"

"None can."

I grinned. "Geesh, Eb."

"Well, I can," Seth smiled.

"Well…" Ebonee just shrugged her shoulders. "I guess you're not a normal man then."

"This mindset, my friend, comes from the foolishness of how the people have placed others in a handbasket. Everyone in this huge place called the world is different. If I were a person who just thought like that man did, why would I want to be married, have a family? All men are not the same, and all women are not the same. It's just a demonic force making people miserable, separated, and hateful—purely against what the Creator intended for their true nature. Just thinking with a flashback, the fool said he had a wife, but all humans cheat. How does that work? His toxic speech may lead to another person believing his mentality and going around thinking every soul is like that. I'll tell you this, which is a pure fact, true men don't cheat."

Ebonee just shook her head slowly, but from Seth's voice, it was clear that he was sincere and seemed to genuinely know and believe in his words.

"Oh yeah, I said it. True men and women do not cheat. Why, you ask Ebonee? Because no true person has the time for foolishness. Both people are there to protect their families. Only little boys and girls cheat and play games. Why, you ask Ebonee?"

"I don't think she likes what you're saying," I giggled.

"These are all his opinions. تو مثل بقیه هستی، پسر کوچک."

"…On the contrary, they are not. Listen, a man puts away childish acts when he becomes a man. A boy never puts away childish acts as he plays with them until they are broken. Cause and effect, my dear. Hell, they grow up with the same mindset and never learn how to take care of anything. Women like to call themselves a princess but want a king. It's called king and queen, not king and princess, vice versa. We've spoken on this before. If you want something real, you have to own up to it and take it. Nothing in this world is free. It's just another prime example, though. I have never been to a strip club. Clubs, yes—but not a strip club. It's not my style. Why do they also call it mainly a gentlemen's club?"

I just shrugged my shoulders, but I could feel what Seth was going to say, and I had to listen to his wise words.

"It is because mostly men…my apologies, boys attend to see women on the poles. Now, there are male clubs for women, but the main types are those mainly for men to see women. Women have always had the power to seduce. I said it proudly and clearly; nothing to hide here. So, her power draws males into those buildings, and if the men who are true to themselves do not attend, the women would not go."

"Cause and effect," I blurted out while Ebonee kept a straight face.

"The shop would close instantly because no business would be walking in. I have never been because someday I may have a daughter. Ha, check this out—if my daughter were to be a stripper, they would say negative things about her just because I do not attend those events. Just because demons love to irritate the pure heart. However, if I were the Saturday night party guy, I wouldn't have anyone say a thing. That energy in a whole, any person can feel it when they walk inside. It's not just me. It's all about instinct and perspective, my friend. Man has ruined many things, yes, but some of us good guys still exist. Those who want to grow old with a family. Just as with women. So, I agree, man has twisted and corrupted so many things, though cut us some slack, kindly?"

Ebonee just got up and left the table. I not only sensed she didn't care for what Seth had to say, but she was bothered by something more severe—something very ferocious in her heart that ravaged every fiber in her being.

"Guess she was done listening."

"I did not mean any harm. The poor girl was probably heartbroken long ago by a boyfriend or someone. How old is she?" Seth asks as we both just stared at her walking away through the crowd.

Of course, the eyes of the other men looked upon her. "I'm not sure. She never told me, and most of us women don't give out our age."

"I see. You know I never asked yours, but I can kind of sense yours. Hers is a bit different. She exudes an agelessness beyond her years. Hmph, like me. So, I know there are many who see as I see."

I can tell Seth felt some type of way for her, and he did not realize that I was still in his face listening to think about someone other than me.

"A black heart is what she has. That is something tough to add color to. The truth will always stand supreme, whether someone likes it or not. Under her breath, she said something in a foreign language, so I assumed my words were tapping a nerve somewhere."

"Right. I think so," I grinned. "Eb knows like five different languages. The first person I know who is like that. Other than that, she's not from here and is all alone in a foreign place. Maybe one day she will tell me. The crazy thing is, why would they bring her to such a faraway place?"

Seth looked at me as though he knew something.

"Tell me, Seth. I know you know something about why she is here."

"I do, but it causes more confusion and is not necessarily needed… it really isn't a big deal. Do you see how some parts of her hair are starting to give off the appearance of green strands?"

"Yes. It's dye, isn't it?" I asked, as it should be obvious. "But she couldn't have done that in here since there's nowhere to get it done."

"A person like that doesn't play with her hair, even if she wanted to. I can read her very well. That serum they give us makes things change into unnatural forms. Yes, she didn't do that to her hair. Something about that serum makes everything reveal more."

"Just like it gave me a black eye."

"You don't have a black eye," Seth replied. "It just darkened it, but you can still see, thank God. For her, it reacted for some reason in her hair. It almost matches her eyes, too. I know you've noticed."

"Yeah… yes, that's right. That does make sense. But why green—because of her eyes?"

Seth shrugged. "Probably. Put two and two together and see S.I.L.O. has an agenda, as we know. They are looking for certain people. They call them Aretenians."

"Ar…tenians?"

Seth nodded. "This is what I have been trying to figure out, as to me, it just sounded like Type A people. What? You've heard of Type A people, correct?"

"Yes, my teacher actually spoke to me about them. Said I was one, along with her."

"Hmm. Well… I've done research while on the computer, but they limit everything you can see in here. They don't say who they are looking for online, but you know how information gets leaked. Before I came inside this building, I thought it had nothing to do with me, but I guess they are truly searching for the *chosen ones*. I know it sounds crazy… it's just how it is. I can't even explain it."

Seth never said a word about these Aretenian people, and I had certainly never heard of them. Only the one Travis told me about. That made sense. "Figure Eights… I have the eighth sense. That means I am a chosen one?"

"Not… sure. But they are testing on people just because they are in this building. The Figure Eights you speak of is a name they gave it—just like many other names they label. For Ebonee, they brought a human being over here for a reason. The Aretenians are the ones they believe are a race from the beginning of time that was never really documented. They are highly intelligent, learning things at an extensive geometric rate. They can get rid of diseases from their own bodies more easily than the average. Even since things beyond the five senses of manipulation. They are unique in their nature—highly valuable to the world and the new world order."

That is why they wanted me. I should have known this with my abilities. Ebonee said it best: they take everything, twist it, and use it for their own purpose. "Anyways."

It was time for me to ask about this true mystery woman. "Seth. Yeah… you said earlier that you had someone. You never told me that before."

"It didn't really matter. That was over ten years ago."

"You still love her?"

"What?"

I grinned, seeing that Seth knew what I said, but I caught him off guard. "I asked you, do you still love her? I know you've never lied to me, so I expect the truth."

"I… I don't know."

I was surprised and didn't think he would play with me like that.

"You don't know? That was a yes or no answer, my friend."

"I suppose you want that story now?"

"I have a few minutes. Go ahead. I need to hear your so… special love story."

Seth smirked, shaking his head. "Now, it was special. But I will try to tell you as much as I can remember."

Before he spoke, I kind of didn't want to hear about another woman. I just needed to see if he had her out of his heart so I could finally be the one moving in.

"About ten years ago, I met someone online. I had been searching for someone overseas since the year two thousand and fourteen."

"Why? So many women here. Oh, you want one like Ebonee?" I frowned.

"Not exactly. I just wanted to try something new. My way of thinking especially did not align with how people think here. I believe you've noticed that. In time, I found this person that I finally traveled to see. We spoke for a year and a half before the meeting. She was very intelligent and understanding. The crazy thing was, she spoke Arabic and, of course, did not understand me unless I used a translator. We became that bond that I had never witnessed before, and I swear it was divine. She was my… best friend."

I squinted, as I could not understand Seth for the first time. "How can that be? You couldn't understand her only through an app using a translator. How does that work?"

"Let me finish. We did things the fair way. She didn't understand me either, so we learned each other's language by taking turns, week to week, speaking English and Arabic. We did that for a year and never became annoyed. Once I booked a ticket to Libya, I—"

"Libya? I knew it! Ebonee is your type; she looks like one of those girls." I laughed but was a little jealous.

"Come on, let me speak," Seth grinned. "I landed, and I was the last person to come out of the passport control area. I saw her, and she got up from her seat."

"Aww," I smiled.

Seth was going to speak on a woman I didn't even care to hear or know about.

"There was a man who helped with the luggage, but I wanted him to record me and her first meeting. He couldn't understand either my Arabic or my English. My soul met hers, and we hugged, grabbed a rental, and from that point on, I was in paradise. We had the time of our lives—especially to me. I saw a new place, met a woman I loved, and saw the beauty of a natural society. I met her brother-in-law and sister, and they were extraordinary people. Then met her mother and aunt at dinner."

"Wait. So, you mean to tell me that you met a full-blown stranger… how old was she?"

"…Twenty years old, if I recall correctly."

"You were thirty, right? Oh my gosh, why so young?"

"Yes, many say that, but in cultures like that, they will marry a man who is thirty years older than them."

"And they let her ride around with you?"

Seth smiled and nodded, sipping his probably cold coffee. "Yes, they did. She spoke so much about me to her mother that it was as if they already knew me before I arrived. The only thing that she talked about… well, I'll tell you that later. Now, the reason I tell you this story is because there were many divine connections from this trip, even though I never saw her again. As I told you, this was paradise when I visited this extraordinary place. We rode around together, and she showed me many beautiful things. I actually went for her birthday on this trip, and that party that night—I dressed in a white and gold African-style attire while she had on a white dress. We arrived at the restaurant, and as soon as we walked in, people clapped and praised as if we had just gotten married. It was extraordinary. I met her mother and aunt that night, and everything was a blessing. I could not love it more, as I had never been to a birthday party for my significant other. Of course, I gifted her a necklace with a type of marble stone—I believe it was called a black opal. Everything was beautiful."

"Did you two get married?" I asked, needing to know.

"Wait. After that, I returned home and went back to my hotel. The following days were even more extraordinary. We walked on a beach, then rode camels—which I almost fell backward on as it stood up. We hung around that area the entire day, all the way until night. We never got bored with each other. We talked using a translator there as well, and it all felt divinely genuine. The night sky came upon us along with the people of the night. There was a small carnival, and the people's happy faces couldn't have been more pleasing to the eyes—faces you would rarely see in a place like this. Anyway, we rode the rides together, and it was my first time ever riding with anyone."

"Wait, really? You've never been on a ride with a girlfriend?"

"I am telling you the truth, my friend. After the rides, the good seafood she introduced me to near the shore—we settled by the water once again. We spoke and looked up to the stars, which you rarely see here anymore due to the artificial light of the city. She said to me: 'When the stars and moon look down on a couple like this, it is a blessing.' I truly felt it. The love from everything there was truly divine. The sun on my face when I arrived, to the moon and the stars on me and her that night."

I could see deep in his eyes that something broke him after that. "So, what happened after?"

"Well, I left her—and before I did, I held her tight and cried with her, as she could not help my departure for the next day. I promised her I would be—oh, almost forgot that. I proposed a promise ring to her as the first step toward our loyalty to marriage. I gave her that so she would know I meant it. I would never break a promise. When I left to come back to America, I knew I would be back soon. I came for my birthday in September."

"Ha, I forgot we're Virgos. Did you marry her?" I asked in my final step of curiosity before exploding.

"When I returned, as promised, it was good, and I did feel the divine connection once again. She gave me flowers when I arrived, and I had never seen that before. I met up with her brother-in-law and sister again, and they threw me a surprise birthday party. I can usually sense when something's coming, but I couldn't sense that. I teared up on camera as her sister recorded me and her together. The love from the people was beyond, and again, a divine connection. They gave me what I needed to keep going when I was in a dark place."

I slowly nodded. "That's nice. Yeah, it is. I never had friends do that for me either. I get you."

"This time, before I left her once again, we traveled around Libya and took pictures together. I loved it all. Soon… I think this is what you've been waiting for. I felt something as we returned to her home area, and as we walked together, I felt that energy that never came to me until then—a sense of doom, if you will."

"…Doom."

"Yes, this doom is what we all feel when something is about to happen. Not just in our dreams, but they come when our angels are telling us to brace ourselves."

"She died?"

"Razaiella," Seth grinned, shaking his head. "When I returned to America the second time, we planned that I would finally meet her father to ask for her hand in marriage. I wanted to do that from the beginning, but I needed to improve my Arabic."

"Because her father wouldn't accept you if you didn't speak the native language."

"Exactly, and that is never a good sign—especially for a foreigner. Before I could return to see her, December came, and that is when it hit. She told her father she was speaking to a foreigner. Her father rejected this, and I kind of felt it coming. She even messaged me saying she could tell I wasn't upset—because I knew it was going to happen. I told her, things happen, and I was upset, but something told me otherwise."

"…What is that?"

Seth smiled and finally wiped a tear from his face as he held his head down and looked back up to me. "I was not ready. Nor was she."

"Ready? Ready for what?"

"All this time, you wanted the answer, but you didn't catch it?"

"Oooh, ready for marriage."

Seth nodded. "I had so much going on, and I knew I didn't want her involved. I had to change myself before I could. But she made that mistake, and I never met the man. Her love for me was so much that she could not keep her mouth closed."

"I understand. You said she told her mother so much about you, but never her father. Why?"

"If I had, we would never have gotten to know each other. We both agreed we needed to learn from each other before marriage—but we needed more time. Ironic—I thought I was ready since I was older, but I wasn't."

"Geesh… I'm sorry. He denied you because you were with her? Did you all have sex or something?"

"Hmph. The most we did was hold hands. I did that because she couldn't see far, and I had to help her cross the street with busy traffic. She hated wearing her glasses."

This man was something else. He traveled all that way and never even kissed her. No, I didn't believe that one.

"You never kissed her either?"

"Razaiella. You've known my spirit for a while now. You know I'm not aggressive. When you love someone, it's not about a kiss or sex, or even thinking about them all day out the window. When you truly do, you want to see them be the best they can be. I loved her, as she showed me—along with her family—what love and the beauty of relationships were all about. So no, I did not kiss her… intentionally."

"Oh my gosh. What is wrong with you? I know you did—"

"It's not as you think."

Seth smiled, turned upside down, and I felt his energy getting stronger from his voice, as if he meant to be serious about this topic.

"The last time I visited her, which was the second, we went to get tea because I felt a little weird—possibly from that all-day flight. As we took our seats together and looked back at the chair, her lips ran into mine. Now, I saw her eyes, and it looked to me like she was aiming for the shot."

"Oh, come on. You expect me to believe that? I'm Ra, not an idiot girl."

"I know who you are, my friend. I tell you this because it matters. On the second trip, when I left her and flew back to the States, I told her kissing leads to other things. I knew it was a mistake, and she said it was nothing."

"I mean… if it wasn't, then it wasn't… right?"

Seth smirked. "Energies, Razaiella, energies. What have you been learning from me this whole time we've been in here together? How do they work? We transmit them—through holding hands, kissing. Sex is the most powerful because it involves soul ties. Once a man enters a woman, she can become so addicted or even become like him."

"So… she became a gang leader?"

Seth just grinned and looked at me, knowing it was a silly question. "My friend. My apologies, I did not mean—"

"No, I want to know the ending of her. What happened? Might as well tell me anyway since I have all the other information."

My heart raced with excitement. I needed to know this person's true ending, but I felt bad for him in a way. He really loved her.

"I never spoke to her after Christmas morning. All I could do was try to keep myself busy, but things came as a surprise. After that kiss, she told me—before we stopped talking—that she dreamed she saw me getting married to another woman. I told her: Don't believe that. That mistake of a kiss brought her mind the fear of losing things—just like I did. That kiss caused her to tell her father about me before I could return. That kiss of energy caused us to not hear from each other ever again. Fear steals and takes everything, including your dreams, with someone. A kiss from the soul—it hits hard. Trust me."

"I understand. Yet, I kind of wish she hadn't done that. She pretty much sabotaged your two's marriage. I'm… I'm sorry."

Seth nodded. "When someone loves you, love can make them do crazy things. Then again, she was very young. We must learn to control our hearts and desires, as they can sometimes go against us. Fear is a sickness. It destroys so many things, believe it. There's always a reason for everything, though. Destiny."

Seth was heartbroken by this. He truly was, and I saw it still in him after those ten years. It was like a scar that had healed, but that bump never smoothed out.

"Lastly. This is what really got me. One night, as I was trying to sleep, I woke up around three in the morning. I had a dream about her that felt so real. She had become someone that I could not recognize, and all I could do was look at her. She began doing drugs to make herself feel good after our separation. Out of my sleep, I tried to contact her, but my message didn't go through. So, the only thing I could think of was something so simple—and if the love was true, that kiss could help with it."

Seth grinned as if he didn't want to tell me. "I grabbed the matching promise ring that I kept in my drawer and placed it on my wedding ring finger and begged her to never give up on herself. To never give herself to this dying world. To find a good husband, someone better than me—and to just never stop going. I taught her that, just like I taught you. Let your mess become your message."

"Razaiella. It's time," a guard said from behind, while I just gazed at Seth's face that I had never seen before.

I felt Seth, and I couldn't help but wipe a tear. Why do good people always get hurt the most? I didn't know anything better to say after that.

"…I'm sorry."

I got up from the table and felt something tight grab around my lower arm. Seeing Seth's sad and broken heart made me cry more on the inside for him—an emotion that was still there behind my hardened heart.

"Whatever you do, Razaiella… do it with love. Never give up on yourself. Never do this. Promise me that. To never gain a black heart or sell yourself to anyone. Once you obtain a black heart, you will be blinded to nature's beauty, and these forces will take everything from you. They did it to me. These demons have twisted everything and used it for evil; they have to be stopped. One day, just one day, it may happen. They took away my business, my family, and then my best friend. Just promise me you will never let them take everything from you as well. Never let fear take away the ones and things you love. Please?"

Seth's eyes watered, and his face changed drastically. I had never seen him this way.

"I… I promise."

Seth smiled with a tear falling. "Good… good. Go."

Walking away with the guard, he then took me down to the lunchroom, where everyone chatted and laughed. Amidst all the commotion, I couldn't stop looking back at the man who claimed to be a gang boss, yet showed me love, compassion, truth, and integrity. All I have been through in this cold, despairing building—his presence gave me the strength to survive and conquer all things. The last test was in the virtual room, and I was out of here. After everything with Seth and his lost lover, I forgot to tell him about my soon-to-come freedom.

"Dr. Sarban?"

"He is preparing for your final exam, and then you are to be released," the guard said.

The room contained all the standard control units to activate the dream machine. I knew this was the end, and I was not afraid.

"This is it, Razaiella," I said, closing my eyes, holding my necklace, and kissing my pendant.

The room became dark, and the darkness penetrated my eyelids. I saw how things were, and it was nothing new to me.

"Nothing I fear, nothing I fear," I murmured with a smirk.

Standing alone in the pitch-black room, I felt the wind getting stronger, and my pupils dilated as the darkness enveloped them. Lightning from afar struck down to the mountains, and I could see the clouds forming. My nightmares were all the same. It could no longer control me, as I am the one. I knew what they were doing, and I could beat this. It was all in my head. Multiple tornadoes formed on the ground from the night sky, and all that could be seen miles away were the zaps of electricity dancing with them. They came in unison. My senses felt them coming straight for me. The winds grew stronger as I stood still in the same spot, waiting. "Nothing we fear."

The skinny black and gray tornado formed right in front of me, then sent itself back to the sky while the four to five continued to come my way, swirling all over the place. It was almost as if they had their own personalities. The skinny one that came down and tried to frighten me was the goofy one. The two skinny twins were the trifling demons just trying to test me. Then the big one was the most serious, as it came down the mountain. "You."

The mile-wide tornado had a face, surely. I looked at it, trying to figure out who it could be. It was a man for sure. It felt like I knew this one, as my spirit told me more than it was just a twister looking down at me. "I don't fear you," I murmured.

It smiled back, continuing toward me while the others went their own way from the East to the West. My hair blew violently all over my face, and the thunder couldn't break me this time with its shocking vibrations. The smiling tornado finally faced me, and I looked up to it. I closed my eyes and bowed my head slowly as it covered me. No more torture. No more lies. No more fear. No more pain. It was all in my head, and it could no longer control me.

I am the one. I am the way. They will never break me.

"Systems offline."

I turned around to see the door open and the guard standing, waiting for me. Seth would be so proud of me. Dad too.

"Are you ready?" the guard asked.

I smirked. "Definitely."

They thought they could break me, but I succeeded. To be a woman and conquer her fears—I was resilient to anything against my spirit. It molded with my very soul, and one day, Seth and I will return the favor for everything they have done.

The X-Wing. To the top floor. I guess we were to be released—definitely. It was a little far-fetched, as I knew it came with a cost.

"Hello, hello, Razaiella," Dr. Sarban said, as he and the other staff stood behind him. "Come in. Been expecting you."

"Oh my gosh, Eb?!" I said, covering my mouth.

Ebonee's body was lying on the table, but I could see her breathing.

"She's just asleep. In another dimension, if you will."

"What did you do—mmmmh."

"Don't fight it. Please, Razaiella! It will be all over soon. I promise. You will be born again."

Seeing everything instantly become blurry as a white rag covered my mouth.

"They got me," I murmured, feeling the cold floor hit my body.

"Sweet dreams, child," Ms. Ava said, standing above me as the room went black.

Sounds of thoughts and voices.

"Who am I… where am I?" echoed in my head.

My dreams—the good and the bad—showed like a movie. Seeing my papa, him, and Mom happy. Doing graffiti with my friends. Running with my little sisters at the nightlife fair. Being taken by S.I.L.O. Tested and tortured. Meeting the second most amazing man of my life. Seeing the tornado in front of me as it took everything away. Leaving me alone and scarred.

"Nothing I fear… nothing to fear. I am ready… for anything."

Finally, the light came—water in my eyes with a light pinkish world. "Mmmh."

Underwater, I floated inside what looked like a tank, breathing, but not knowing how, as the pink liquid surrounded me. The cables attached to me felt like they were on my skin for hours. My breathing felt off with the pinkish water as well as the fact that I could not speak or scream. I couldn't believe I was breathing it in. The glass that surrounded me left me in shock as my fingers slipped and slid across it. Noise was coming from below, and it was violent. Ebonee's body was right next to mine in another tank, and all alone, like me. She just wasn't waking up. This couldn't be another dream. "Mmmh."

The roof caved in, breaking my tank glass, allowing my naked body to rush to the floor with the cables snatching off easily. "Hack-hack. Hack-hack!"

I threw my head back as I got on my knees gasping for air, and my body immediately followed, throwing up the pink liquid in front of me. What were they trying to do to me? The flickering of the lights and the true colors of this place came to me. The sound of the alarm was almost unbearable. My senses seemed so much higher—like I could hear a pen drop through all the ruckus. "Oh God, hack-hack. They're… shooting."

My clothes, along with the smaller ones for Ebonee, were on the table. "What the?"

White, yellow, and violet, rose gold, and even black colors of lighting zapped down from the ceiling to a crystal pyramid sculpture on the table. One behind both of our tanks. The neon electricity was breathtaking to watch, almost making me forget what I needed to be doing. I couldn't tell if it was all in my head or truly there. What were these people trying to do to us?

"Ebonee?" I said, tapping on her glass tank. "Eb! Can you hear me?! Wake up!"

I couldn't just leave her. She was a good friend of mine. Even though we only got to know a little about each other, she needed me. Grabbing the chair with a metal leg wouldn't break the glass—or I just didn't have enough strength.

"Eb, come on! We have to get out—eygh!"

Throwing myself to the side as the gunfire grew louder and bullets came from underneath, hitting her tank. The glass was so strange, it looked like it was trying to heal itself or something. Nothing I'd ever seen before—or maybe the liquid left in my system was making me hallucinate. "Eygh!"

The next part of the roof fell, almost hitting me, but thankfully, it broke her glass. "Ebonee? Are you okay? Hey, can you hear me?"

Just like me, she threw up the liquid and couldn't stop coughing. Her eyes glowed brighter, and I finally figured it out. We were nothing but test subjects. That was all. "Ebonee, come on, get up."

"What… is happening?"

"No idea. They're shooting, and everything is falling apart. We have to get out of this building. Come on."

Both of us were so weak and partially numb, she could barely put her clothes back on, while I could barely hold her up. This place was not going to keep me, Ebonee, or Seth here any longer. I had to find him, too, and make sure he was okay. Opening the door, smoke rushed in and made us both cough and wonder if we truly would get out of here. We were helpless girls in a man's war. The worst part was that we were on the highest floor. It kind of felt like my voice was still talking in my head. So many screams and yelling with rapid gunfire. However, how were we going to get out of this mess? "Please… ancestors, guide my feet."

Rapid gunfire to my left and to my right, with smoke in between. "Hey… is that… Seth?! Oh my gosh."

My eyes widened as I tried to hold up Ebonee the best way I could through the mayhem. Seth's bloody face dripped red and black blood from the guard's neck as he took a chunk of it.

"Hey! I was just looking for you two! You girls need to get out of here!" Seth said, throwing the guard's body to the floor. "Down this way."

"What about you?" I asked.

"I'm okay. A little banged up, but I'll be alright. Now, keep moving. This place isn't going to last long. Agh!"

"Seth? Seth?!" I shouted as Seth hit the floor.

"I'm alright, I'm alright. Just get to the bottom floor!"

Seeing my best friend shot like that, I wanted to help. "Oh no. What is that?"

"Razaiella," Ebonee whispered. "Walk… slowly. It's a hybrid."

The beast-like creature I had never seen before—or even heard anything about—crawled like a lizard and had a tongue similar to a snake. It was the size of a crocodile with spikes on its back. Rapid fire knocked the lizard from us, and its bluish-yellow guts spilled on the floor. Our feet were bare, and we had many floors to go. There was no point in taking the elevator, as the lights kept flickering on and off.

"I think… I can walk alone," Ebonee murmured. "Let's go."

She was strong—I definitely felt it. We both ran down the side stairway. Some parts had already fallen apart, obstructing our way. From the highest floor—the twelfth—it seemed like something was guiding me, and we were going to make it. Just something in my spirit gave me a bad feeling. Some floors, like the one we were on—floor five—were not that bad. Just the shooting became more violent. "We're almost there, Eb. Eygh!"

"You little whore! You thought you could get away, did you?!"

"Run, Eb! I got this bitch!" I said as Ms. Ava held me down. I wanted her all to myself. Everything happens for a reason.

Ms. Ava and I tussled as the bullets and explosions surrounded us, but my mind was all on her.

"You… won't leave."

"Stupid… bitch, eygh!"

We fell down the middle stairs of the building, and the fire from the bottom made my face feel like it was melting.

"This is the end, Razaiella."

Ms. Ava again tried to choke me on the floor. My hand felt the very thing I needed in the moment. I grabbed a piece of sharp glass and felt my grip bleed. "I've had enough… of your bullshit!"

Blood gushed from the witch's throat onto my clothes. I got back on my feet and could never feel better. "I win; you lose."

Her eyes stayed wide open as blood spilled to the floor. One demon down, so many others to go.

"Razaiella! What are you doing up here? Come on! Oh, I see her debts have been repaid."

I smirked, but then Seth pulled me—as if to say it was nothing new to him. The place was collapsing fast. I just wondered who the people were who caused this destruction. Seth grabbed a dead guard's assault rifle, and we ran together down the last few floors.

"We're going to make it."

I knew we were going to get out of here together. I always felt it.

"The ground is shaking," Seth said, holding me down along with the rail of the stairway.

Dust and debris fell all over my hair and face, along with other objects crashing down.

"Hold on!" Seth says as the staircase came down.

"Eygh!"

I thought I was crushed as the glass and steel environment came down with us. "Hack-hack-hack. Seth?!"

Looking for Seth—as he had just been next to me. "Oh no," my heart skipped a beat, and it felt like nothing good would ever come to me. "Seth!"

"I'm… I'm pinned. I can't get my legs free. Oh, Creator… forgive me. Razaiella, get… get out of here."

"No-no. There must be a way. Hold on!"

"Razaiella! You have to—"

"Eygh!"

The burning building above us began to fall, and it seemed like it didn't want me to help my best friend.

"Listen to me… Razaiella. You—"

"No! I won't leave you," I said, getting behind Seth and attempting to pull him.

"Try and pull your legs out! Come on!" I cried.

"Razaiella," Seth said in his calm and beautiful tone. "Please, save yourself. Please… for me, okay?"

His warm smile—a feeling better than anything—soothing from the flames around us.

"Never give up on yourself. Remember that. Now go!"

"I love you," I said, kissing his cheek.

Seth smiled. "It's all love. Egh, be sure to follow your heart… no matter what it is. See you soon."

This time, I walked away without someone actually forcing me. The gunfire still surrounded the area—even outside—but none of it fazed me. I felt this man was definitely not from this world. I didn't care if he said he wasn't. To me, he was my guardian angel. I came to this place for a reason: to meet the greatest person who has shown me everything in life.

Looking up at the ceiling, I watched as it collapsed, crushing my friend's body. It just didn't seem real. I couldn't help but cry as I covered my mouth in tears and ran away from the smoke and debris from the flames engulfing the building. He had been with me from the beginning. My ancestors never left, and I knew that this was a divine experience. He wanted me to witness this place burning so I could burn everything else that harmed—or intended to harm—Mother Nature's beauty. Being inside showed me that you never know who you will meet and who you will become.

I will never forget, and I am ready for anything…

EPILOGUE

There are no more strings. I control my own destiny. I am free. I am divine.

There is no fault in being there, but there is a fault in staying in my demise. I am a new being. I will deal with these toxins poisoning the souls of the pure. My soul is restored, but my heart seeks vengeance for what they took from me. Seth told the truth: no forces can hold us back. My days will be brighter, as the sun's rays grant us another blessing each day—dreams to nightmares, nightmares to dreams. Peace in nirvana will be my destiny. Everything will be clear, and they will see what I will do to mark the earth with divinity, peace, and love. The healing of the world will be from those who are not afraid. Nothing we will fear, as there is nothing—only humans. Rewiring my thoughts and desires to what matters most: freedom.

Mom and Lakia—those two are dead to me. Munisha was the most innocent, and if she ever crossed my path, I would show her how life should be. There is nothing more important than family when they are true to you.

This new place in the woods, called The Village, located in Acadia Park, is where we reside; it is only temporary. It's run by a man who thinks he's in charge. Eb and I know weak men when we see them. This lifestyle is only temporary. Wes wants to be my lover, but my heart belongs to another man. I thought giving myself to someone else would help in a way, but it only gave me more reasons to never lie to myself about my feelings—just as Seth warned me. The truth is the only truth. My heart was buried beneath the rebel, where it belongs. No man was like him.

I met his brother at a club in Bar Harbor, Maine, just as he told me. He is nothing like Seth, but he is very respectful, as he never looked at me in a way that was wrong or touched me in any way. He showed signs of what his heart truly desired, and that was okay. As long as his character was right, it didn't matter who or what he was interested in. He knew I was coming, but Seth said he never contacted his brother from the inside. Caesar claims Seth was always to himself, but taught him how business works. Money working for you is the key to your control over your own life. Second, freedom in this new world order is the only thing I plan to have beneath my feet. All I really wanted was to get back at those who had taken everything from me.

My future is still bright, and the storm is coming. I just have to believe and see my vision become a reality. We have borrowed a few cars and food to keep our energy up. Then there's someone who managed to escape from the prison walls of S.I.L.O. with us. He was brought here from Asia and, unfortunately, lost his voice—but he is one of the most superb hackers in the world. All we needed was a laptop and a few fake cards to borrow a few credits from generous souls.

The world has become so topsy-turvy, but it has its advantages. They wanted to eliminate paper funds, but that only gave us more opportunities to take from those who had more than what they needed through digital currencies. One small step after the other, and we will have all that we desire in this world. To do as we want and take as we please. To be strong is never to show weakness. So, no matter what, these demons won't have me, and I plan to expose every single last one of them from their matrix of lies and confusion. That is my promise to Seth, for what they did or what they will try to do to anyone else like us. It is only right to, no matter what you do, do it with love…

Special Thanks
Quelenia and Fraline